C000230988

JACK BYRNE

BEFORE THE

STORM

Northodox Press Ltd
Maiden Greve, Malton,
North Yorkshire, YO17 7BE

This edition 2023

1
First published in Great Britain by
Northodox Press Ltd 2023

ISBN: 978-1-915179-19-7

This book is set in Caslon Pro Std

Praise for the Liverpool Mystery Series

'A love letter to Liverpool
with a touch of Peaky Blinders.'
SE Moorhead, Author of Witness X

'A thoroughly enjoyable debut.'
Catherine Fearns, Author of the Reprobation Series

'A truly British and Irish thriller.'
Readers' Favourite, Reviewer

'I was hooked from the first chapter.'
Readers' Favourite, Reviewer

JACK BYRNE was born and raised in Speke, Liverpool to an Irish immigrant father and grandparents. He is an advocate of Irish and Liverpudlian history.

The Liverpool Mystery Series, including *Under the Bridge*, *Across the Water,* and concluding in *Before the Storm* follow our heroes, Vinny and Anne, across Liverpool and Ireland as the mysteries of the past collide with their investigations in the present.

Follow Jack on Twitter @Jackbyrnewriter
And find him on jackbyrnewriter.com

For sisters
Yvonne, Carol, and Debbie

.

Chapter One

DI Cooper

12.10am, Friday, June 24th, 2016

Swirling, flashing, blue and red lights lit up the empty streets as the ambulance raced. No siren blared, but lights screamed through the darkness, waking neighbours in quiet dread as the engine roared through to the end of the estate, the end of the street and the end of a life.

'Junkie, Sir. But you said to let you know.'

'For Christ's sake, I had to get out of bed for him? What did the paramedics say?'

'Not much, but syringes in the living room, marks in his arm and his heart had stopped. Body cold, grey skin, blue lips. If Dulux did junkie it'd be this colour.'

DI Cooper shivered. 'Cold is right,' he said, walking through the disorder. Chaos was normal for an overdose.

He came down the carpeted stairs and gave his instructions. 'Tape up the door to keep the rats out. There's plenty of crime here, but not the overdose. The Coroner will write it up as accidental. The paramedics can take it to the Royal to join the queue for the pathologist.'

'Can you sign off on it?'

He scribbled his signature on the waiting paperwork, then

walked toward the front door, but something about the quiet, empty house made him stop.

'Who called us?'

'Paramedics, dead on arrival.'

'Who called them?'

'Don't know, Sir.'

Lights enlivened the chill night air as the ambulance filled the road outside. There would be an audience for the removal; neighbours in dressing gowns and behind curtains watching the living drama. *Better than the TV*, he thought. He pulled away in his unmarked service car, heading away from the estate. A warm bed in his clean, organised flat awaited. He left death behind.

Chapter Two

Helen

9.15am, Friday, June 24th, 2016

Helen dropped Charlie at school, late again. On the drive home, her phone buzzed, she took her eyes off the road to swipe the screen.

Stay away

She dropped the phone on the passenger seat. The second message from Macca this week.

In her peripheral vision, a black car veered towards her out of a T-junction. 'What are you doing? No!'

She swung her wheel to the left to avoid it. Her front wheel hit the kerb and bounced up. The steering wheel wrenched out of her hand as the car smashed into a lamppost with a deafening crunch. Thrown sharply sideways, her head struck the window. A flash went off behind her eyes, in front of her still silence. The shattered windscreen splintered the harsh, bright sunlight. Dust eddied and swirled. She gagged, petrol fumes stinging her throat and nostrils. The black car disappeared down the road. 'Bastard!' A thick ribbon of blood ran down the side of her face. She tried to raise her arm, but the movement sent stabs of pain across her chest. Unable to move, the last thing she heard came from within the car. The phone buzzed and the screen lit up.

Stay away

Chapter Three

Vinny

10.30am, Friday, June 24th, 2016

Vinny glanced at his watch. Time was running out. He had student papers to mark, but the all-consuming news distracted him. Britain would leave the European Union. Leave voters had won the referendum. The Guardian's front page declared, "Britain sets course for Brexit." Anger rose in his gut. He should have voted, but it was too late now. Like so many things, the realisation came too late.

The slightly open sash window brought a warm breeze into his study, disturbing the undergraduate essays on his desk.

At 9.30 am, his phone lit up. He tried to ignore the vibration, but his eyes wandered over the flashing screen. Unknown caller. Telecom, or Power companies, selling shit he didn't want. He turned his attention back to an essay on historiography. If he had to read one more cliché about history being written by the winners, he would go crazy. Two minutes in, and it was a refreshing change. He returned to the front page. Aliz Novak. Well done, Aliz. A Polish name. He wondered if she was first or second generation. He also wondered how long it would be or even if she would ever feel British. How would the vote affect her? Would the victors of this referendum write their history?

His mobile buzzed again. Merseyside Police. Vinny put the

essay down and transferred his attention to the incoming call. He swiped to answer and leaned back in his chair. He picked up another paper.

'Hello,' his eyes took in the title of a new essay *Climate Change - A Crisis in Time.* He smiled at the ambition of the essay. 'Mr. Vincent Connolly?'

The authority of the voice set his nerves on edge.

'Yes, speaking...' Something was wrong.

'I'm sorry to disturb you, Mr. Connolly...' He rested the paper on the desk. 'There's been an accident.' Vinny's thoughts went to Charlie.

Shit, Shit, Shit. No, don't be sorry. Sorry is bad. No. It had to be serious. Something about the speaker's slow, careful delivery unnerved Vinny.

'This is Sergeant Collins from Merseyside Police.'

The surrounding air grew cold.

'Okay, what is it?' his words came rushing, tripping over each other to get out of his mouth. 'What? What's happened? Is it Charlie, Helen, both of them?'

'There was a traffic incident...'

The pace of the voice killed him. 'Just tell me,' he interrupted.

'Your wife is in the Liverpool Royal Infirmary, Mr. Connolly.'

He breathed out, 'And Charlie? My son, Charlie?'

His phone buzzed with an incoming call. He ignored it, waiting for his answer. 'Are you still there? What happened to my son?'

'I'm sorry, Mr Connolly...' Vinny's legs weakened. He felt sick.

'...I have no information on anyone else in the vehicle. As far as I know, your wife was alone.'

'Oh fuck. Okay, Okay...' *That's good, isn't it?* He checked the time. Charlie should be in school by now.

'You will need to arrange for the recovery of the vehicle.' *Sod the car.* Vinny rang off. He needed to get to the hospital.

The screen flashed, and the buzzing started again. Work. He swiped to reject it.

He rushed down the hallway and grabbed his jacket from the coat hanger. His phone buzzed again.

'Mr. Connolly, I think the call cut out. This is Merseyside Police.'

'Yes, I'm sorry. Okay, I got the message. The Royal.'

'I have to inform you that we will recover the vehicle as it is currently blocking a roadway.'

'Yeah, sure, okay. Do whatever you have to. Can you just let me know where you take it? Look, I'm sorry, I have to get to the hospital.'

'Central vehicle compound will contact you when they receive the car, and you can make arrangements with them for its recovery.'

'Okay. Thanks for letting me know.' He rang off.

Vinny stepped into the street, his eyes scanning the tidy row of Victorian semis in Ensworth Road, just round the corner from the busy Liverpool suburb of Allerton Road. They were ten minutes' drive from the Speke Estate, where he grew up, but a world away in atmosphere and lifestyle. The morning sun was intense, but a freshness hung in the air, under a blue sky. Not a day for accidents or anxiety. What did he mean? Brexit day was one big accident. He turned the ignition and drove out onto the main the road.

Vinny pulled into the car park of the Liverpool Royal Infirmary. Making his way through the multi-storey lot, he ended up on Prescot Street. The Royal was grey and dirty, a concrete block similar to the worst of sixties housing schemes. He walked through to the main reception desk. He passed a collection of bandaged, wheelchair-bound patients accompanied by family members — all of them a reminder of human frailty. At least Charlie remained safe.

He approached the reception. 'Helen Connolly... Dwyer, the paramedics brought her in this morning after a car accident.' He didn't know what name she would've used for the police or paramedics.

The receptionist ignored his lack of courtesy. 'How long ago?' her fingers, practiced at protecting her painted nails, expertly floated above and tapped the keys.

'I'm not sure. An hour? Forty minutes?'

'She's probably not in the system yet. You'd best go down to A&E. I'm sure they'll be able to help you.'

'Shit. Okay, where do I go?'

'The easiest way is to go back outside, turn right, and follow the building round. You will see it.' She pointed out the main door, using her fingers and nails to full effect.

He followed her directions and left the building. He hurried round to the right, pulse racing. In front of him, the traffic edged its way into the town centre. They were close enough to the river for stray scavenging gulls to be circling overhead. He didn't know what to expect? Blood, stitches, broken bones?

Vinny turned the corner and saw the Accident and Emergency. More functional and less imposing than the main entrance, the business end of the operation. Diagonal yellow lines marked the front of the hospital for ambulance arrivals. The sliding double doors lead to a short corridor that opened into a wide waiting room. An ambulance pulled up, lights flashing, but no siren. The sight took him back. Sammo and Jaime in Garston as kids. He walked straight on and through a set of swing doors into the medical area. He knew behind those doors people were suffering, maybe even dying. A room full of the bruised and broken, of all ages and colours, representing Liverpool in all its desperation. He walked past two trolleys, one holding the figure of an elderly man, his dignity absent as he lay back half-dressed on pillows, breathing heavily through an oxygen mask, his thin, grey-haired chest rising and falling with the rasping breaths. Vinny caught his eye; he could see no emotion but blank endurance. Fuck this.

He kept his eyes on the reception window in front of him,

refusing to notice details of the person inhabiting the second trolley, except it was someone younger. An anxious mother stroked the smaller shape under the blanket.

'Helen Dwyer. Car crash, about an hour ago?' he asked.

The admin behind this desk was older and more harried. Nurses and orderlies were coming and going, leaving or collecting files and checking or writing on a large whiteboard behind her.

She swivelled effortlessly in her seat. 'Cubicle five, beyond the double doors.'

He nodded in thanks. She acknowledged him and picked up the phone.

Vinny prepared himself and went through the swinging doors. He didn't want to see blood and guts or hear cries of pain. He didn't. Instead, he saw the hustle of the reception repeated. Nurses and orderlies criss-crossed the area in a scene of controlled efficiency. The disinfectant smell of all medical facilities hit him. Voices rose and fell in urgency and volume, but never panicked.

A blue-uniformed woman stopped his progress. 'Yes?'

'Cubicle five?'

She pivoted and pointed straight ahead to the left. He walked on, each curtained area contained a casualty. He avoided the gaps between the curtains. Instead, his eyes focused on his destination, third up on the left. He looked through the curtains of number five. Helen lay immobile. Not a good sign. A shockingly white bandage threaded round her head, trapping her dark bedraggled hair and forming clumps. Her eyes were closed and puffy, her breathing regular. She looked peaceful. No blood, no scars, but a large, bluish purple patch ran down the side of her face. Vinny's pulse slowed, and he exhaled heavily. Her arm in a sling. He could see the fingers of her left hand poking out at the end.

He swished the curtain open and then closed it behind him.

He approached Helen, reaching out to touch her shoulder.

'Helen, Helen.'

Her eyes remained closed. He leaned in, his head next to hers, touching cheeks. He pulled back and stroked her shoulder.

'Excuse me.' The words and the swish of the curtain behind him were simultaneous.

He moved around and sat on the edge of the bed. 'I'm her husband.'

'Ok,' the nurse looked at the clipboard on the end of the bed. 'Mr Dwyer, your wife needs rest.'

'How is she? What's going on?'

'You'll have to speak to the doctor.'

'Ok, well, where is he?' Vinny looked around.

'She is with a patient. If you wait, I'll let her know you're here.'

'Excuse me.' The curtain was pulled open again and a police officer put her head inside. 'Mrs. Dwyer?'

'Yes.' Vinny answered.

'It's about the traffic incident. Can we have a word?'

Vinny moved to stand beside Helen. The officer opened the curtain fully, revealing her uniformed colleague. They stepped forward, and the nurse moved out of the way and let them through. Her colleague stood at the edge of the curtain with his helmet in his hands, fidgeting.

'I'm PC James, and this is PC Cartwright. We're here to get a few details regarding what happened this morning.'

'Well, as you can see, my wife is in no condition.'

'Can you take this outside, please?' asked the nurse.

'Of course.' Vinny moved out into the ward.

'Outside, please.' The nurse pointed to the double doors.

'After you.' The officer waved Vinny ahead. Beyond the swing doors, PC James spoke first. 'Can I just check the basics: make of car and registration? And just to confirm the driver?'

'Do we have to do this now?' asked Vinny

'It's just to confirm the basics.'

'I haven't even seen the doctor yet.'

'I'm sorry, sir, but we need to establish what happened.'

'Ok, so what happened?' asked Vinny.

'Excuse me?'

'You're the police. You tell me, what happened?'

'Sir...'

'Sir nothing, have you been to the scene?'

The officer stepped forward. 'We're not here to answer your questions. Now—'

'Suzuki Swift, registration KLM 342,' Vinny finished.

'And the car's registered to Ms Dwyer, your wife. Can you confirm she was the driver?'

'Yes.'

'I'm sorry, but we have to ask. Had your wife been drinking?'

'Really?' Vinny asked. 'You know she's a registered social worker?'

'I'm sorry. It's a formality. We have to check with anyone involved in a road traffic incident.'

'No, she hadn't been drinking. She was on the school run, on her way back since my son wasn't in the car. Thank God. What happened to the other car? How badly is it damaged?'

'What other car?'

'It was an accident. Who was driving the other car?'

'No other car involved, Mr Dwyer.'

'The name is Connolly,' Vinny said.

'The car's registered to Ms Dwyer.'

'That's her maiden name. So what happened?'

'That's what we are trying to establish Mr...' the officer paused. 'Connolly.'

'Your wife's vehicle left the road and hit a lamppost.'

'Why did her car leave the road?'

'We aren't sure yet.'

'So, no one else was involved?'

'As far as we can tell at the moment.'

'Where did it happen?'

'Menlove Avenue, just past the junction with Springfield Road.'

'She would have been coming back from the school.' Vinny rubbed his hands over face.

'Jesus. What the hell's going on?'

'Can you think of any reason someone might want to harm your wife?'

'No, of course, not. Why would you ask that?'

The officer didn't answer. For the first time, Vinny got the feeling something was going on.

'Okay. I see. Is there anything else you want to add? Anything that could have contributed to the accident?' the officer asked.

'No, of course not.' Vinny shook his head.

'Have you spoken to anyone else? Were there any witnesses?' Vinny asked.

'If you need anything else, my name is on there.' The officer smiled for the first time since her arrival. 'I hope your wife recovers soon. Be grateful she'd already dropped your son at school. How old is he?'

'Fourteen,' Vinny said.

'Okay, well, all the best.' She turned and followed by her colleague, walked out through the main doors.

Vinny stood and watched the police leave. He waited until they were through the double doors.

The nurse in the blue uniform appeared in front of him again, carrying a large manila envelope containing Helen's personal effects from the paramedic.

'The doctor will be with your wife in about five minutes.'

She handed him the envelope.

'Thanks.'

Vinny made his way through the waiting room; the older man hadn't moved from the trolley. The harried receptionist made a flicker of eye contact, and then he was back on the street.

The noise of the street contrasted with the quiet inside the hospital. Vinny could see the growing structure of the new Liverpool Royal Hospital being built up the road. There were rumours of cracks in the infrastructure, but public money was still being poured into it. He remembered the quote from Marx: 'All that is solid melts into air.' How did it end? Something about man being compelled to face his real condition?

Cars and buses negotiated the busy road into the city centre. Liverpool bustled with activity. Instead of making his call, he opened the envelope containing Helen's handbag and contents, nothing important: phone, some makeup, lipsticks, and a compact, tissues. He looked for keys but couldn't find any. He turned on the phone after swiping in Helen's symbol, and it went straight to its last position, showing an open text.

Call me

He swiped to see who sent it. Steve McNally. What? Vinny stared at the screen. He let his hand drop, but didn't know what to do or think. Why is Helen getting texts from Steve McNally? First, the headcase Sammo shows up, then the crash and now Macca. A seagull swooped and stabbed at a piece of mouldy burger bun near his feet. What the fuck!

Chapter Four

Macca

10.30pm, Thursday, 2nd July, 1981

The time was right. Macca knew if you wanted something, you had to take it. He stepped over the low wooden gate, careful not to rattle the latch. He marched up the path and darted into the entry. Quick and quiet. The light was fading. Looking down the end of the street, he could see the sun disappearing beyond the houses into the river.

The streetlights were on, the orange glow fighting the remains of the day. Kids had been called in, football and skipping were over, the street fell quiet. TVs blared behind curtains up and down the road. Hale was better than Speke because they had more, much more, cash, even jewellery, but the walk to it from the estate was dangerous. The bizzies knew kids from Speke going to Hale at night were not out visiting friends or family. This should be easy. Macca relaxed in the entry, safe in the knowledge he remained unseen from the street. The entry ran between the two houses, giving access to the back gardens. At the end, there were two gates at forty-five degrees to each other. He moved down the entry cautiously; he knew there were no dogs next door.

Sammo was somewhere in the street and would give a whistle if anything looked out of order, so there was no rush. This was about patience and nerves.

Before the Storm

Old man Doyle turned out the light in the living room and made his way upstairs. Macca watched as the light from the living room went out. He moved down the entry to the back gates. The old man would be in the bathroom above. Macca looked up and saw the light through the window. He should wait until this light went out, too, but fuck it, he liked the danger. He grabbed the top of the gate, which wouldn't budge. Locked. He pulled himself up smoothly and eased on top of it. He was just feet away from the bathroom window. The light went out. Macca dropped silently to the ground.

The back door was half glazed, four square panes above waist height. He tried the door, but it was locked. The bottom left window in the door had a crack. Macca's lucky night. He pulled a pair of socks out of his pocket and slipped them over his hands. A precaution learned watching Kojak and Columbo, as police in Speke didn't bother fingerprinting for burglary. He pressed against the crack with his elbow pushing firmly, then relaxing, pushing, then relaxing. Each time the glass moved, it separated from the putty holding it in place. Another push, harder this time, and a new crack appeared. Now he could push and pull a triangle-shaped piece to loosen it, until he could lift it out of the frame, and discard it on the grass. Macca guessed the old man would be in bed by now. Rolling up his sleeve, he slid a hand, then an arm, through the gap in the glass. The key sat in the lock halfway down the door. Macca turned it and let himself in. His eyes had adjusted to the darkness. The kitchen was tidy; a single cup and plate were on the drainer next to the sink, a knife and fork in a glass next to them. The air was still. A dog barked in the distance, sounding an alarm for better-defended homes.

The kitchen table was against the wall. Macca reached for a shelf above it. He picked up the first of three tins, turned the lid, and his fingers went inside. Sugar. He emptied it out onto the floor. The second tin held tea. Maybe he would be lucky with the third. Biscuits. He took a bite of one and let the others fall. He picked up a tea towel from the drainer.

Mr. Doyle coughed and turned over. The bed creaked as he tossed and turned, seeking comfort. Macca opened the living room door. He knew these houses well. They were all the same, and he had been in this house with Helen. A cupboard occupied the space under the stairs in the hallway. Everyone had a utilities cupboard, and everyone had a lecky and gas meter. Shillings fed the meter until the money changed. Now they were ten pence pieces.

He crossed the room quickly when he heard the cough from above. He wasn't worried. If the old man came down, he could be out the door in seconds. Small padlocks fixed the coin collection tin under the meter. Macca pulled out his screwdriver and wedged it through the gap. A strong twist and the loop of metal holding the padlock bent. The padlock would hold, the collection tin was weaker. One arm of the loop snapped off with barely a sound. Macca slid the padlock off, laid the tea towel down on the ground and eased the collection tin from its place. The coins slid out with tinkles, a sound Macca loved. He repeated the exercise with the gas meter. Holding the corners of the tea towel, he enjoyed the weight of coins. He was happy. Everything was still and quiet, nothing stirred. He put the tea towel down, stood in the living room, and spun, smiling, with his arms outstretched. He bent down, picked up the tea towel, and tied the corners together, closing it tightly. The kitchen door was open, and he could see straight out to the back garden. His way out was clear, but he didn't take it.

Chapter Five

Vinny

11am, Friday, 24th June, 2016

Vinny made his way back through the hospital. Why would Helen be talking to Macca? The last time he had seen Steve McNally was years ago. Before his trip to Ireland with Anne. His recent visit from Sammo was out of the blue, and now this with Macca. He swished the curtain aside and entered the cubicle. Helen was awake, and the doctor was leaning over her, pressing her stomach. 'Hey.' Helen's smile turned into a grimace.

'How are you?' he asked.

'I've been better.'

The doctor turned toward Vinny.

'My husband,' said Helen.

'Your wife has had a serious accident. The x-ray results show fractured ribs and significant bruising.'

Vinny didn't know what to say. 'Ok.'

'We'll be keeping her in for a few days. An accident of this kind can cause trauma to the internal organs. We want to make sure there are no complications.'

'Of course,' Vinny said.

The nurse from earlier entered the cubicle. 'We'll get you onto a ward as soon as we can.'

Before the Storm

The doctor nodded to the nurse and turned. 'I'll call by and check you again when you're settled.'

'Thank you,' said Helen.

Vinny handed Helen the envelope. 'Your stuff from the ambulance.' He waited for a few seconds. 'Is something going on?' he sounded harsher than he meant. Helen opened the envelope with one hand and began awkwardly searching through it. Vinny reached over and held the envelope open. He held up the phone. 'Are you looking for this?'

She leant back. 'Yeah.'

'Anything you want to tell me about?'

'Yeah, just give me a chance. And can you stop being so dramatic?' Helen ran her hand through her hair as much as she could and then began pulling out strands that were trapped by the bandage.

Vinny thrust her phone forward with the message "Call me" displayed. 'From Steve McNally. Really?'

Helen tried to move forward and groaned in pain. 'What are you doing, looking at my messages?'

'What's going on?' Vinny was poised between jealousy and anger. How could she do this? Secret messages with Macca?

Vinny swiped to the message again.

'Why are you getting texts from Macca?'

'Oh.' Helen closed her eyes.

'Come on. Macca, really?' There was an edge in Vinny's voice.

'It's not about him. It's not what you think.'

'Stay away, the one before says? Have you been seeing Macca?' he asked, but he didn't believe it. Not with their history.

'No. It's about Sammo.'

'What the hell has this got to do with Sammo?'

'He's been having a rough time. I bumped into his sister in town. We had a chat. She was desperate to help him. Thought you might help, too. She put me in touch with his daughter.'

'Help? How could I help? And why didn't you tell me?

Keeping secrets, really?'

Vinny paced up and down in the small space beside her bed. He could've told Helen about his visit from Sammo, but he was still angry with her.

'Will you calm down? I was going to tell you, before all this.' Helen spread her hands to show everything around them.

'Jesus Christ. Sammo, Macca, what is this..? Scallies reunion class of '81?'

'That's why I didn't tell you... because of the way you are. You never talk about them, and when you do, it's nasty. You wouldn't think they were your friends. Stop pacing around. You're making me nervous.'

'Yeah. We were friends, past tense.' Angered, Vinny knew whatever it was, it wouldn't end well. His gut churned at the thought of what might come out. 'So, what's going on? You went to see Macca?' he stopped pacing and sat down. 'Okay, look, I'm calm.'

'I didn't see Macca. Like I said, I went to see Sammo. He's in Speke on Dymchurch.'

'Yeah, I know where he is. He's been in the same house since he was a kid.'

'Well, after I met his sister, I thought I would go round. He's been trying to sort himself out. Desperate.'

'I know.'

'How do you know?' she asked.

He waved his hand at her. 'It doesn't matter now. So, when did this start? And what the hell is the text about? Is that a threat? Why didn't you tell me?'

'All right, give me a chance,' Helen said. 'Look at when Macca was on the telly... how you reacted. Do you remember?'

'Yeah, I do. He's an arsehole, a bully. He's always been the same.'

'And you wonder why I said nothing?' Helen's eyes widened.

'I just can't believe you've been doing all this behind my back.' said Vinny.

Before the Storm

Helen sighed and shifted position. 'You're a great one to talk about secrets. What was all that about your dad? Gallivanting round Ireland with Anne. So stop it, will you? Stop feeling sorry for yourself. I didn't tell you because you can be an arsehole, too. Maybe that's the problem. You're more like Macca than you realise.'

'That's not fair.'

'What's fairness got to do with it? Let's be honest. You haven't been listening to me… us… for a while. Your meetings and your students always come first.'

'It's called work.'

'Yeah, and I wouldn't know what that is, would I?'

The nurse appeared again. 'Hi, is everything okay here?'

'Yeah,' Helen replied and with a roll of her eyes. 'Panicking husband.'

'Oh, don't tell me.' The nurse winked at Helen. 'And women are supposed to be the ones who go to pieces.' She smiled and turned to Vinny. 'Your wife is fine, but it was a car crash. She needs to rest and recover her strength.'

Vinny held his hands up in mock surrender. 'All right. All right. I get it.'

'We're sorting out a bed for you now. You should let your wife rest.'

'Yes, sure.'

Vinny waited until the nurse left. 'So… what happened?' he had a bad feeling about this.

'Nothing. I saw him last week. He got himself a little dog. Then the Social sanctioned him, which messed him right up. He kinda got paranoid. Everyone against him, that kind of thing.'

'And Macca?' Vinny asked.

'They fell out, him and Sammo.'

'Have you been seeing him?'

'No… I met him once. Macca said Sammo had lost it: his family situation, the drugs, PTSD,'

Vinny was quiet for a minute and then, in a calmer voice, asked,

'Why? Why did you put yourself back there, in the middle of all that?' Vinny had spent half his life getting away from it.

'All what?' Helen looked confused.

'That shit: Speke, Macca, Sammo.'

'Jesus, we grew up there, with them. What's wrong with you?'

Vinny couldn't hide his annoyance. 'With me? Really? You are asking what's wrong with me? I'm not having it,' he declared.

'Having what?'

'Him, them, interfering in our life.'

'They aren't,' she protested.

'Then what are we doing here? Car crash, texts, telling you to stay away. Talking about heroin and PTSD. That's their lives, not ours.' Vinny stood again. 'I'm going to see him… them… tell them to back off. Sammo. Then Macca. You're getting out of this. What the hell is wrong with you? You've got a fourteen-year-old son to look after.' He tried to sound definite, final. 'Whatever's going on has nothing to do with us. It's not our problem.'

'Let me get out of here. I'll call him, explain,' Helen said.

'No. I'll sort it out.' Vinny stood.

'Don't forget to pick Charlie up.'

Vinny instinctively checked his watch. 'Of course.'

'And you have to meet with Mrs Kane, the headteacher.'

'Oh shit, really?'

'Yes 3pm, don't be late. A chance to do some real parenting.'

'Oh, right, Thanks.' Vinny moved toward the curtain.

'And can you bring my nightclothes, underwear, and buy a new wash bag with toothpaste, soap, and shampoo?'

'Jesus, alright. Anything else?'

'Yes. Don't do anything stupid.'

Helen's words followed him out of the cubicle and hospital.

Chapter Six

Vinny

12pm, Friday, 24th June, 2016

He drove to Speke. This needed sorting out. The first port of call would be Sammo. If necessary, he would find Macca. He wasn't looking forward to that part, but if it had to be done, he would do it. He edged his way through town, passing the neoclassical columns and portico of the once grand and now shabby Adelphi Hotel. Then the famous Lewis's department store, empty now. Stuck behind the 82c bus, he remembered the joke. 'How do you get a parrot to speak? Put it on the 82c.'

There were two ways to Speke from town — through the Dingle or Toxteth. The bus took the Dingle route, and as a kid, he had done this many times. As a driver, he always chose Toxteth, then the bottom of Smithdown, down through Allerton past Penny Lane. Between the town centre and Smithdown Road, buildings were showing their age; peeling paint and untended entrances, but from Penny Lane on, it was nicer. He drove on past the parks, Calderstones, Woolton, Camp Hill, and through Hunt's Cross to the estate where he grew up.

For Vinny, it was a drive back in time. Speke was the last area of Liverpool before Cheshire; the edge of the city. He turned off the Boulevard. To his left was once the largest industrial estate in Europe. The golden years for the area were from the mid-sixties to the early seventies because there was work. Vinny's family moved from the terraces under the bridge in Garston to good family houses. He turned on the radio to drown out his thoughts and caught the end of the news. A vote in favour of leaving the EU was fifty-two to forty-eight per cent remain. A breathless reporter talked of crisis and tension. The big question was, what would Prime Minister David Cameron do?

* * *

Sammo's house was a modern redbrick at the end of the block, built in the late '70s. Flat and functional, with no architectural flourishes or individuality. A modern box that kept out wind and rain, along with any sense of style or taste. It had walls, a door, and three windows.

Dog ends and litter covered the path and a small patch of grass that was his front garden. This looks bad. A couple of youths loitered on the corner watching him, one on his mobile. A piece of wood replaced the central glass panel on the front door. Police tape hung from the bent door jamb, where the lock had shattered when forced. The guys, probably the ones that busted the door, were still watching him. He pushed it open further with growing anxiety. 'Sammo… Sam, are you here?' he pushed it open wider. A pile of brown letters lay unopened in the hallway. The door had swung to the left, and immediately on the right was the staircase.

'Sammo,' he called again up the carpeted stairs.

Nothing. A musty, damp smell came from the house.

It was quiet, strange. Vinny had been in the house as a kid. Nothing had changed. The dirty carpet was the same, the wallpaper, too. He walked along the hallway; he could see into the kitchen. 'Hello…' The smell grew stronger and stale, air gone bad.

No answer.

Everything was old and used, including the enamel on the gas cooker, stained yellow around the eye-level grill. Vinny hadn't seen one for years. Besides the back door, someone had pushed a pine table and benches up against the wall. The edging on the kitchen countertop had chipped and curled. A cupboard door hung askew with one hinge missing. He retreated from the kitchen and pushed open the living room door, revealing a sparse but liveable room. Sammo had been surviving. The three-piece suite was serviceable, and a small wooden coffee table was in front of it. It was depressing and made him appreciate the comfort of the home he had built with Helen.

'Hello?' The voice shocked him, and Vinny spun round. 'Who are you?' he asked.

'Detective Constable Peter Crowley.' The well-built man in his early thirties held out his warrant card, then dug in his breast pocket and produced a business card. 'And you are?'

'Vincent Connolly.'

'What are you doing?' The tone was sharp.

'Looking for Sammo, Sam Maddows. The door was open. Broken.' He pointed.

'Are you a friend… family?'

'Neither, well, friend, maybe, from years ago,' Vinny said.

The officer paused before saying, 'You shouldn't be in here.'

'Why?' Vinny asked.

'I'm sorry, but we found Mr. Maddows last night. I'm afraid he's dead.'

'Dead… Jesus. How?'

'It looks like an overdose, but we will have to wait for the Coroner's report, to be sure.'

Vinny leaned against the back of the sofa.

The police officer walked into the kitchen and back to the living room to rejoin Vinny. 'Looks like kids have been in. Must have seen the ambulance. Come in to see what they could find, probably after meters.'

'People don't have electricity meters anymore.'

'They do if they can't pay their bills. The lecky, sorry, the electricity company installs them, so they pay as they go, some cash, some payment cards. If they run out of money, no electricity. Anyway, there's nothing in here for them. I will get the house secured, get the council to tin it up, or they'll be setting fires, turning it into a crack house.'

'Lovely.'

The officer ignored Vinny's sarcasm. 'Are you from round here?'

'Used to be,' Vinny said. He was still processing the news of Sammo's death. 'You said overdose?'

'Yeah, that's what it looks like. He was in here, on the sofa.' The officer had led the way down the hall. He pushed open the living room door. 'No reason to think anything else.'

'Does that mean accidental?'

The officer shrugged. 'Probably. There's no note. His stuff was all over the coffee table.' He pointed.

The living room was dirty like the rest of the house, a threadbare settee and armchair filled the space, a coffee table strewn with debris, rizla papers, a broken cigarette, a scrunched up fag packet an overflowing ashtray two syringes lay at an angle pointing at each other, the dark residue of blood visible in one of them.

'Not suicide?' The syllables were difficult to produce for Vinny.

'Who knows? Sad, eh? Looks like the guy was ex-army, too. Shame.'

'Yeah, a shame.'

'Anyway, you shouldn't be in here.'

'Yeah, of course, it's just the door was open.'

The officer shook his head. 'Fucking kids.'

Vinny was heading for the front door when he stopped and turned. 'What happened to the dog?' he asked.

'What dog?'

'The last time my wife saw Sammo, she said he had a little dog.

There's a food bowl in the kitchen.' Vinny pointed down the hallway.

'Oh, right? I haven't heard about a dog, but I'll make a note of it. Thanks.'

'No problem,' Vinny replied, walking back through the open door.

He recognised the figure walking up the path. Older, greyer, but still a big man. The suit and tie didn't sit right on him. But he was a councillor now, a man who demanded respect. Not that Vinny would ever respect him. He knew far too much about Macca.

'Well, if it isn't Vinny. Vincent Connolly, long time no see.' Macca held his hand out.

Vinny ignored it. 'You sent Helen a text?'

'I was worried about her. Sammo has been so unstable recently — sadly, as we can see.'

'How did you know I would be here?'

'I didn't. Pure coincidence,' Macca said.

Vinny glanced sideways, unconvinced. The guys on the corner were still watching. He was lying.

'But I'm happy to see you, just sorry about the circumstances. What brings you here?'

If Vinny had spider senses, they would be tingling. Macca came to see what he was doing. Was he worried, hiding something?

'I came to see Sammo,' Vinny said.

'After so many years?'

Yeah, he was definitely worried.

They stopped, facing each other.

'Who's in the car?' Vinny asked.

DC Crowley had come out and interrupted the conversation. 'And you are?' he asked Macca.

'McNally, Steve McNally, local Councillor.'

'What can I do for you?' The officer inquired.

'Oh,' Macca stumbled for a second. 'I'm an old friend, only found out this morning, and well, I thought maybe he had something of mine. I was just going to check.'

'No, I'm afraid I can't let you into the house now. What were you looking for? I can ask the family.'

'Nothing really, nothing important. Just something of sentimental value.'

'Well, you came here to get it, so it must have some importance?'

'Yeah, it was… a book. A book I lent him. You know we served together.'

'An old friend dies, you hear about it, and come to get a book back? Vinny could see the answer didn't convince the officer, either.

'I don't remember seeing any books inside, to be honest,' the officer replied.

'Yeah, never mind,' Macca said with a wave of the hand. DC Crowley stood his ground. Vinny moved to go past Macca towards his car, but Macca turned to follow him.

Vinny felt a hand on his shoulder and spun round. 'Get your hands off me!'

'Woah, what's this? Eh?' Macca stepped back, hands raised, palms forward. 'This isn't the Vinny I know.' Macca smiled.

Vinny knew he was being taunted. He walked towards his car.

Macca followed. 'Maybe that university made a man of you?'

'Piss off,' Vinny opened his car door. Over Macca's shoulder, he saw DC Crowley go back into the house.

'Nice as it is to see you, let's just say you are better off staying in Allerton.' Macca reached out and held the car door.

'I'll go where I want,' Vinny said. 'I was here to tell Sammo, and you, to stay away from Helen.'

'It's not me you should be telling. She's the one who's been sniffing round. Maybe you should have a word with your missus.'

Vinny wanted to get away now. The whole discussion was pointless. 'Stay away from us. We want nothing to do with you.' Vinny pulled the door away from Macca's grip and got in the car.

'Yeah, go on, back to Allerton. You don't belong here. This is ours.' As Macca spoke, his hand swept forward and flicked Vinny on the side of his head. Not a punch, or even a slap, but a flick. It made Vinny feel thirteen again.

Macca walked over to a waiting black BMW.

Vinny closed the door and turned on the ignition, flushed with embarrassment and shame.

Bastard, how did he do that?

Chapter Seven

Vinny

8.45am, Friday, 3rd July, 1981

Alderwood Avenue, Speke, Liverpool

Macca built the tension like a magician. He drew the chain out of his pocket, teasing his audience. Golden links appeared one by one.

'C'mon, what is it?' Vinny asked. 'A necklace?' he never really trusted Macca. He had latched onto him when he arrived at All Hallows Secondary Modern a month earlier. They lived close to each other, and Macca was hard.

'No.' Macca was grinning, his eyes bright with pride.

The chain was six... seven... eight inches long, and it kept coming.

'Fuckin'ell, we'll be rich,' Vinny said.

It was nearly twelve inches long. They were thick links, too, not the tiny ones you'd see on a girl's necklace. Finally, a golden watch, shiny and smooth.

'Wow. It must be worth hundreds, thousands,' Vinny said to please Macca. Vinny always tried to stay on the right side of him. 'Can I hold it?'

'Yeah, but I'm not letting go of the chain.' Macca carefully placed the watch on Vinny's open palm. Vinny's hand lowered to accept the weight.

Before the Storm

They were huddled in a dank stairwell, opposite All Hallows Secondary Modern in Speke, a council estate on the edge of Liverpool. The maisonettes had a common doorway and entrance. In the grey drizzle on this Friday morning, it was the first point of escape. They met just before school. Macca and Vinny came from near Western Avenue, so they usually met on the way to school. Instead of turning left through the school gates, they turned right and were waiting in the entrance of the flats.

'That's amazing.' Vinny meant it. He had never seen or touched anything gold, not real gold like this. The whole thing was glistening. He could run his hands over it, feel the weight of it all day long. He moved his hand up and down, enjoying the sensation.

'Giz it back.' Macca didn't want to let it go.

'Does it open?' asked Vinny.

'Course it does. We should wait for Sammo, though.'

Sammo was Macca's sidekick. Vinny thought Sammo was sneaky. The bell from the school rang out across the road, its dull tones reverberating through the damp air.

'Why?' asked Vinny.

'He kept dixie for us. The bell's gone. Where is he?'

Vinny cracked the door. 'Here he is.'

Macca popped his head out, too, and they could see Sammo running across the road, head down against the morning rain. His school tie flew over his shoulder. The drizzle had soaked his uncombed hair, splaying it out in all directions.

'All right?' Sammo pulled the door open.

'Yeah. What happened to you?' asked Macca, his square face set in a frown.

'Mister Thomas saw me. I had to pretend I was going in.'

'He'll notice if he doesn't see you all day,' Vinny said.

'Nah, we don't have him today. He won't know. Beep said he would cover for me, if anyone asked.'

'Let's have a look at it then,' said Sammo.

Macca kept hold of the chain but allowed Sammo to hold the watch.

'Here, let me open it.' Macca slid his thumbnail into a groove that ran around the edge of the watch. He gently pried open the cover to reveal a curved glass face that covered a white background.

'What are those numbers?' Sammo pondered.

'They're Roman numerals,' said Vinny.

Two intricate black hands pointed out the time. Inside the cover of the watch, there was an inscription. '*Faugh A Ballagh*.'

'Is that Roman as well?'

'You mean, Latin? I don't know. It doesn't sound like it.'

'C'mon, smart arse? You passed the Eleven Plus, didn't you? You went to a posh grammar school. I used to see you getting off the bus with your little briefcase.'

'Piss off.' Sammo was pointing out what Vinny always knew — he was different, and the embarrassment showed.

'Shut up, knobhead,' said Macca. 'At least he knows something. What was your school called?'

'Cardinal Allen,' Vinny answered.

'And who kept dixie for you? While you screwed the house. Eh… made sure no one was coming?' Sammo answered his question. 'Yeah, that's right, me.'

'Where's the dosh?' Vinny asked.

'I hid it. We can get it later,' said Macca.

'How much did you get?'

'Not sure. We didn't count it.' Macca replied.

'Anyway, that school was shit. They didn't want me, and I didn't want them,' Vinny said. This wasn't true, but it had become Vinny's way of rationalising his failure.

'Okay. Right, are you ready?' asked Macca.

'What for?' asked Sammo.

'We have to swear.'

'Fuck off… Bastard… Twat—' Sammo had a lot more, but Macca cut him short.

'Not like that. Like a promise.'

'An oath,' said Vinny. 'Like in court.'

'I swear to tell the truth, the whole truth, and nothing but the truth.' Sammo had placed his hand over where he thought his heart was.

'But not that,' Macca said. 'Vinny, you make up the words.'

'What for?' asked Vinny.

Macca uncovered the watch again and held it in his palm in front of the other two. 'We have our gold, our—'

'Treasure,' Vinny smiled. He knew Macca would like the adventure of it. Macca was always the hero in his own story.

'Yeah, treasure.' Macca said. 'And we have to swear to stick together.'

'Okay, let me think,' said Vinny.

'You robbed it,' said Sammo. 'I kept dixie. What did he do?'

'He's my mate,' said Macca. 'And he's going to make our oath.'

'And I'm going to find a buyer,' said Vinny. He wanted to fit in, be a proper part of the gang.

'Okay, what do we say?' asked Macca.

'Put your hand on the watch,' Vinny directed. Macca held the watch while Sammo and Vinny placed their hands on top. Then Macca sealed the clasp with his other hand. 'I swear I'll protect the treasure, and my mates, against all enemies and obstacles.'

With their hands on the watch, Macca and Sammo repeated Vinny's words in unison. 'I swear I'll protect the treasure, and my mates, against all enemies and obstacles.'

'All for one and one for all!' said Sammo. 'Like the three muscleteers.'

'Musketeers,' Vinny corrected.

'Who gives a fuck?' Sammo replied.

'And we split the money three ways,' added Vinny.

'That's not in the oath,' said Sammo.

'It is now,' said Macca. 'I'll split the money three ways. Your turn.'

'I'll split the money three ways,' said Sammo reluctantly.

A regular click echoed through the stairwell. 'What are you lads doing here? Sagging school?' A woman came down the stairs; the wheels of her shopping cart clicked as they bounced down each step.

Macca quickly put the watch back in his pocket.

'Nah, we're just on a message,' Sammo said. 'I've got to get some things for me mam. My mates are helping me.'

'Well, you'd better get on with it then, or I'll be right over to that school. You shouldn't be hanging around this doorway. You don't live here.'

'All right, missus,' said Sammo.

'Don't give me any of your cheek. Go on, out.' Her wheels clicked as she came down the last few steps.

'We're going. Don't get your knickers in a twist,' added Sammo.

Vinny opened the door, and they stepped into the street, laughing.

Heads down and blazers pulled tight, they scurried through the rain along Alderwood Avenue, towards The Parade. The Parade was the centre of Speke. Built in the mid-60s, it was the main shopping and leisure area. Austin Rawlinson's swimming baths were just along from Speke Police Station, and both opposite the shopping area.

Macca dug around under the hedges. 'It was here.'

'I don't know. It was dark. Maybe it was further up?' Sammo suggested.

'No, it was definitely here. Come on, help me look. It's in a brown cloth.'

The three boys poked about at the bottom of the hedgerow.

'Bingo. Here!' Sammo pulled out a tea towel tied at the corners. The coins inside clinked together as he swung it around.

'What are you doing, dickhead? Give it here.' Macca grabbed

it and felt the weight of money between his fingers. 'I could only get the lecky meter. Then I thought I heard something, so I got out of there quick. On my way out, there was a sideboard. I pulled open the drawers, and there it was waiting for me.'

'Good find.' Vinny nodded.

'Come on, let's spend some of this.' Macca ran off, the other two in hot pursuit.

Even with their ties off, their blazers, white shirts, and black trousers gave them away as All Hallows students. So, the shopping centre was the worst place for three truants to hang out.

Vinny didn't like The Parade. In his thirteen-year-old mind, The Parade was outside his safety zone, a place for older and harder kids. It was okay today because of the money from the meters, the sweet shop was their destination. Usually, it was just a bit too far from his home near Western Avenue. Vinny existed in a state of semi-fear wherever he went on the estate, and since it was where he lived, fear was a constant.

For Macca, Speke was his playground. Full of confidence and without Vinny's fear, at thirteen he swaggered about like he owned the streets. Sammo would have been a happy-go-lucky boy if he had anything to be happy about. As it was, he made the best of everything.

Chapter Eight

Macca

10am, Friday, 3rd July, 1981

Loaded up with Mars bars, Kit Kats, and crisps, they walked down Central Avenue, the three-storey family houses on the right and Speke Comprehensive on the left.

'Where are we going?' Sammo spluttered through a mouthful of crisps.

'My cousin's. He'll know a buyer for us. Maybe he'll make an offer.' Vinny tried to sound like he knew what he was doing.

'He would need a few quid to get the treasure,' Macca said.

After Speke Comp, they took a right onto Lovel Road. The red brick houses had front and back gardens. An entry ran between houses, allowing access to the rear. They displayed their status and privilege through well-kept privet hedges, verdant front gardens, and gates.

'Here we are.' Vinny stopped. The misshapen privet hedge fronted a three-metre square of patchy grass. 'We'll go round the back.' Vinny led the way between the houses. The dark entry led to gates at the end. Vinny almost jumped out of his skin as the entry filled and reverberated with angry dog barks.

'For fuck's sake.'

'Woah.' Sammo was at the back. 'What the hell has he got in there?'

Before the Storm

'You first,' Macca said, pushing Vinny forward.

'Thanks a lot.'

'He's your cousin.'

Sammo backed off. 'I think I'll wait out here, keep dixie.'

Vinny lifted the latch and pushed the gate open. The back garden was in no better state than the front. There was an old sofa and a fridge in the middle. The broken fridge door hung at an odd angle, and the guts of the sofa were scattered across the garden. There was also an Alsatian dog tied to the washing line post. It was straining at its lead, snarling and barking at Vinny, it's dribbling jaw a foot away as Vinny edged towards the back door with his body pressed against the wall. Macca followed him, both boys hoping the dog wouldn't snap its restraint.

Safely in the back kitchen, they stood nervously. The sparse room was dirty and smelled of grease. Vinny looked through to the living room. The curtains were closed, and the blue light of the TV flickered with pictures of a procession. Dust motes danced in the half-light. A voice rang out. 'Who's there?'

Vinny replied, 'Me... Paul? It's me, Vinny.'

'Come in, then. What are you doing lurking out there?'

Macca pushed Vinny forward again and followed close behind. Paul splayed out on the sofa and raised himself as they entered. 'Open the curtains,' he instructed over the sound of the television.

A news reporter was speaking into the camera. 'The funeral of the latest Hunger Striker has seen huge numbers of people pay their respects for this the ultimate sacrifice.'

'And turn that shit off.' Paul pointed at the TV. Vinny crossed the room and pressed the off button, then moved to the window and pulled the heavy material aside, letting the morning light flood the room. The coffee table was full of bits, tobacco, dead matches, and cigarette butts. The room was thick with stale smoke.

'What do you want?'

'We've got something you might be interested in.'

'Let's see, then.'

Macca pulled out the watch and let Paul hold it, but he kept the chain wrapped around his fingers.

'Not very trusting, are you?' said Paul.

'Just careful,' Macca said.

'Yeah, right? Well, yeah, it looks good.' He squinted at the chain. 'Looks like solid gold, not sure about the watch.'

'Of course it is.' Macca pulled it back into his hands.

'Okay, don't get shirty.'

'What do you think?' Vinny asked.

'Yeah, I could probably get rid of it for you.'

'Where'd you get it?'

Macca replied, 'A place in Harefield last night.'

'Okay, right?'

'The very end, near Damwood,' he continued.

Paul's expression changed. 'On the right or the left?'

'The left. Why?'

'The second to last house?'

'Yeah. Why?'

'Fuck, that's Joey Doyle's grandad's.'

'Who's Joey Doyle?'

'Fuck. He's a mate.' A loud rapping at the front door set the dog barking again, interrupting them.

'Who's that?' Paul got up and lifted the corner of the curtain. 'It's him, quick get out of here. Get in the kitchen.'

Vinny and Macca scrambled into the kitchen and hid behind the door. The knocking rang out again before they heard Paul say, 'Hey, mate, what can I do for you?'

Paul had brought him into the living room. 'I want you to keep your eyes open for me. Someone robbed my grandad's place last night.'

'Shit, that's bad, mate,' Paul glanced over at the kitchen door. 'What did they get?'

'Not much, the meters and a watch. Can you keep an eye out for the watch? Someone might try to pass it on. It's gold. Only thing of value he had.' Joe shook his head. 'He brought it from Ireland.'

'Yeah, sure mate. I'll let you know if I hear anything.'

'Little bastards,' said Joe. 'You know who it was?' asked Paul.

'No, of course not. If I did, I would be round there. No, but it's got to be kids, hasn't it? They got the lecky meter.'

'Yeah, probably,' Paul agreed.

'The thing is, whoever done it will regret it big time.'

'When you get hold of them?' Paul said, looking at the kitchen. 'No, not just that… grandad died last night.' He paused again, as if he was struggling to understand.

'Shit, what happened?' Paul's tone shifted to genuine concern.

'A stroke or a heart attack. They're not sure yet. But it happened sometime overnight. Probably while those bastards were robbing the house.'

Vinny and Macca stared at each other, eyes wide with shock.

Chapter Nine

Vinny

2pm, Friday, June 24th, 2016

Vinny drove from Speke along the Boulevard and turned right at the traffic lights. He was waiting at the next set of lights and banged his fist against the dashboard. Fuckin' bastard.

In one simple gesture, McNally had reminded Vinny of everything he hated about the place. Bastard.

Years of achievement and success lost. He had written books, lectured at prestigious universities across the country, and yet an ignorant arsehole like McNally had reduced him to this? There was anger, but alongside anger, there was shame. How had he let that bastard embarrass him? What was he supposed to do? Sink to his level? Start fighting in the street like dogs? He hated such a juvenile confrontation. Helen was digging up his past. A landscape of secrets and lies, better left buried. As he waited at the traffic lights, his anger and frustration grew. When they changed, he slowly pulled away. He needed to stop. Needed some air. He pulled off the road into the entrance to Allerton Cemetery, Vinny turned down the long drive. He parked on the verge and walked the twenty or so metres to a grave. It hadn't been intentional, but here he was, standing in front of his mother's plot.

The place was quiet. He put his hand on the headstone. Its

coolness felt reassuring. He breathed deeply, and the air filled his lungs. He knew, as he had known for years, this was where his problems began. It took him a long time to find his father's grave in Ireland. He couldn't have done it without Anne. Now he was a parent and understood the frustration of kids. He felt guilty about not being there for Charlie when he was born, but he had never hit him and knew he never would. The outbursts of rage that resulted in physical violence had never been a part of him. He had seen it too often and suffered from it. As a boy, whenever it surfaced, he panicked, trying to shield himself from the lash of a mother's anger. The impotence, helplessness, and anxiety that coursed through his veins in the face of violence began here, and here it was back again with Sammo's death. He knew he couldn't deal with this on his own. Returning to the car, he called Anne. After two rings, she answered.

'Hey, how did you know?' she asked.

'Know what?' Inquired Vinny.

'That I was back in Liverpool.'

'I didn't.'

'Oh, right?' There was a pause. 'So, what can I do for you?'

'Well, now I know you are back. Fancy a coffee?'

'You don't drink coffee.'

'You know what I mean.' He could hear her smiling.

'How's Helen?'

'In hospital, actually. That's partly what I want to talk to you about.'

'Oh, right, anything serious?'

'It could be.'

'Okay, where and when?'

'After work today, in town. I'll message you.'

'Later then.'

Vinny climbed back into his car. The road to the past was opening up in front of him.

* * *

Vinny flashed his parking pass to raise the barrier. He was late, so he'd be lucky to find a space. He drove slowly along the lines of the car park. With a town centre campus, he didn't know why so many people drove. The world is going to shit. Selfish bastards don't care about anything.

The university was a cash machine these days, churning out degrees to middle-class kids who didn't understand or care about history. Even worse was the opportunism, cashing in on China, supplying overpriced courses to the sons and daughters of China's new elite.

Movement caught his eye, and he saw a white SUV reversing out of a space. A small sporty SUV, less than a year old. The driver was a young guy, blond crew cut with a rugby shirt and shades. He didn't recognise him. Lucky bastard.

If he was one of Vinny's students, his marks would suffer for this. Vinny would get revenge. He pulled in just along from the reversing car, his five-year-old Fiat Punto ticking over like a fucking lawnmower. He didn't make eye contact. The student waved his appreciation for Vinny's patience as he reversed. Fucker.

Vinny climbed out of the car and slung his bag over his shoulder. The day was warming up. The online timetabling system logged him as available for consultation for the next two hours. Students were supposed to book ahead, but most didn't. He would check his messages when he got into his office.

He entered the building, a low-profile concrete construction that edged the paved quad. Designers saw it as a modern equivalent of the gothic quads of Oxford. Instead, it looked like a poorly serviced shopping centre in a 70s era new town.

He said hello to Roger, the concierge. Concierge, porter, or security? Every building had to have them these days to keep the nutters and drunks out. You couldn't go anywhere without being conscious that they turned mentally ill people out of shelters and social care accommodation like overstayers at a cheap bed-and-breakfast. What was the point of teaching history in a society without a future?

Security everywhere — not that they would be much use, badly dressed and badly paid. He wondered if one required the other. He supposed the only skill they needed was to get on the radio. If a real lunatic, terrorist or madman ran amok with a kitchen knife, then Roger wouldn't be much use. Arse glued to the chair in his little room next to the entrance, he slid the window closed, glasses perched above his escaping eyebrows.

'Morning.' Roger waved as Vinny walked by. 'What about that result, eh?'

'What result?' he asked, although he already knew.

'Brexit, that's upset the apple cart, hasn't it?' he said with a smile.

'Yeah, and that's what we need, eh? Apple carts upset. That's really going to make things better, isn't it?'

'Can't get any worse, can it?' Roger shrugged.

'You know what department this is?'

Roger lifted his glasses and put his paper down. 'History,' he said confidently.

'Yeah, that's right.' Vinny nodded. 'And are you sure you want to stick to that statement about things not being able to get any worse?' he walked off, leaving Roger bemused.

Vinny fumbled the key into the lock and pushed the door with his shoulder. His office was little more than a broom cupboard. It was three metres wide by five metres deep. Longer than it was wide. His desk was at the bottom, facing the window. In consultation with students, he would swivel his chair and face the door. There were two chairs for students, although he only usually had one at a time. Bookshelves lined the left-hand wall. This is where he kept his most frequently referenced material, and, of course, titles on the student reading lists. The University supplied his desk, like the bookshelves, made of cheap pine. Functional, but without the gravitas of professorship. A small landline phone sat between the letter trays on his desk. His desk wasn't tidy, and it wasn't a mess. He knew where to find things — it was busy. But not too busy. Now he needed some space. He put piles on top of piles to clear a spot. Most of the papers needed filing away properly, and he would get to it, but not now. A large, plain clock hung on the wall, its black hands and letters standing out against a white background.

There was a knock on his door. Oh, shit. His appointment was here.

'Hey, come in. How are you, Aliz?' Vinny made a point of remembering the names of students where he could.

She took a minute to remove her jacket. Her black, shoulder-length hair bounced as she hung her coat over the back of the chair. She reminded him of a young Anne. 'How is your work going?' he asked.

'Good. I think. Your clock is wrong.' She waved towards the timepiece on the wall.

'Yeah, don't worry about it,' he replied.

He didn't keep files on his students; working on the principal that he would remember those who were worth it, and the others would have to remind him of their existence or work if they wanted his attention. He kept a sizeable hardbacked notebook on his desk. In this, he entered the time and date, the name, and then any notes from the meeting. That way, he could always look back and find earlier conversations. He had a stack of them now, covering the five years he had been in the department.

'So, how can I help you today?'

'It's the essay for the end of term,' she said.

'You have the list of options?' Vinny asked.

'Yeah, I was thinking about Creativity in History. I like the idea of it, but I am not sure I understand it exactly.'

'Okay, what do you think it means?'

Before the Storm

A look of doubt passed over Aliz's clear features, and her dark eyes narrowed. 'Well, I know it's not about making things up — history has to have a basis in truth or fact.'

'Yeah, but whose truth? Whose facts?' he asked. It was a standard question to get students thinking.

'I know we can self-select — confirmation bias — where we choose the facts that support our version of history and ignore the rest.'

The discussion was going in the right direction, and it was a salve to the wound inflicted by McNally. 'Can there be objectivity in history?' he asked. The more he asked, the more his own situation rose to the surface.

She paused, narrowed her eyes, and her forehead wrinkled. 'In that, we can verify facts and agree on those facts, yes. But the meaning we give to those facts is different,' she said.

'Can you give me an example of that?'

'Well, we can agree about lots of things. That X happened on a certain day in a certain place. But how we explain that or its consequences depends on the view we have. For example, the invasion of Iraq; if you are an Iraqi, you could see it as an occupation. If you are a supporter of UK policy, then it is an act of liberation. So history is not independent, not in the sense that one truth serves all people.'

'Okay, all that is good, except it's not just the view someone takes of an event, but who and what they are, materially, determine the impact of events. So, where does creativity come in?' he asked.

'Well, I thought it was like finding facts and then extrapolating from those facts.'

'Yeah, good.' He paused. 'What time is it?' Vinny asked. He regularly used the clock to make a basic point.

Aliz smiled. 'Twelve.' She looked at the clock on his wall again. 'The clock is right!'

'Yeah, and…' Vinny was glad she'd noticed.

'Well, it means that even a stopped clock is right twice a day.' Aliz smiled. 'That's a pretty common observation,' she said. 'And…'

She screwed her face up as she worked through the idea. 'Okay, that if the clock is right twice a day, maybe there is a right time for things.' *There is indeed*, thought Vinny, and maybe this was the right time for him.

Aliz paused. 'Like in Ecclesiastes; there is a time for everything, a time to be born and a time to die.'

'Okay, good… but what's different in the way a historian would see that?' he prompted.

'It's not "time" in the abstract, but the conditions create the time. So, the time is right when the facts and circumstances are right. An idea can be right, say, for example, "democracy," but if people don't have the power to enforce it, then it makes no difference if the idea is right. The time also has to be right. Time is not independent of material conditions.'

'That's great. What does this mean?' his internal voice was shouting, the watch, the watch. Sammo, Macca and Jaime.

'It means that a strategy has to include time. Ideas, time, and material conditions have to be aligned for something to happen.'

'I think you're doing really well,' he encouraged, also aware that everything she was saying related to his childhood.

'You're so good at helping,' she paused. 'This is so simple. Okay, so the time has to be right.'

'And how else can we be creative with history?' he asked.

'You said in the last lecture: history is about the present, not the past. I thought about this for a long time. Studying history tells us how we get to the present. We can't understand what's happening now without understanding the things that got us here.'

'Go to the top of the class.'

Aliz smiled. 'Have you read Anton Chekov's 'The Student'?' she asked.

'No, I can't say I have. Why?'

'There's a bit in it. Can I read it to you?'

'Yeah, sure.'

'Okay, well, there's this student, as in the title.'

She was using her hands to articulate, and he liked the graceful flowing movements.

'Anyway, this student meets a couple of widows on a cold, dark night…'

'Ooh sounds scary,' he said, regretting it immediately as infantile.

'No, not like that… Anyway, I think it's near Easter or something because he talks about how St. Peter denied Christ three times, and about how frightened he must have been to do that.'

He knew he should be bored, but somehow she was speaking about his past.

'And the women start crying, feeling empathy with St Peter. Then Chekov says…' She held her notebook open and read, 'he realised the past was connected to the present in an unbroken chain of events flowing one out of another, which seemed to him that he had just seen both ends of that chain. When he touched one end, the other quivered.' She looked up at him, her dark eyes on his, and he could feel her enthusiasm for the idea.

'That image of an unbroken chain of time, not only that everything is connected, but that we can grasp both ends at the same time.' The image broke through to him. Is that what's happening? The broken links are being rejoined? Is that what this is? Sammo and Macca, but who is holding the end of the chain?

'Okay, I'm definitely impressed. It is an interesting quote. I will look the story up. And what do you make of it?'

'The one that I thought of is Boris Johnson blaming the EU for imaginary rules on bananas and prawn cocktail crisps at one end, and leading a campaign to leave the EU based on fears stoked at the other.'

'Sounds like you have a great basis for an essay.'

'You think so?'

'Yeah, seriously. I think you have identified something

intriguing. Use "The Student" example and draw out the implications.' As he spoke, he knew the implications of his own history were about to rise to the surface.

'I look forward to seeing the essay.'

'Thank you, Professor Connolly.'

Vinny turned back to his desk and heard the door click as she left. He leaned back in his chair, his legs stretched out, and closed his eyes. Maybe the time was right for him. The stopped clock of his life was about to be the right time. He knew something had to change. The morning had left him angry and frustrated. McNally had deliberately tried to wind him up. He also tried to warn him off? He leaned back in his chair and closed his eyes. Why?

His phone vibrated. It was a call from Anne. He sat upright. 'Hey... how are you doing?'

'Fine, when are you free?'

'I can get away any time now,' he said.

'Okay, great. Cafe Tabac? Bold St.'

'Sure. I can be there in an hour. I'll just finish up here.'

He collected his things. All thoughts of Aliz had faded. Now he had Anne, Macca, and Sammo on his mind. Now, Sammo's recent surprise visit to made more sense. Vinny hadn't followed it up or paid much attention. He had just hoped he would go away, but now it was clear Sammo wanted to tell him something. The questions about what happened to Sammo were becoming larger than his anger towards Macca. He was determined to resolve both. How much should he tell Anne?

As he left the building, Vinny nodded to Roger, who held a hand up to attract his attention.

'Yeah, I get it. Things can be worse. But we're sorting it out now, eh?'

'That's the idea,' said Vinny. Time to sort things out.

Chapter Ten

Vinny

'You look well.' Vinny meant it. Anne looked bright and fresh, while he felt old and tired in comparison.

'Thanks. I've ordered tea.'

'One step ahead, as always.' Vinny pulled up a chair.

Anne didn't respond. As Vinny sat down, the waitress appeared with the tea things on a tray.

'How's work?' Anne asked.

'You know, students, essays, lectures.' Vinny looked round. The cafe was pretty busy.

Anne smiled. 'Enthusiastic as ever.' She nodded in thanks as the waitress retreated.

'I haven't been in here for a while.'

'We used to meet here all the time.' Anne poured the milk.

'Maybe that's why.' A half-smile passed over his lips. 'And what are you up to these days?' he asked, to change the subject.

'A bit of everything, really. I'm on a retainer from Novo Media. I freelance for a few magazines and have just started video blogging. That looks like it could really take off.'

As she spoke, Vinny knew why he had been with Anne for so long. She was attractive, smart and independent. All those raw feelings from their time together flooded his unwitting mind, and he felt like a twenty-something again.

'Bloody hell, keeping busy, then?' Vinny raised his cup.

'Yeah, it's a weird time, media is changing so quickly. So come on then. What's the problem? Sorry, I should've asked. I meant to. How is Helen?'

'She's ok, still in hospital, she was banged up pretty badly. Broken ribs, they're keeping her in for observation.'

'What happened?'

'A car crash.' Vinny rattled his cup back onto the saucer. 'You can ask for mugs, you know?'

'Yeah, I forgot.' Anne smiled. 'So this crash, is that what you want to talk about?'

'Yeah, that and someone I know has just died.'

'Oh, I'm sorry... who?'

'Sammo, a mate from when I was a kid.'

'I think I heard you talk about him. How did he die?'

'An overdose.'

Anne took a drink of her tea.

'He was in a bad way.'

'But you think something more is going on?' she asked.

'I don't know. It's just weird how things have started happening. First the crash, then the message from Macca, then when I find Sammo, he's dead.'

'What message?'

'The hospital gave me Helen's stuff. I opened her phone and there was a message from Macca saying "*Stay away.*" Then another saying "*Call me.*" What the fuck... I know something is going on, but…'

'You don't know what.'

'Exactly. See, I knew you'd understand.'

'Have you spoken to Helen about it?'

'A bit, but she doesn't know Sammo is dead.'

'A bit of a mess,' said Anne.

'You're not kidding.'

'What does Helen know about us?'

'Everything. She knows we were together. We went to

Ireland.' He took a gulp of tea. 'She kinda thinks I dumped you to go back to her and Charlie.'

Anne raised her eyebrows. 'You finished with me?'

'Well, yeah.'

'That was nice of you.'

Vinny pulled a face. 'Well, you know what it's like…'

Anne laughed. 'Don't worry, I can play the broken-hearted ex. Ok, so tell me what you know about the crash.'

She pulled out a notebook and pen.

'Nothing really. The weird thing is that there was no other car involved, well, not directly.'

'What do you mean?'

'It sounds like someone forced Helen off the road, or at least forced her into the kerb and then she hit a lamp post.'

'Where?'

'Somewhere near the junction of Springwood and Menlove Avenue.'

Anne scribbled in her notebook.

'What are you writing?'

'Thoughts, things to check.'

'So you're gonna help?'

'You sure you want me too?'

'Yes absolutely. Why wouldn't I? Oh shit…' Vinny looked at the clock on the wall and then checked his watch.

'What's up?'

'I wasted time, and now time doth waste me.'

Anne smiled. 'Shakespeare really? You can be so pretentious.'

'I have to go. I've got things to sort out for Helen, and I've got to get Charlie from school. Do you want to come with me?' Vinny finished his tea.

'You are kidding, aren't you?'

'What do you mean?'

'Your wife is in hospital and you want to turn up at the school to collect your son with your ex in tow?'

Before the Storm

'Yeah, when you say it like that...'

'Ok go. You've got my number. You can call me if you need to.'

'Thanks.' Vinny stood. He leant down as if to hug or kiss Anne.

She waved him away. 'Go, you'll be late.'

Anne put her notebook down. 'If I help, are you ready for whatever we find?'

Vinny gave a half smile. 'The truth will out.'

Outside the cafe, Vinny uncrossed his fingers.

Chapter Eleven

Vinny

10am, Friday, July 3rd, 1981

Vinny pointed at the back door. Macca nodded. They crossed the kitchen quickly and went outside. They ran past the barking dog and up the entry.

'Come on!' Macca shouted at Sammo as they raced past him.

They crossed the wide Central Avenue derisively called Central Africa because a couple of Speke's few black families lived there.

'Hey, wait up. What's going on?' asked Sammo.

Vinny looked over his shoulder, saw Paul and Joe come out of the house and down the path. The boys didn't stop running until they reached the end of Lovel Road.

'What's going on?' an out of breath Sammo asked as he caught up with them.

Everyone was gasping for breath. Vinny leaned over, hands resting on his knees. 'We've got to get off the street.'

'Why?' Sammo asked urgently.

'The old man you robbed was Joe Doyle's grandad,' Vinny said.

'So?' said Sammo.

'Come on, let's go.' Macca urged them on.

They turned the corner onto Damwood Road. Vinny saw her first. Helen Dwyer was coming down the path of her house.

Before the Storm

Vinny had always liked her. Helen had long brown hair and hazel eyes. There was something in the shape of her lightly freckled face and the fullness of her lips or the brightness of her eyes. Something different.

'Hi. Where are you lot off to?' she had a quizzical look on her face.

'Hey, Helen.' Macca marched over to her, put his arm around her waist, and kissed her on the lips. 'What's my girl doing off school?'

Vinny's heart sank, and he looked away.

'I'm just going in now; had to wait for the Lecky man. I've got a note for school. What about you, lads?' she asked.

'We're going down the shore. Do you wanna come?' Sammo asked.

'You're sagging school?'

'Obviously, if we're going down Oggy,' Macca said.

Sammo laughed. 'Yeah, it's not like school would let us.'

Vinny saw the embarrassment flash across Helen's face as her boyfriend, Macca, made fun of her. He felt her pain, and he wanted her to know he felt it.

She tossed her hair and turned to walk away. 'Well, I hope you don't get caught.'

Macca doesn't deserve her.

'They won't catch us,' Macca boasted. 'Come on, let's get out of here.'

Vinny watched as Helen crossed the road. She turned to look in their direction, and Vinny waved. He thought he saw a half-smile on her lips, and it warmed him. Macca led them across Damwood and Hale roads at the edge of the estate and into Critchley Woods.

Two large purpose-built pubs, The Pegasus and The Dove and Olive, marked each end of Hale Road. Both were under the flight path of the new airport runway. Critchley was a collection of silver birch saplings, rough ground, a few ponds, and a pathway, which led along the airport fence to Dungeon Lane and then down to Oglet Shore.

They were off the street and could relax a little. The boys followed the path in a single file, with Macca leading the way as usual. The sky had cleared, and the sun was breaking up the grey clouds.

'What are we gonna do? Did he know it was us?' Sammo asked.

Macca stopped and turned to face them.

'Will your cousin tell him?' he asked Vinny.

'How am I supposed to know?' Vinny shrugged.

'He's your cousin.'

'Yeah, but I don't know what he's gonna say. Do I?'

'This is shit. We could give the watch back,' Sammo said.

'You haven't heard the worst of it yet,' Macca said. 'He only went and had a heart attack. You two only went and killed him,' said Vinny.

'What do you mean, we killed him?' Macca asked. 'You heard him. It was nothing to do with us. He had a heart attack or something.'

'He's dead, isn't he?' Vinny replied, the gravity of the situation dawning on him.

'Double shit,' said Sammo.

'Hey.' Macca was in Vinny's face. 'What do you mean, we killed him?'

'I'm not saying anything,' said Vinny. 'I wasn't even there.'

'Oh, it's like that, is it?' Macca was whipping his stick against bushes.

'You're blaming me and Sammo?'

'I'm not blaming anyone. Just saying.'

'I was only keeping dixie. I didn't go in the house,' said Sammo.

'What?' Macca thrust his fist forward and punched Sammo in the shoulder.

'Ow, that hurt.'

'Hurt? It'll hurt worse if you say that again. You, too, Vinny, fuck blaming me. You heard him just like I did. A fucking heart attack.'

Sammo rubbed his shoulder and looked down at the ground. Vinny started stripping a branch to make his stick. He avoided eye contact because he didn't want Macca to hit him.

'Great mates, you two are. We swore an oath and everything.'

'Yeah, I didn't mean anything,' said Sammo.

Vinny, stripping his branch of twigs and leaves, added, 'Me neither.'

'Okay, we've got to work out what to do. The old man died. It's not my fault. I didn't even see him. He could've died any time. Nothing to do with me.'

'What do they call it when you don't mean to kill someone?' Sammo asked.

'Manslaughter,' Vinny offered. 'When killing someone is kind of accidental, but wouldn't have happened except for you.'

'Like drunk driving,' said Sammo. 'If you accidentally got drunk.'

'Don't be a knob. You can't get accidentally drunk. Anyway, it's not even manslaughter; there was no accident or nothing. He just died,' Macca said.

'Maybe he died before you even got there, and his ghost was watching you,' Sammo said. 'That would really piss him off.'

'All right, enough. We can't do anything about that now.' Macca turned and started walking again. 'What do we do with this thing?'

'What thing?' asked Sammo, falling in line behind him.

'The thing.' Macca turned and gave him a dirty look.

'The treasure,' offered Vinny, bringing up the rear.

'Yeah, the treasure,' Macca repeated.

'Ahh, the treasure,' Sammo added. 'We could just throw it away?'

Macca stopped again. 'Okay, let's sit down. We've got to work this shit out.'

'Go forward a bit,' said Vinny. 'There's a bit of a clearing.'

They sat facing each other, Vinny on a tuft of grass, Macca on a rock, and Sammo on an old log. 'We need a plan.' Macca brushed the sandy ground with his stick.

'We could bury it? That's what you do with treasure, isn't it?' suggested Sammo.

'We're not fuckin' pirates.' Macca rejected his idea.

'He's right, though. We could just hide it somewhere,' said Vinny.

'How much is it worth, anyway?' Sammo asked.

'Maybe a hundred quid or more. That's what our Paul reckoned,' Vinny said.

'It's a lot of money. More money than my old man earns in a week probably, and he's on good money,' Macca said.

'He's at Ford's, isn't he?' Vinny asked.

'Yeah, what happened to your dad?'

'He died,' Vinny said.

'What of?' asked Sammo.

'Not sure, in the war.'

Sammo squinted at him. 'Which war?'

'The big one, stupid. That's right, isn't it?' Macca said.

'Yeah. That's what my mum said.' Vinny hated talking about his dad. He guessed the story about the war wasn't true.

'Mine got redundant,' said Sammo.

'Standards?' Vinny asked,

'No, Dunlops.'

'Shutting everywhere. That's why we should get our own back. We have to look after ourselves. That's what my dad reckons.' Macca said.

'But your dad's working,' Sammo objected.

'Yeah, well, it's not like I get anything off him. The fucker. This could be worth a lot of money,' said Macca.

'We can't sell it to anyone we know,' Sammo said.

'I've got it.' Vinny stood and paced. 'There is a pawnbroker by me Nan's.'

Before the Storm

'Where's that?'

'In Garston. King Street. She lived at twenty-six. I know because me mam is always going on about Kett's, the pawnbroker. How me Nan would take me grandad's winter coat down there, in and out every week, she said. Said they buy anything.'

'Not bad, not bad. No one knows us in Garston,' said Macca.

'We could go in your Nan's for a cup of tea?'

'No, we couldn't. We're sagging school. She's bound to tell his mam,' said Macca.

'She wouldn't tell me, mam.'

'See.' Sammo puffed his chest out a little at his very rare victory.

'But we can't go, anyway.'

'Why not?' he asked.

'She's dead,' Vinny said. 'But there was a pawnbroker.'

'Okay, look, the choices are hide it or try to get the cash,' Macca said.

Everyone was quiet for a second. Then Vinny said, 'Sell it. If we can get rid of it, then any link between you,' he stumbled over his words quickly adding, 'or us… and the old feller, is gone.'

'True enough. Except your cousin,' replied Macca.

'But we don't know if he's said anything.'

'We're going to have to find out later, but the first problem is—'

'The treasure,' interrupted Sammo.

'Exactly. Okay, we should stay off the road. Don't want to be seen,' Macca said.

'Right,' Vinny said.

'Right,' Sammo agreed.

Macca drew a line in the loose earth. 'We go along here, down Dungeon Lane to Oggy shore, behind the runway, along the river to Garston. Then up, do the deal. Agreed?'

'Yeah, sounds good,' Vinny said.

'Yeah, me, too,' said Sammo.

Macca pulled out the watch. In the late morning sunshine, it shone brighter than earlier. He placed it carefully on the ground.

'What are you doing?' Sammo asked.

'It's your turn. We all have to carry it part of the way. We are all in this together, remember?' Macca wanted to lead but didn't want to do it alone.

'Nah, it's okay. I'm good,' said Sammo.

'No, you're not. It's your turn to carry it.'

'Vinny can go first. I don't mind,' said Sammo.

Macca grabbed Sammo. He bunched his blazer up at his chest as he held it. 'No. I'm the leader of this expedition, and I say it's your turn.'

'Right. Yeah, sure.' Sammo leant down and gingerly picked up the watch. He slipped it into the inside pocket of his blazer. 'Right, come on, let's get moving.'

The boys followed the airport fence through Critchley Woods till they reached the end, then turned right at the Dove and Olive. The Dove — like The Pegasus, The Fox, and The Orient — was a purpose-built pub. Speke was a new estate, so there were no old Victorian pubs with ceramic tiles or stained-glass windows. Functionality was the overriding architectural motif. Alcohol and punters supplied the atmospherics.

The walk down to the shore was around half a mile. The lane passed the end of the runway. When planes took off, people could stand on Dungeon Lane and feel the roar of engines as they passed yards above their heads.

The boys walked three abreast down the lane, blazers tied around waists as the sun rose higher, burning the morning mist off the river and revealing a patchy blue sky. Leaving the estate behind, a buzz of insects filled the air and the scent of the wildflowers that lined the lane. They rolled their shirt sleeves up. Sammo transferred the watch from his blazer to his trouser pocket, and he looked at his reflection as the gold glinted in the sunlight.

'What would you do with the money?' Sammo asked as he slipped the watch into his pocket.

'I would get a bike,' said Vinny. 'A chopper. I always wanted one of those.'

'Choppers are shit. No speed in them. I had one. All show,' said Macca.

'I know, but they look cool. All I get is frames and wheels from the council tip.'

'Same here, but built some great go-karts,' said Sammo.

'I'd order everything at one go from the Chinese — number one to number fifty. That'd be boss.'

'Yeah, imagine that…'

Sammo looked behind him. 'Shit, police!'

Looking back over the curve of the road, they could see the distinctive chequerboard of yellow and blue with the lights on the roof.

'Fuck, hide.'

The three boys dove into the bushes and undergrowth beside the lane. Vinny lay flat against the ground. He waited a minute, then raised his head.

'It's okay, they've passed,' he said.

Macca and Sammo stood.

'Think they're after us?' asked Sammo.

'I don't know, but I don't want to find out either,' said Macca.

'What happened to your arm?' Sammo asked, pointing to scratches on Macca's arm.

'Fucking bushes,' said Macca, rolling his sleeve back up.

'What do we do then? Turn round, go back?' asked Vinny. 'Do you think it could be a murder hunt?'

'No one was murdered,' Macca insisted.

'But the old fella died,' Sammo said.

'He would've died anyway, sooner or later,' Macca said.

'I want to go quickly, without knowing,' Vinny said. 'No hanging around, smelling of piss and covered in dandruff.'

'Who was that?' asked Sammo.

'Mrs. Dunlap across the street. She was disgusting.'

'Okay, come on, guys, focus. The police are up the road. If we turn round and they come back, they'll definitely see us. Let's carry on. Be careful, though, try to keep hidden when we get closer to the shore,' Macca said.

They walked on in a single file, past a group of four single story cottages, homes to farm workers in days gone by. The road ended at the shore, so the police would have to come back the same way.

'What the hell are they going to the shore for?'

'Maybe just ducking off work,' said Sammo.

'Yeah, what else would they be doing down there?' Macca said.

At the end of the lane, the scene opened up; they were above the actual shore. Wooded paths led off in either direction along the river. Straight ahead was Oglet Shore. It ran steeply downhill to the riverbank itself. Generations of Speke kids had made swings from trees over the slope. It was a favourite place to escape the streets of the estate.

They approached the end of the lane carefully. Macca led them to the right, through some bushes and a little along the path, until they reached a vantage point where they could look back. The police car had stopped at the top of the ridge above the river. The shore was down the steep drop of slippery earth, and below it, about thirty feet or so, lay the river. Trees lined the riverbank on both the left and right sides. Sammo and Vinny followed Macca through the trees and hid out of sight of the police.

'Are they looking for us?' Sammo asked.

'Can't be. Paul wouldn't grass like that.' Vinny defended his cousin. 'Anyway, he didn't know we were coming here.'

They had a good view of the police car parked at the top of the embankment. The right-hand rear door opened.

'What's going on?'

'Shhh.'

Sammo pulled the watch out of his pocket and tried to hand it to Vinny. 'Your turn.'

'What? Now?' Vinny put his palms up in refusal.

'Yeah, now.'

'You bastard,' Vinny said.

Sammo threw the watch. Vinny caught it and threw it back.

Sammo, afraid to let it fall to the ground, caught it and put it back in his pocket.

A copper got out the rear door of the car and moved round to the right-hand side. He reached inside and pulled out a black bag. It was a Puma school bag. He threw it down the slope in front of him, and schoolbooks flew out of it. The copper then reached back in and pulled someone out — a black kid in a school uniform, black trousers, white shirt, and black blazer.

'What the fuck?' Vinny said. 'What the hell are they doing?'

'Shut up,' Macca said.

The copper pulled the kid out and pushed him towards the slope. He was slipping and sliding down on his arse and feet. The copper got back in the car. The car engine whined as it reversed and swung round, before heading back up the lane and towards the estate.

'Shit, what was that about?' Vinny asked.

'Fuck, I dunno,' Macca responded.

'Poor kid. Did you see what they did?' said Vinny.

'What's your problem?' Macca looked at Vinny. 'That's nothing. You wanna see my old man when he's had a few.'

'Maybe we should help him?' asked Sammo.

'Why? He's not our problem,' said Macca.

'It's not fair, though,' said Sammo.

Macca turned and walked along the path. 'Come on, let's get moving,' he called back. 'We've got a mission to complete.'

Sammo looked at Vinny. Both stood waiting for the other to act.

Macca stopped and turned. 'What the fuck? Come on.' He waved his arm. 'Vinny, get your arse over here.'

Vinny stood his ground. He was too far away for Macca to hit immediately.

Sammo turned to face the kid. 'We shouldn't leave him. All for one, remember?'

'That's for us, not others, not outsiders,' Macca bunched his fists and called again, 'Come on.'

Vinny shuffled his feet, trying to put off a decision. Macca moved towards him, Vinny broke and moved towards Macca. Sammo moved away from both of them and towards the kid, struggling back up the embankment.

Chapter Twelve

Vinny

3.15pm, Friday, June 24th, 2016

Vinny turned into the parking lane on Allerton Road. The afternoon light was just fading in the busy streets. He liked the Allerton suburb, four or five miles from town, despite it being a cliché of suburbia and the inspiration for The Beatles' song "Penny Lane." The lyrics were all around him — the TSB Bank, the shelter in the middle of the roundabout, the barbershop. And, of course, the people who "stop and say hello." Well, maybe not so much the latter.

He entered the lane, but he couldn't see any vacant spaces, so he came to a stop. A black BMW SUV waited behind him. The driver was barely visible because of the angle of the windscreen and storefront reflections. Vinny's only concern was he would start beeping. Impatience was a condition of the times, and Vinny suffered as much as the next person. He checked his watch. It should still be okay to meet Charlie on time. An older man appeared further up the line and placed shopping in his boot. Relieved, Vinny watched him get into his car and waited for him to reverse out so he could get into the spot. This was the worst part for Vinny. What do people do when they get in their car? Put your key in the ignition, seat belt on, start the car, reverse. Thirty seconds max. For Vinny, between five and ten.

Before the Storm

Okay, any second now. Come on. Vinny checked his rearview mirror and saw the guy in the BMW. He was calm, which was good because he was younger, bigger, and looked like he could handle himself in a scrape. He had a shaved head, square jaw, and the defined features of someone who worked out. In front of him at last, the reverse lights went on, still a twenty-second delay. Someone further up the parking lane had returned and left already. There was a space waiting. He thought of passing this guy, but no doubt, he would reverse right into Vinny if he tried now. Vinny waited. Okay, here he goes.

Vinny followed him, passing the newly vacated space. He checked his mirror to nod to the BMW guy, but he was looking away. Vinny moved forward until he could swing into the gap. As he locked his car, he saw the BMW go into the first space. He walked along the pavement towards the pharmacy. Since he would pass the BMW, he intended to give a neighbourly nod. He noticed the driver didn't make any move to get out. Probably picking someone up, he thought.

On his way back to his car, having bought Helen's toiletries, he noticed the vehicle and driver were still there. When he reversed to leave his space, he felt a chill as the BMW also reversed. Okay, maybe he pulled in to use his phone, or whoever he was waiting for wasn't coming now. Whatever.

Vinny pulled back out onto the busy Allerton Road. He headed south towards Mather Avenue and Springwood School. Buses, lorries, traffic lights, and the black BMW filled his thoughts. Inside lane, outside lane, the black BMW was still there. Okay, now there's no way he is also picking a kid up from Springwood, but if he is, I will see the kid, so all's good — one way or the other. Turning off Mather Avenue, the BMW followed. Vinny took the next exit towards the school entrance, but couldn't see if the vehicle was still behind. He parked halfway on the pavement and walked towards the school gate. The BMW was nowhere in sight. Helen usually dealt with Charlie's school pick-ups and drop-offs, so Vinny didn't know the other parents. Uninterested in faux-socialising or networking; he wasn't keen on small talk. He waited for Charlie outside, then they could go back in together.

The kids filed out. He peered over others, looking for Charlie, who waved when spotted.

'I thought Mum was coming?'

'No, not today. My turn.'

'But you never come.'

'I know, but I'm here now. Okay?'

'Yeah, I guess.' Charlie remained unconvinced.

'How about you tell me what's going on before we go in there? Come on over here.' Vinny led the way to a small wall and sat down. Charlie sat next to him.

'So,' Vinny said.

Charlie's school bag was at his feet, his legs swinging, kicking it softly. 'I don't know. I guess I'm not doing so well.'

'What's wrong? Don't you like it here?'

'It's okay, I guess.' Boys streamed past on their way out of the school gates. The sound of excited voices and high spirits contrasted with Charlie, head down, shoulders hunched, kicking the bag repetitively.

'I've got to go in and see Mrs…'

'Kane,' Charlie said.

'Yeah, Mrs. Kane. What's she going to tell me? I would rather hear it from you before I get in there.'

'I don't know. Maybe that my marks are not so good.'

'Come on, then. If that's all it is, then it's not the end of the world.' Vinny ruffled Charlie's hair.

Charlie smiled, picked up his bag, and swung it over his shoulder.

'Puma, they've been around for years,' Vinny said.

'Yeah, it's retro, from the olden times.'

'Come on, get in there.' Vinny playfully pushed Charlie in

front to lead the way.

Against the stream, they made their way into the school while everyone else was leaving. They entered through a set of glazed double doors that was a separate entrance for teachers. Once inside, the atmosphere of order and regulation was striking. A glass cabinet contained cups and medals won by former students. Another had a series of certificates. The polished floors and long corridor amplified sound.

'Here.' Charlie knocked on the first of two doors on the right.

Vinny read the plate on the door: "Secretary." There were two chairs against the wall between the doors. Charlie put his head briefly inside. 'For Mrs. Kane.'

'We've got to sit and wait,' Charlie said, pointing.

Vinny took the chair next to Charlie. He felt as if he were the one waiting for punishment. They sat in silence.

After a few minutes, the door opened. 'Apologies, Professor Connolly, administration in the burden of educators these days. But you would know all about that. Come in, please.' Mrs Kane waved them into the room.

'I was expecting Mrs. Connolly, but please sit down. I am honoured. History, isn't it? At the University?'

'Yes,' Vinny replied.

Mrs. Kane was around his age, a tall, slim woman in a tight black skirt and flowery blouse. The bonhomie and welcome felt odd, overdone. 'Well, it's good to meet you at last. I'm sure they keep you busy up there. *Booming*, I believe, Liverpool University, it's what I hear.' The words were a constant stream, hardly allowing interruption or comment.

'Now, Charles.'

Vinny had to do a double-take to realise she was talking about Charlie.

'Charles… so much potential. No wonder, of course, he could progress, and no doubt emulate you in his academic success, but at the moment, that's not exactly the picture, is it, Charles?'

she didn't wait for an answer. 'Here at Springwood, I would rather be proactive, not wait until a problem occurs. No, that would be too late. If we are having this discussion after Charlie has not performed as well as expected at GCSEs, then we would indeed be in trouble. It wouldn't just be Charlie and his burgeoning academic career, but the school would also suffer. I'm sure I don't need to remind you that league tables are everything these days. So you see, that for all our interests, we need Charles here to pick up the baton, the academic and intellectual baton, as it were, so ably passed over from yourself.'

She stopped. The sudden silence was surprising. He got the general message that she wanted Charlie to work harder. 'Yes, of course—'

'Charles is a bright boy, clearly capable if he applies himself. Application is required now. These next two years, he'll be preparing for his GCSEs. There is no room for inertia or even worse, lethargy. No, what is required is at the risk of repeating myself, application. I know you understand that, professor. Application is the basis of all achievement. Don't you agree?' Vinny shook his head as they walked to the car. 'What the hell was that?'

'That was Mrs. Kane.' Charlie smiled.

'Okay, look. You're not stupid, you know the score: to get anywhere, do anything, you're going to need your exams for whatever you want to do after school. The starting point is getting good grades.'

'You didn't get GCSE's or A Levels,' Charlie said.

Vinny stopped. 'That's different. I had to do a lot of catching up, begging, and pleading to get into Uni. It would have been a lot easier if I'd studied at school. Believe me. If I could go back, I'd do things differently.'

'You would study?' Charlie wasn't convinced.

'Yeah, I would, but not for the teachers, or the headteacher, or even the exams. I would do it for myself, so I could say, "here's the challenge, here's the task, and you know what? I can do it. I can learn it." To prove I could. I kinda always knew I was clever, but never proved it. If you take control, the exams will follow. Don't do it for the teachers, or for me and your mum: do it because you can. Then, whatever else comes after, you will be in a stronger position because you know you can handle things. You don't back down or run away, you face challenges.'

'Nice speech,' Charlie said. 'Was that for me or you?'

'You know what? You're not stupid, are you?' he smiled and shook his head. 'Get moving.'

Vinny's eyes scanned the cars in the street. The rush was over, so it was pretty clear.

'Come on, then.'

'Can I go up front?'

'Yeah. Come on, get in there.' Vinny moved Helen's bag into the back. 'Strap yourself in.'

They were back on Mather Avenue, heading up towards Allerton Road, when he saw it again. Was that it? Was it the same car? It went out of view behind a bus.

'Why didn't Mum come for me?'

'Oh, something happened with her car.'

'What happened?'

'Your mum is fine, but she had a crash.' The words echoed inside his head.

The black BMW emerged behind him in the outside lane. It had overtaken the bus. He must know I can see him? He wouldn't be so stupid. Shit, I didn't get his registration.

The BMW increased its speed. A blue car was parallel with Vinny, and he hoped it would stay there, but it didn't — it moved ahead. They weren't far from home. Surely, they could make it. He started feeling hot.

'Is something wrong?' Charlie asked.

'No, it's fine,' he lied.

The BMW was beside him on the right. Shit.

He couldn't see the driver. The SUV was too high. He braked to slow down, let him get ahead. But the BMW matched his pace. They remained side by side. Shit. What the hell?

He put his foot down and increased speed. His turn was coming up. Come on, 50 yards more.

The BMW increased speed rapidly and swerved in front of Vinny.

'Bastard!' Vinny shouted.

Charlie jerked forward.

'Sorry,' Vinny apologised.

'Who? Dad, who are you shouting at?'

'No one, mate, it's okay.'

The BMW was directly ahead. He prepared himself for sudden stops. Vinny's foot hovered over the brake. You're not getting me like that.

'At last, we're here.' Vinny indicated, slowed, and turned right. The BMW continued ahead. After pulling round the corner and into his normal parking space, Vinny checked the rearview mirror. Jesus, what the hell was that?

'Come on, mate, let's get you inside.' Vinny led Charlie into the house. 'We're home,' he shouted to announce their presence before he remembered no one was there. 'You run up and get changed, mate.'

Vinny went through to the living room. Macca was following him, threatening him. What the hell's going on?

Charlie came bounding back in, wearing tracksuit bottoms and a T-shirt.

'You can put something in the microwave. I've got to go back to the hospital to see your mum.'

'Can't I come?'

'No, she'll be out soon. They won't keep her in that long.'

'That's not fair. Why can't I see her?'

'It's not a show. She's injured.'

'I know, that's why I want to see her, see how she is.'

'She's all bandaged up and I have to talk to her.'

'I'm not a kid dad.'

'Yeah right.'

'I'll call her.' Charlie pulled out his phone.

'No, don't do that. Go on then, get your coat.'

They were directed from the main reception up to the fourth floor. Helen had moved onto a ward.

'Are you ok?' Vinny asked.

'Yeah, bit weird seeing all these sick people.'

Vinny rolled his eyes.

'Should we wake her?' Charlie asked.

A passing nurse stopped. 'No, I'm sorry guys, you should let her sleep. She's been sedated.'

'Why?' asked Vinny.

'Hold on.' The nurse retreated to an office near the ward entrance. Vinny unpacked Helen's things. They had picked up some flowers from a garage and Charlie arranged them on the bedside cabinet.

'Is she ok?' Charlie spoke softly as he tucked the blankets in around his mother. The white bandage around her head and the bruising on her face had shocked him.

The nurse returned. 'She was in pain from the bruising to her ribs, so the doctor decided she would benefit from some rest.' The nurse spoke to Charlie. 'Don't worry, your mum will be fine. Did you buy the flowers?'

Charlie nodded. 'I'll tell your mum when she wakes. It's probably best if you let her rest now. With a bit of luck, she might be ready to go home tomorrow.'

'Sure thing.' Vinny nodded. 'Come on, mate.'

She might be ready to come home tomorrow, but would she be ready for what was waiting for her? Sammo dead, Anne back in town and the black car still on the road.

Chapter Thirteen

Vinny

11.30am, Friday, June 3rd, 1981

The kid was scrambling back up the slope. Sammo stepped out and started moving towards him.

'Sammo,' Macca shouted. 'Wait. What are you doing?'

Sammo didn't wait. Vinny watched, impressed by Sammo's independence, as he ran to the top of the slope.

Macca waited, then frowned. 'Fuck it. Come on.'

He and Vinny followed Sammo.

Sammo reached the top of the slope and started collecting the kid's books. He picked up his bag and put the stuff back in. When the kid was near the top of the slope, Sammo reached down to give him a hand. Vinny and Macca joined them.

Macca spoke first. 'Why did the bizzies throw you out here?'

'I don't know.' The kid was around their age. He had a brown freckled face and a short, loose afro. His clothes and shoes muddied from sliding down the slope.

'Bastards,' Sammo said, then asked, 'Where did they pick you up?'

'On my way to school. I was going in late, and they pulled up next to me. Then they searched my bag, and when they didn't find anything, told me to get in the car.'

'What did they say in the car?' asked Sammo.

'Nothing, they were just calling me darkie, laughing, and saying I would have a long walk home.'

'Bastards,' Sammo repeated before asking, 'What's your name?'

'Jaime,' the boy said. He accepted his bag from Sammo and checked the contents.

'Where are you from?' Vinny asked.

'Liverpool 8.' He looked around. 'Where am I now?'

'Speke,' said Vinny.

'Oh, fuck. I've never been to Speke.'

'Well, you have now,' said Macca, pointing up the lane. 'You'd better get going.'

'Have you got any money for the bus?' Sammo asked.

'No. I'm skint,' said Jaime.

'No dinner money?' Sammo asked.

'On free dinners,' Jaime said.

'Snap,' Vinny and Sammo both said.

The three boys smiled. Sammo reached into his pocket and brought out a Marathon bar.

'Here, are you hungry?'

'Thanks.' Jaime reached out for it.

'You'd better get going then,' Macca repeated. 'You go back up Dungeon Lane, you'll get to the estate, and you can find a bus stop there.'

'He doesn't know his way,' said Sammo.

Vinny could see the standoff brewing.

'Not our problem. We have a mission to complete,' Macca replied.

Jaime shrugged.

'He can come with us,' Sammo said. 'When we get to Garston, we can show him the bus stop.'

'He's not with us. He's not even white. He's a you know...' said Vinny. His face flushed as the word came out. He drew circles in the dirt with his foot. His attempt at getting in with Macca left a sour taste.

'He can be in our group if we want him to. Do you want to

join us?' Sammo asked.

'I don't know. I don't fancy walking through Speke,' said Jaime.

'I don't blame you,' said Vinny, trying to undo the word he used.

'Hey what's your problem?' Jaime chided, looking directly at Vinny.

'I didn't mean anything. It's just a word, isn't it?' said Vinny, aware of how stupid he sounded.

'Well, you're not English. We can see that,' Macca said. Vinny knew Macca was taking his side, but he didn't want him to.

'Of course he's English. He's from Toxteth,' Sammo said.

'My dad's from Gambia, and my mum's Chinese, and I was born in the women's hospital on Myrtle Street,' Jaime said.

'Wow, that's fucking amazing,' said Sammo.

'Being born in Myrtle Street?' Macca asked.

'No, China, and the other place.'

'Gambia,' said Jaime.

'It's not so special — all your family was from Ireland.' Macca gave Sammo a push.

'Well, China's a bit further than Ireland,' said Sammo.

'My dad's a sailor,' Jaime said.

'Well, sailor boy. You'd better get on your way.' Macca turned to signal the discussion was over.

'I vote he comes with us.' Sammo looked at Vinny.

'Yeah, me, too.' Vinny half-smiled at Jaime.

Macca turned back. 'This is not for voting. I'm the leader here, and I say he's not coming with us.'

'Right then, I'm going to show him.' Sammo walked towards the lane.

'Come on, Jaime. I'll show you the way to go.'

Jaime moved after Sammo.

'Stop, you can't go. You've got the treasure.'

'I'm going.' Sammo turned.

Macca rushed forward and grabbed the back of Sammo's shirt. He spun him round. 'Don't make me do it.' Macca formed a fist.

Vinny and Jaime stood back. Vinny didn't want Sammo to get hit. Sammo pulled his head away and tried to get free. Macca punched him hard in the upper arm.

'Ouch, fuck. That hurt,' he complained.

'I meant it to, now, do as you're told.' Macca pushed him in the direction away from the lane. 'Get going.'

'What treasure?' Jaime asked.

Sammo, head down and sulking, suddenly perked up.

'This.' He reached into his pocket and pulled out the watch.

'You bastard.' Macca launched himself at Sammo, who dodged to the side.

Although scared, Vinny moved forward to get between them, his palms raised. 'Let's all calm down, eh?'

Macca reached around Vinny.

'Yeah, why don't you back off,' Jaime said, supporting his new friend Sammo.

Jamie moved forward. He and Vinny were now between Macca and Sammo.

'Yeah, back off,' said Sammo, holding the watch high.

Macca was outnumbered and took a step back. He held his hands up. 'Okay, Jaime can come. He's seen the treasure now, anyway, hasn't he?'

'Really?' Sammo asked.

'Yeah, you can come if you want.' Macca directed this at Jaime.

'And when we get money for it, we'll give him the bus fare, right?' Sammo looked at Macca expectantly.

Macca made a show of thinking about it. 'Yeah, that's okay. Fuck them bizzies, eh?'

'Might as well,' said Jaime.

Everyone except Macca grinned.

'Come on then, let's get going.' Macca tried to show he was back in control and led them off along the path.

They followed the top of the embankment. The Mersey was tidal, and it was coming in. The river had retreated to a silver stream in the centre of the mudflats, but now the water was rushing back in from the Irish Sea.

'We should go down to the triangles,' said Sammo.

At the bottom of the hill, broken concrete slabs and large concrete pyramidal structures covered the shore.

'They are pyramids,' Vinny said.

'What? Like Egypt?' asked Sammo.

'No, just the shape. They look like dragon's teeth, like an amazing fight took place in the sky between good and evil. This is where the Welsh dragon lost its teeth,' said Vinny.

'Wow, is that true?' asked Sammo, who then clarified, 'I mean, I know it's not true, but is it a legend?'

'No, of course it's not. We're staying up here. What are they really for?' Macca asked.

'Something to do with the war, to stop tanks,' Vinny said.

'Tanks coming up the river? That's stupid,' said Macca.

'Well, maybe they come up on boats, then got off here?' Sammo suggested.

Macca ignored him and carried on the path. The shoreline ran to Garston Docks, a walk of about three miles. To their left was the wide-open river basin with the Stanlow oil refinery visible on the opposite shore.

They walked in single file. Macca was in front. Next came Vinny, Sammo, and Jaime. The sun was warm, and the wind was blowing lightly off the river. Seagulls screamed and squawked overhead. The air was fresh and foul in turn with the scents of the river, the direction of the wind, and fumes from the planes at the airport.

'We should have a marching song like the marines,' Vinny said.

'You make one up then,' Macca said.

A few seconds later, Vinny said, 'I got it. Are you ready?'

'Yeah, come on, everyone, march in time.'

'Left, right, left,' Vinny called. 'Left, right, left.'

The boys fell into the rhythm.

'I just know what I've been told.' He broke from the rhythmic chant. 'You have to say it back. I call it out. You say it back,' said Vinny.

'I just know what I've been told.'

Jamie, Macca, and Sammo shouted out in harmony. 'I just know what I've been told.'

'We're gonna sell this watch of gold,' sang Vinny.

'We're gonna sell this watch of gold.' The boys' voices carried over the river.

'Left, right, left.'

'Left, right, left,' they answered.

'I just know what I've been told.'

'I just know what I've been told,' they answered.

'We're gonna sell this watch of gold.'

'We're gonna sell this watch of gold.'

'Left, right, left.'

'Left, right, left.'

'On our way to Garston, sell the watch and have some fun.'

'On our way to Garston, sell the watch and have some fun.'

'Okay, enough,' Macca said. 'This is stupid.' Everyone fell out of step. 'Who wants to be in the fucking army, anyway?'

'Whoa, look.' Sammo pointed.

A plane was coming in to land. They followed its progress through the sky, gently turning through the clouds, swooping down over the river, growing in size and sound as it neared. The roar of the engines flooded over them like a wave as the plane bounced along the runway and touched down. They all stood, hands gripping the chain-link fence as they marvelled at the power and beauty. The smell of jet fuel wafted over them a second later.

'Wow, not the army, but maybe the air force, though,' said Macca.

'How far is it to Garston?' Jaime asked.

'Not far. About half an hour,' Sammo replied.

The plane turned off the end of the runway and taxied towards the terminal and control tower.

'Does this go all the way to the Pier Head?' Jaime asked.

'Yeah, but the docks at Garston are in the way, so you can't go by the river there,' said Vinny.

'That's a shame. I could get all the way home.'

'It would take you forever, though,' said Sammo.

'Yeah, true.'

'What's all this about the treasure and the watch, then?'

Vinny turned round and replied, 'We can't tell you. We swore.'

'Not about telling we didn't,' said Sammo.

'Doesn't matter. We're not telling anyone anything, right?' Macca insisted. 'Sammo, come here,' he continued.

Sammo edged past Vinny on the narrow path.

'Give me the treasure.' Macca held his hand out.

'Why?'

'I don't have to tell you why, because I'm the leader. I decide. Give it to me.'

Sammo looked at Vinny, who shrugged. Sammo slowly reached into his pocket, pulling out the links first and then the round, shining watch. Macca snatched it off his hand. The chain caught on Sammo's finger and snapped.

'Oww.' Sammo shook his hand.

'Look what you've done, you arsehole.' Macca pushed Sammo. He lost his footing and fell down the embankment towards the river.

'Fucking idiot.'

Macca held up the two ends of the chain for inspection.

'It doesn't matter. They can fix that easy,' Vinny said as he watched Sammo clamber back up.

'Yeah, he's right.' Jaime moved over the edge of the embankment and offered his hand to Sammo.

'Well, here, it's your turn.' Macca gave the watch to Vinny. He accepted the watch and his new position with some satisfaction.

Vinny held it up to his face, looking at his distorted reflection in the smooth gold. He went to the front and took the lead. 'Come on, we need to get moving, or it will take us all day.'

They set off at a steady pace, Vinny first with Macca behind him, then Jaime with Sammo making up the rear. 'We need to stick together more. You know, all for one and one for all,' Vinny said.

'That's for fairy tales and stories. It doesn't happen in real life,' said Macca.

'It can if we make it,' Sammo shouted from the rear.

'We're not all together, though, are we?' Macca said.

'Why not?' asked Vinny.

'Don't be stupid. We've got him with us… Jaime.'

'I don't care what you do. I'm not interested in your stupid games. I just want to get home.'

Macca turned to face Jaime. 'It's not stupid.'

Jaime wasn't intimidated. 'Talking about "treasure?" You sound like a bunch of kids playing at pirates.'

'No, it's not like that,' Macca insisted.

'So, you robbed a watch, big deal. Hardly crime of the century.'

'Yeah, but someone died,' Sammo added.

'Fucker. Why did you tell him that?' Macca glared.

'You killed someone?' Jaime asked.

'No, no, someone just died,' Vinny said.

'How?' Jaime looked shocked.

'I don't know — natural causes, got too old, heart attack, cancer, what the fuck do I know?' Macca snapped.

'But you were there, right?' Jaime said.

'Macca was.' Vinny shrugged.

'Hey, what happened to all for one?' said Macca.

'He's just telling the truth,' said Sammo, who took his opportunity for revenge.

'That could be manslaughter. That's when you don't want to kill him, but he dies anyway. If they wanna get you for it, they will. They can do anything they like,' said Jaime.

'No, they can't,' Vinny objected. 'It doesn't work like that.'

'Yeah, it does. When they came for my grandad, there was nothing anyone could do.'

'What do you mean, came for him?' asked Sammo.

'One day, he was here, next day gone. That's what my mum told us. She knew him when she was younger, but doesn't remember much. Always tells us, "be careful of the police. They can do what they want."'

'Did he do something?' Vinny asked.

'No, he was a sailor. A Chinese sailor. He came over during the war. A lot of them did. Worked on the boats 'cos all the English men were off fighting and that. Not just him. There were loads, hundreds of Chinese sailors.'

'Let's have rest,' Vinny announced.

He moved off the track to the grassy area near the airport fence.

'Who made you the boss?' Macca asked.

'This did,' said Vinny, holding out the watch.

Macca slumped to the ground. 'Whatever.'

They sat, backs against the chain-link fence, looking across to Ellesmere Port.

'Did your ma see him again?' Sammo asked.

'Nah, right after the war, it was. The police come and took some men from houses, put them on a ship. But me mam said her dad just disappeared, went off to do a job, never came back.'

'He probably just left, ran off with a tart,' said Macca. 'Like Vinny's dad.'

Vinny flushed, he realised no one believed his story about his dad dying in the war. A wave of shame washed over him. He dug his fingers into the earth. *Fuck Macca, what a twat.*

'Nah, they were Shanghaied,' said Jaime.

'What's that?' asked Sammo.

'Kidnapped.'

'Who's talking about pirate shit now?' said Macca.

'It's not shit. It's real. You can see the photo at me mam's. A Chinese sailor and a baby, the baby's me mam. It's got a date on it. Me mam and me Nan go down the pier head every year on that day to throw a flower, a rose or something in the river.'

'What for?'

'To remember him, I guess. He came from the river, and when they took him, he went out through the river.'

'Fuck, that's not right,' said Vinny in a show of support for Jaime.

'That's shit,' Sammo agreed.

'Yeah, well, it shows if they want to do something, they can,' Jaime said.

'Like they threw you out in Speke. What was that for?' asked Sammo.

'Cos they can. They have the power.' Jaime pulled a blade of grass and split it. He blew air through it to make a whistling sound.

'Well, fuck 'em. We have power, too.'

'What?'

Macca picked up a stone and threw it towards the river. 'Power to fuck em up, get into their posh houses and steal their shit.'

'But you didn't, though. You robbed someone in Speke,' Vinny said.

'Not this time, I know, but I want to. That's what I'll do — like a cat burglar — diamonds and shit. Like the Pink Panther.'

'The Pink Panther was the cop. Clouseau,' Vinny said. 'No, Pink Panther was the jewel thief.'

'You could be a black panther,' Macca said to Jaime.

'Yeah, that's cool by me,' said Jaime.

Sammo said, 'I'd be—'

Macca didn't let him finish. 'You'd be a raggedy arse stray cat.'

'And you? A Pink…' Sammo put on an effeminate voice. 'A Pink Panther?'

'What's in Garston? Why are you guys going there?' Jaime interrupted.

'We gonna sell the treasure. Come, let's get moving,' Vinny said. He didn't want Macca to kick off on Sammo again.

Vinny led the way, and they walked in a single file. The

embankment had eroded, and the grassy path they were walking on had crumbled away. They went down to the river's edge. The ground became sandier with dried silt and mud from the riverbed. They walked on in silence.

'Eww. Look at that,' Vinny pointed, as the head of the group he spotted the carcass first. Bulging eyes and bared teeth in the distorted face produced a hideous effect. Half buried in the mud, a cow's shoulders, head, and neck were exposed to the sunlight. The rest of the body was half submerged. It lay in a shallow channel of water, one of many that were rapidly filling as the tidal waters lapped against its body. It would soon disappear again as the river filled, and what was left of marine life devoured the creature. Sammo picked up a stone and threw it at the head. He missed. The water splashed. Macca tried next and scored a direct hit.

'Bullseye,' he shouted, arms raised. They took turns using the cow as target practice. The smell thrown up by the disturbed water began to reach them.

'Eww, who was that?' Vinny asked, putting a hand over his nose.

'That's the cow. It stinks.'

'Wonder how it got in there?' Jaime asked.

'Probably went for a swim and got tired,' said Macca.

'Really?' asked Sammo.

'No, it must've fallen in somewhere up near Widnes when the tide was high and got washed down here,' said Vinny through his hand.

'It's disgusting,' said Jaime.

'That cow was as happy as Larry a few days ago, walking round, eating grass, mooing to his mates,' said Sammo. 'Look at the poor bastard now. Just goes to show.'

'Show what?' asked Vinny.

'Show that we all end up as stinking mush,' said Macca.

'Or that things change quicker than we think,' suggested Vinny.

'No wonder you went to grammar school,' said Macca.

Before the Storm

Vinny picked up a stone and threw it. It hit one of the cow's eyes, which exploded on contact, producing a small spray of blood and eyeball.

'Now that's a bullseye,' said Sammo to cheers and laughter.

Jaime led the line next and noticed something up ahead. 'What's that?' he rushed forward.

He stopped, and the others joined him. 'Look up there.'

A short distance away, the sun glistened off something on the shoreline. The path they were on turned to the right, away from the river and into Garston. This was the furthest they could go. Ahead, they could see the cranes of Garston Docks. A little way out into the water was a rusting hull, neither ship nor wreck, but a partially destroyed carcass being eaten away by men from the breaker's yard.

'That must be the glass bottle shore. I've heard of it but never seen it,' said Vinny.

'It looks cool. Look at the colours,' said Sammo.

The shoreline from water's edge up to the wall of the bottle works was composed of green, brown, blue, and even some orange pieces of glass. They weren't spread out on it or covered it, but for a stretch of fifty yards, they were the shoreline.

'Can we get to it?'

'Yeah, come on.'

They had to leave the path that swung round to the right. At the water's edge, the incoming tide was pushing the river in, rising from the shoreline. They picked their way across the broken ground. The shore was a couple of inches deep in glass fragments and pieces of all shapes and sizes. Erosion from the tide and constant friction meant the sharp edges had largely disappeared, in some places leaving smooth coloured pebbles of glass. Sunlight created a sparkling water's edge, lapping at the tide.

'This is crazy.' Sammo filled his hands with the glass and threw them into the air in a shower of colour.

'Like jewels,' said Jaime, inspecting the pieces, rejecting some and putting others in his pocket.

'What are you doing?' asked Vinny.

'These are smart. I'm gonna give some to me mam. She won't believe where they come from.'

'Okay, guys, come on. We've got real treasure to sort out, remember?'

Macca led the way off the shore and back on the path to Garston. Vinny turned to look back at the almost magical scene behind him. Leaving it, he knew something had snapped between him and Macca. He wasn't just leaving the shore; he was leaving friendship and youth with it.

Chapter Fourteen

Vinny

10am, Saturday, June 25th, 2016

'Are you okay?' Vinny held the door as Helen eased herself into the seat.

'It hurts, but yeah, all good.' She moved slowly to fasten her seat belt.

Vinny moved to the driver's side and waited before turning the ignition. 'Did they give you anything for the pain?'

'Enough for now, but I need you to fill a prescription.'

'Yeah, sure.' He started the car and eased out of the parking bay. He crawled through the car park until he reached the barrier.

'So, are you going to tell me?' she asked.

'Tell you what?'

'Something's going on. I can feel it. You've hardly said a word since coming to collect me.'

'I wanted to wait till we got home, got you comfortable.'

'Was it the school? What has he been up to?'

'No, that was fine. He's doing OK, needs to work harder, but who doesn't?'

He looked across at her. The barrier rose, and he moved out into traffic.

'So?'

'Can't we wait?'

'No, if there's something going on, I want to know what it is.'

'Apart from you getting messages from Macca?' he looked across at her.

'Really? You're gonna go there?'

'I just didn't know what to think.' Vinny paused as he manoeuvred the car through traffic.

'Anyway, I saw him yesterday.'

'Saw who?'

'Macca.'

'Where?' Surprise filled her voice.

'Sammo's.'

She rolled her eyes at him. 'What were you doing there?'

'I went to warn him off, but I think some local lads let Macca know because, within minutes, he was there. But first… there's no easy way to say this… I've got some bad news. We can wait till you get home?' his head moved to keep eye contact as he delivered the news and watched the traffic.

'What do you mean..? Sammo? You went round… What about him? Is he all right? He's not using again, is he?'

'It's worse.' He paused. The weight of the silence briefly matched the dread. 'I'm just going to say it straight…' He turned to face her for a second. 'He died.'

'What?' her hand went to her face, and she winced at the physical pain. 'Aww shit, what happened?'

'I saw the police at his house. It looks like an overdose. That's what the Detective Constable said. I've got his card somewhere.'

'That's awful. Overdosed?'

'Well, maybe he had a bad day.'

Helen's voice was sharp. 'Had a bad day? He's dead. You are a cold bastard sometimes, aren't you?'

'No. I didn't mean it like that.' He tried to explain. Frustrated that things weren't coming out in the way he meant. 'Yeah, it's shit, but what do you want me to do?'

Helen was quiet. Vinny drove on in silence. He looked

sideways at Helen every minute or so. She was staring out of the window. He reached across with his left hand and placed it on top of hers. She responded warmly, turning her hand over to squeeze his.

A tear slid down her cheek, followed by a slow trail. She didn't move or say anything. Vinny had to let go of her hand to change gears. His eyes darted from the traffic to Helen. 'I'm sorry, love.'

She turned to look at him. He could sense the pain she felt, emotional and physical, as she raised her hand to stroke his hair. Her arm dropped heavily, and she let out a slight grunt of pain.

'Let's get you home, eh?' Vinny patted her knee.

'What's happening with Charlie?'

'Nothing, he's at school. He's fine.'

* * *

Vinny brought her coffee and placed it on the table next to the arm of the sofa. He set up her laptop on a small table in front of her. He sat down heavily, nursing his tea.

Helen leaned across for her coffee, raising it to her lips and taking a sip. 'This is good.'

'Look, I have to tell you something else as well.'

Helen shook her head. 'Go on then. What have you done?'

'Nothing, well, I phoned Anne. She's back in Liverpool.'

'Your ex, Anne?'

'Yeah, you were in hospital. I didn't know when you were coming out. It felt like things were getting out of control.'

'And…?'

'Nothing really, we met and had a coffee. Well she did, I had tea.'

'I don't care what you drank. Did anything happen?'

'No, of course not. She said she would help. She is a journalist. Knows stuff.'

'Unlike me, you mean.'

Before the Storm

Vinny's phone buzzed. He swiped the screen. 'She's on her way.'

'Now? Look at the state of me.'

'It was her idea. She wanted to see you as soon as you came out, everything up front.'

'You could have warned me.' Helen scanned the room. 'At least tidy up. The place looks a mess.'

'She's not doing an article for House and Home.'

'I hope she won't be writing anything about us.'

By the time the doorbell rang, Vinny had tidied the room. 'Hey, come in.' He led Anne into the living room. Helen sat up straight. 'Excuse me for not getting up.'

'No, of course. How are you?'

'Please sit down.' Vinny indicated a chair.

'Battered and bruised, as you can see, but still here.'

'A fighter,' said Anne.

'I'm not so sure about that.' Helen changed the subject. 'So we finally get to meet. I've heard so much about you.'

'Me too. All he ever talked about were you and Charlie.'

Helen smiled. 'I don't believe that for a minute.'

'Can I get you anything?' Asked Vinny

Anne sat in the armchair. 'No, I'm fine.'

Helen looked directly at Anne. 'Can I ask something?'

'Of course.' She answered.

Helen continued. 'You're not here for a story? I mean, this situation.'

'No, of course not,' Vinny asked for help. He thinks something is wrong. 'What do you think?'

'I don't know, honestly. You know how you question yourself, but there was something about that car before I crashed.'

'The black BMW Mark 5.'

Helen raised her eyebrows. 'I don't know what make it was.'

'Vinny told me where the crash was. You were on your way home from the school run. So I went this morning. Turns out the crossing patrol guy saw everything. He didn't get the car registration, but he did say,' Helen pulled out her notebook. 'The BMW went straight at the Suzuki, the lady swerved, that's when she hit the kerb, lost control and hit the lamp post. I called the ambulance.'

Helen lifted her coffee. 'Wow. I'm impressed.'

Anne closed her notebook. 'Don't be, it's just the basics.'

'I told you I would never have worked out what happened to my dad without Anne,' said Vinny.

'Vinny told me all about Ireland. You know my grandfather was from Wicklow too?'

'No, I didn't know that. What was his name?'

'Doyle, his brother, died in the war over there.'

Anne looked sideways at Vinny. 'Didn't we hear about a Doyle that moved to Liverpool?'

Vinny dismissed her. 'No, you're thinking of someone else.'

'Oh, right?' Anne looked confused. She paused before speaking to Helen. 'Look, I understand if you're not comfortable having me around.'

'No, it's fine. Seems like it's time for exes to come out of the woodwork.'

'You mean Macca?' asked Anne.

'Yeah, although we were kids, really. It wasn't a proper relationship.'

'What was going on with Sammo?' Anne asked.

'I saw his daughter Claire in town. She asked me to speak to Vinny. I knew it would be no use. Vinny hasn't had a good word to say about them in years. So I checked on Sammo myself. I'm not sure what I was going to do or what I expected. But I couldn't ignore her.'

'And how was it?'

Helen put her drink down. 'He was in a bit of a state, to be honest. Still in the same house. It's a bit bare now. His mam and dad have gone, so he's there on his own. I think that place has made all the difference, a bit of stability in a chaotic world.

But the big thing is, he said he was clean. No drugs.'

'Are you sure?' Vinny remembered the coffee table strewn with drug equipment.

'I've seen enough people damaged by drugs to know when someone is using. He said he was clean, and I believed him. He was tired; you know the guy's been through a lot. But there was a bit of sparkle. Sammo was always a bit of a chancer, you know, having a laugh, pushing his luck. There was still a bit of that spark there. He talked about doing something for his daughter's birthday one minute, the next he was hyper and paranoid.'

'What kind of paranoid?'

'You know, people were after him. He was being followed. His house was being watched.'

'Why would anyone be watching him?' asked Vinny.

'Did you ask?' Anne had her notebook open again.

'He was up and down, MI5 Military Intelligence, you name it.'

'Well, something happened,' said Vinny.

'An overdose?' Anne asked.

'That's what the police said.'

'Is that an official cause of death?' Anne moved her fingers in air quotes.

'I don't know. You mean a Coroner and death certificate?' asked Helen.

'Yeah. These things have to be done properly.'

'I guess they're doing all that.'

'I could check on that if you want me to?'

'You said you had his card, the DC's?'

Vinny stood and began going through his pockets. 'Yeah, here it is.'

'I'll keep this.' She slid the card into her bag. 'If that's okay?'

'Yeah, sure. I've put it in my phone, anyway.'

'I should call his daughter Claire,' said Helen.

'Have you got experience with this kind of thing? Addiction, overdose?' Vinny looked for words of wisdom or advice from

Anne.

'Not yet, but my job is to find out, so leave it with me. The chance is that it will turn out to be what it looks like, an accidental overdose.'

Helen looked directly at Anne. 'I don't know what he's told you, but something happened when they were kids. They were all mates together, then suddenly, nothing. Vinny never saw them, talked about them, like they didn't exist anymore.' Helen was talking about Vinny, not to him.

'It was a long time ago. It doesn't matter now.' Vinny tried to steer the conversation. 'I'm sorry Sammo is dead. I don't know what happened. No one deserves to die like that, even if he was a smack head, junkie, or whatever.'

'There you go again, making judgments,' said Helen.

'It's not a judgement. It's a statement of fact. He was an addict. I saw the needles.'

'Actually.' Helen put her cup down. 'He was in recovery.'

'So he had a relapse, misjudged the amount.' Vinny opened his hands wide. He was drawing the conversation to a close.

'Yeah, it's possible, of course, it is, but we shouldn't jump to conclusions before we even start.'

'Needles?' asked Helen. 'More than one?'

'Yeah, two on the table. Maybe he meant it.' Vinny turned toward Helen.

'You mean suicide?' she asked.

'Well, yeah. Regrets and all that. His life wasn't exactly a glowing success.'

'Unlike yours, you mean?' she paused before adding. 'The man who didn't see his own son for four years?'

Her bitterness shocked Vinny. 'That's not fair. I saw him.'

'Barely,' Helen snapped.

Anne sat back in the armchair.

'I know you're upset. But that's not fair. I had all that shit about my family.'

'Yeah, and while you were "finding yourself," I was raising your son.'

'You don't get it, do you?' his frustration erupted. 'It wasn't a choice for me. I was fucked up — I needed to sort myself out — stop myself going crazy.' He leaned back in his seat, hands pressed against his face.

'Perhaps,' Anne spoke quietly, 'We should take a break here?'

Vinny shook his head. 'No, this needs saying. I don't talk about it because I don't want it in my head.' He took a deep breath to calm himself.

Helen remained quiet, staring into the coffee mug.

'I know you liked Sammo. I can't stand the mythologising, turning him into some kind of victim. The guy was a scally who joined the army because he couldn't do anything else. Here's one of the most vivid memories I have of Sammo. Do you want to hear?'

'No, I don't. I don't care. We have all done things we are not proud of,' Helen said.

'Should I go?' Asked Anne. 'Let you two talk things over?'

'No, stay. Vinny invited you,' said Helen.

'Things we're not proud of,' Vinny said. 'Try this… A couple of guys from Wavertree came down to a disco at St. Christopher's, invited by some girl, who knows? The word goes round that Wavertree boys are bigging it up in Speke. Local idiots spread the word and demanding that we help chase them out. I was with Sammo, doing nothing much. I'm crapping myself. What am I supposed to do?'

'Refuse to go?' said Anne.

'Yeah, well, I should have, but I didn't. Anyway, a group of bigger lads caught up with these guys near the lights at the top of Western Avenue. They were trying to get out of Speke, terrified. One runs up a path knocks on the door to ask for help. A woman took one look at what was happening and closed the door in his face. They dragged him down the path and kicked the shit out of him. His head was going back and forward like a ping-pong ball. Bleeding and comatose, seventeen-year-old, splayed out in the street, and then what happens? What happens next?'

Helen shrugged.

'Sammo. Sammo is what happens. He's carrying this long twig or branch that he stripped off a tree, and he sits down next to this kid. Legs crossed like he's doing fucking yoga and starts whipping the kid across his bloody face with this stick. Like nothing in the world, looked as serene as a fucking monk. Slap, slap…'

'What did you do?' Anne asked.

'I got the fuck out of there. Ran home. Locked myself in the toilet.'

Vinny finished his tea. 'It was serious enough to have made radio Merseyside News the next day. Three kids in hospital, two in intensive care, one with stab wounds. So excuse me if I don't get out the violin for Sammo.'

'That sounds horrible. But we're adults now. You can't hold what happened as kids against him. Do you know how many traumatised kids I've seen? We're ankle-deep in them. Parents without jobs, motivation, even the basics to survive these days, money, food. No one cares, that's the bottom line. Every year they cut budgets and close offices. Austerity is killing people, death by a thousand cuts. So, I know all about problems, but there was something else. You, Sammo and Macca, there has always been some strange bond, connection, or I don't know.'

'We knew each other as kids, knocked round together. That's all it was.' Vinny was tired and wanted to close the discussion.

Helen shook her head in exasperation. 'This is me. Vinny. I knew you then, and I know you now. What is it you are running away from?'

Vinny stood. 'Jesus Christ, I'm not running away from anything.' The more he protested, the more things came to the surface. He knew exactly what he was avoiding.

Helen and Anne shared a look. Vinny was hiding something.

'I should go.' Anne stood.

'Thanks for helping.' Vinny said, 'I really appreciate it.'

'You made the call and I'm here, but if I carry on with this, it won't just be for you.'

'What do you mean?' Vinny asked.

'I'm just letting you know, if I carry on, it will be because Helen deserves the truth.'

'Thank you,' Helen raised a hand.

Anne nodded toward Helen and walked to the door.

I'll see you out, Vinny followed her.

Anne pulled her coat together. It was June but a chill wind blew. Vinny followed her toward her car. 'What was that about?'

'The watch and the guy who left Wicklow for Liverpool, you knew him? Or something about him? He was part of the ambush in Ireland.'

'This,' he spread his hands. 'Has got nothing to do with that.'

Anne opened her car door and slipped inside. The door was still open when she said, 'I meant it. Helen deserves the truth.' She closed the door and turned the key to start the engine.

Chapter Fifteen

Vinny

12.30pm, Friday, July 3rd, 1981

'Does anyone know the way?' Macca asked.

'Yeah, I do. My nan lived here.' Vinny led the way as they scrambled up from the shore.

They were at the back of the estate, at the industrial end nearest the river. 'We go through the factories, and we're there.'

They walked up Brunswick Street and took a left at Blackburne Street. The road ran parallel to the river. Industrial buildings crowded both sides. Vinny didn't like it. Unlike the steel shed factories built in the early '60s in Speke, high brick walls and black chimney stacks marked their progress. They looked like figures in a Lowry painting, buildings darkened by the smoke and dirt of decades. After Window Lane, things improved, and the terraced housing ran in lines. At the end of Blackburne Street on the left were the docks. King Street faced the docks at one end and ran straight out through Church Street, under the bridge and into Garston village.

'Are you sure you know where you're going?' Macca asked.

'Yeah,' Vinny answered, but as he got closer to the dock end of Blackburne Street, he realised something was different.

'It should be up here: turn right at the dock gate, and bit further in — that's where me Nan's house was.'

Before the Storm

'Come on lads, nearly there, nearly rich. We'll be loaded. We'll get you on the bus… we might go into town with you,' Macca said to Jaime.

'Yeah,' Sammo added. 'It'll be great. We can go to the pictures. Go to Saint John's market.'

'It should be up here.' Vinny pointed, and his heart sank. 'But this looks new.'

'What do you mean?'

They were standing in front of the dock gates. Facing them was King Street, the parts furthest away were as Vinny remembered old terraced houses on the right. His Nan lived at twenty-six, and on the other side, three pubs: The Cock n Trumpet, the Kings Vaults, and there was another one that was boarded up. All the old houses were closed up, too. Windows and doors covered with sheet metal. What remained of King Street was empty, and they had built new homes in the space nearest the docks.

'Where's the pawnbrokers?' Sammo stood in front of Vinny.

'I don't know. It was all here or used to be here, called Frank Ketts. You used to go down the entry next to me Nan's, but it's all gone.'

'For fuck's sake.' Macca kicked a stone down the road.

'What do we do now?' asked Sammo.

'I need to get the bus home,' Jaime said.

'With no bus fare?' said Macca.

'I can bunk it.'

'Let's go into the village. If we can find a jeweller, they might buy it,' Vinny said.

'I guess we've got no choice,' Macca replied.

Vinny led the way, crossed the road, and started up King Street.

'All this fuckin' way. I can't believe we walked all the way from Speke to Garston.' Macca moaned. 'It's hot, and I'm starving.'

'It's not his fault the place has changed,' Sammo said.

'Yes, it is. He should've known. He's full of shit, that's what he is,' said Macca.

Vinny strode ahead. He heard what Macca said, and he hoped something would turn up in the village. As they moved towards the bridge, traffic increased. Banks Road was the main street through the area.

'Where can I get a bus?' Jaime asked.

'In the village, we're going that way anyway,' said Sammo.

Ahead of them was Saint Michael's church, and to the right of it, the grey gas tanks that dominated the skyline away from the docks.

Vinny led the way under the railway bridge. 'Can you hear that?'

'What is it?' asked Jaime.

At first, it sounded like a train, way off, rumbling. As they emerged from under the bridge, it became clearer. 'Maggie Maggie Maggie, Out. Out. Out.' The chant was rhythmic and insistent, voices loud and clear.

Ahead, they saw a group of marchers coming down Saint Mary's Road. The front of the march had a large banner, a green background with yellow lettering: 'People's March for Jobs.' Behind this banner were around a hundred youths. Then lots of Trade Union banners and placards demanding 'Jobs not Dole.' The entire scene was one of movement, colour, and noise. People with megaphones led the chanting. 'What do we want?' 'Jobs not dole,' was the shouted answer.

The front of the demonstration moved past the boys and continued up past the public wash house and baths. People ran alongside the marchers with collection buckets and sold newspapers.

'There are police everywhere,' Macca said.

'Yeah, but they are not interested in us. They've got this lot to deal with,' Vinny replied.

The police controlled the traffic in front of the march and at the rear. A queue of cars was building up on Saint Mary's Road. In the village, there was enough room to shepherd the cars past the marchers and keep some kind of flow.

'Come on,' Vinny said. 'Let's join in.'

Vinny stepped onto the road and began walking alongside the marchers.

'Fuck,' Macca complained. 'Come on.' He caught up to Vinny. Sammo and Jaime were behind them. 'What are you doing?' Macca asked.

'If we're with the marchers, the cops aren't gonna take any notice of us.'

'Yeah, okay, but what about the treasure?'

'If we see a shop, we can nick off and get it checked out.'

The truck leading the demonstration pulled over opposite the job centre. The marchers stopped, and everyone gathered around the vehicle. A second van came up, parked beside the truck. Within seconds, a trestle table arrived with tea and sandwiches for the marchers.

'Come on, let's get some. I'm starving,' Jaime said.

'They won't let us,' Macca replied.

Jaime approached a woman giving out sandwiches. 'Can I have one?'

'Shouldn't you be at school?' she asked.

'Yeah, but we wanted to march for a bit, so we missed our dinners.'

'Yeah, sure, come on.' She handed Jaime a sandwich. 'Here, bring your mates over.'

As she said this, a voice boomed out over the crowd. 'Welcome, friends and brothers. This is the first day of our long March to London, two hundred and eighty miles to tell Margaret Thatcher that we do not accept mass unemployment as the price for her policies.'

The boys collected a sandwich and tea each and regrouped at the back of the crowd. They sat on the ground, eating and drinking as the speaker's voice droned on.

'We demand an end to this government of spending cuts and unemployment...'

'Our John had to go to Bournemouth to get a job,' said Sammo. 'He comes back between jobs. He's been there ages now.'

'Loads of people are doing it. Maybe these lot will stay down there,' said Macca.

'Wait, look over there.' Vinny pointed to where the speaker was.

'Let me introduce comrade Joe Doyle, coordinator of the Speke Area Trade Union Committee.'

'Look who it is?' Vinny nudged Macca.

'What?'

'Look at the guy on the back of the lorry.'

'Oh, shit,' said Macca.

'Who is it?' Sammo asked.

'It's the guy from this morning whose grandfather you robbed,' said Vinny.

'Good afternoon, comrades and friends. As Chairman of the Garston and Speke Area Trade Union Council, let me welcome the People's March for Jobs on the first day of their long march for justice.' There was general applause. The metallic voice rang out through speakers. 'There are over four million unemployed in Britain today, and we have the most vicious Tory administration in modern times, a government that is determined to destroy effective trade unionism in Britain. Make no mistake, working-class communities all over this country are facing a life and death struggle.'

'We should get out of here before he recognises us,' Vinny said.

'He didn't see us earlier,' Macca said.

'Even so.' They stood and worked their way through the back of the crowd. As they snaked their way through the audience, the speaker's voice followed them. 'The government watches as we turn our anger, our frustration on each other, destroying the very communities we live in.' the speaker paused.

'He doesn't half go on.' Macca pushed Vinny in the back. 'Come on, get a move on.'

'I am! There are people in the way,' Vinny said.

Before the Storm

Joe continued, 'the choice is whether we tear ourselves apart and create a dog eat dog society—the employed against the unemployed, the healthy against the sick, the young against the old. A society where we destroy the values of trade unionism and solidarity for the profit of the elite, whether we fight each other instead of fighting them. Or we fight for our class interests against a government and state that wants to take us back to the 1930s — private railways and transport, where we have to pay for education and health care. Make no mistake, these things weren't given to us as a charity. Our forefathers had to fight for them, and if this government or the next can take them away and turn back the clock, they will.

The boys reached the edge of the crowd and turned to face the speaker.

'You know what this means beyond the politics,' he said. 'For our communities, our estates? With no work, no future, no unions, we fight each other. English against Irish, black against white, women against men, British against foreigner. Young against old.' He paused for a second.

Vinny thought he was looking straight at them.

The speaker's voice was booming out over the crowd. 'No solidarity, no community, no humanity.' He raised his fist. 'Solidarity is humanity.'

The crowd clapped and cheered. The organiser moved toward the speaker, but Doyle held on to the microphone.

'One more minute.' The crowd waited, the microphone screeched in a feedback loop,

A chill ran down Vinny's spine. He stopped and turned.

'My dad died last night.' A conversational tone replaced the sing song delivery. The crowd was quiet. Chanting or clapping faded. The speaker's arm dropped to his side, head flopping forward.

The organiser reached for the mic. "Okay Joe, that's enough.'

'No, wait...' Joe raised the mic. 'My dad fought for Irish independence. I will go to his funeral in the next few days, just like Bobby Sands' family and the Hunger Strikers' families who are still fighting the British Emp... today.' Scattered applause and a murmuring of boos followed as they snatched the microphone from his hand, while they led Joe Doyle away.

'Come on, let's get out of here,' Vinny said.

They followed the slope down towards the centre of the village and the bus stop outside Woolworth. 'What are we gonna do now?' asked Sammo.

'I can get the bus into town,' Jaime said.

'We can walk back with the marchers. Their next stop is Widnes, so they will have to go through Speke.' said Macca.

'What about the treasure?' asked Sammo.

'I could sell it for you,' Jamie said.

'How could you do that?' asked Macca.

'I know people.'

'You're bullshitting.' Macca replied.

'No, seriously.'

Vinny took the watch out and gave it to Jaime.

Macca reached to grab it, but Jaime pulled back. Macca launched forward. 'Give me that.' He lunged at Jaime's arm.

Jaime and Macca pushed and pulled each other. Macca let go. Jaime stumbled back. He missed his footing on the kerb and fell backwards into the road and into an oncoming car. A woman waiting at the bus stop screamed. Jaime bounced off the front right corner of the car and hit the bonnet. There was a screech of tyres as the driver slammed on his brakes, and Jaime was thrown sideways, landing half on the kerb and half in the road, about five feet in front of the car. The watch skidded along the pavement. Sammo picked it up.

'Shit, what have you done?' Sammo pushed Macca.

A crowd gathered around Jaime. Police ran over from the march. Vinny could hear someone on the microphone. 'Where's the march doctor? A kid's been hit. Quick!'

'Here.' A man ran over to the group. Police pushed people

back. 'I'm a doctor.'

'Who is it?' A copper asked. 'Does anyone know him?'

'He was with those lads.' The woman who screamed pointed at Vinny and Macca. Vinny and Macca backed away. Vinny shivered with the dread of capture.

'Do you know who he is?' the copper asked.

'No,' said Macca, shaking his head.

'How about you?' The copper looked directly at Vinny.

Vinny shook his head. 'No.'

'They're lying.' The woman at the bus stop screwed up her face in disgust.

'We don't know him.' Macca denied Jaime for the third time.

'He's with me, he's my mate,' Sammo stepped forward.

'Come here.' The copper pulled Sammo through the group of bystanders.

Macca led Vinny in the opposite direction. 'Come on, let's get out of here.'

Chapter Sixteen

Anne

10am, Saturday, June 25th, 2016

Anne took Aigburth Road and then the bypass. Garston village wasn't even on the route now. She looked down to her left. St Mary's Road was a shadow of its former self. There was something about this city. The past was never over here. Like the city itself, the past refused to be quiet. She had arranged to meet DC Cowley in Speke; it wasn't her first visit to Speke police station. Her first big story back in the days when everyone read the local paper was a body discovered under the bridge in Garston.

The station itself was the same squat corner building, detached with no immediate neighbours. It surprised Anne that The Old Noah's ark pub was now an evangelical church. She rang the door buzzer on the police station and looked into the camera.

'Anne McCarthy here to see DC Cowley.'

A loud click opened the door, and she stepped inside. If anything, the reception area looked smaller and grubbier. In one step, she was behind the counter. The uniformed officer nodded. Good morning. She was about to speak when the door to her left clicked open with the same metallic buzz.

'Good Morning Ms McCarthy.'

Anne turned and was shocked to see a smiling Dave Cooper. 'DS Cooper?' Anne managed to get his name out.

'Detective Inspector these days, if you don't mind.' DI Cooper enjoyed the moment and waited for Anne's response.

'I'm supposed to see DC Cowley.'

'That's right, you were, but not now. Shall we have a chat? This way, please.' He stepped back and held the door open.

'Of course.' Anne's mind was racing. Why hadn't she expected this? She had thought of him when arranging the meeting, but she didn't expect him to still be around. Dave Cooper was the only copper she had ever slept with.

In front of her were the cells and interview rooms. She also remembered those.

'This way,' DI Cooper turned left and led her up a flight of stairs. He entered a security key at the top and opened the door to an open-plan office. A couple of uniformed officers were tapping away at keyboards. The space felt empty, under-used.

DI Cooper opened the door to a private corner office. The windows looked out over the construction site that used to be the main shopping area of Speke The Parade.

He swept his hand across the vista. 'Ch… Ch… Ch… Changes, as David Bowie would say.' He laughed at his own joke.

'Sit.'

'You look incredible.' His eyes scanned her.

Anne pulled her jacket closer and sat down on the straight-back chair facing a large oak desk. 'This is not what I was expecting.'

'Expectations can cause so much trouble, that's why they have to be managed.'

Anne needed to refocus.

'How'd you know I was coming?'

'DC Cowley reminds me of myself. How long ago was it, ten, twelve years ago?'

Anne looked around. The door was closed. 'Can we cut the

crap? I'm not interested in whatever game you're playing.'

'Who says I'm playing anything?'

'I do. I'm here as a journalist. A man died on this estate and I am here to find what happened. I do not know what your game is. But you being here makes me think something is going on.'

DI Cooper stood next to the chair behind the desk. 'Don't get on your high horse. I'm a Detective Inspector, of course. I know about deaths in my area, and this is part of South Liverpool District. What is it with you people?' he sat down heavily in the chair behind the desk.

Anne raised her eyebrows and made air quotes. 'You people? Really?'

'I meant journalists. I thought you'd left? Leeds wasn't it? What are you doing back, and here of all places?'

'I didn't realise you were keeping tabs on me.'

'I wasn't, just gossip. You know how it is.'

'No, not really.' Anne opened her notebook and placed her digital recorder on the desk.

'Like that, is it?' he asked.

'Like that,' Anne replied. She opened her notebook.

'In that case, Ms McCarthy, you know where the door is.'

Anne closed her notebook. 'Okay, have it your way.'

DI Cooper nodded at the recording device. Anne picked it up, turned it to face him, and pressed a button. The machine beeped before going blank.

'Thank you.'

'Sam Maddows?'

DI Cooper opened his hands. 'Overdose. But why are you interested?'

'He was a friend of Vinny.'

'Looks like we are repeating history here, your student friend.'

'History professor.'

'I stand, or sit corrected.' He leaned forward over the desk. 'Ok I get it. You want to show due care and attention, but honestly, from our point of view, death is accidental when the drug was taken accidentally, too much of a drug was taken accidentally. The wrong drug was taken or given accidentally.'

'Are you still connected to Special Branch?'

'Are you still a conspiracist?' he shot back.

'DI Barlow?' Anne asked.

'He's passed now. A good officer, you'll never know how much he did to defend this country.'

'That's what bothers me. Not knowing what he did.'

'Apparently, Sam was afraid of military intelligence?' said Anne.

'You need to be careful. From his medical records, it looks like Mr Maddows had a number of problems, including Post Traumatic Stress. I would be cautious about reading too much into anything he said.'

'You've checked then?'

'Excuse me?'

'His records, you've checked them?' she paused before adding, 'For an accidental overdose?'

'Of course I have. He died in my district. I know you think we're all cowboys, but we are a professional service, probably the most; watched, overlooked and regulated public service there is.'

'The pathology report was sent to his doctor, the cause of death has been recorded as an accidental overdose of heroin, the Coroner will certify that a post mortem is not required and a death certificate will be issued allowing the family to make his funeral arrangements.'

'Bish, bash, bosh, all done.' She said.

'Procedures have to be followed.'

'Ok, I get it.'

'Do you? For you, everything is a story, a mystery, an investigation. Sometimes life is just boring, there is no excitement, no mystery, just an overdose.'

'Isn't your job to investigate?'

'Yes, crimes, not social questions. If you want to run a feature on the reasons for addiction, you will have our full support.'

'But not in looking at individual cases?'

'I didn't say that.'

'No, you didn't,' Anne agreed.

'Things could have been so different, you remember?'

'Of course I do, and no, they really couldn't. It was a one-night stand.'

'For you maybe.'

'Yes, for me.' Anne stood to leave. 'I should be going.'

'I'll walk you out.'

They walked out of the office and down the stairs, through the buzzers and clicks. He held open the station door.

Anne paused. 'One last question.'

DI Cooper shrugged.

'Who called the ambulance?'

DI Cooper pursed his lips. 'A neighbour, I think. Yeah, a neighbour.'

'Name? Address?'

'Anonymous,' replied the DI.

'Shame,' said Anne.

'It is, isn't it?'

The DI turned and allowed the door to close behind him.

Anne sat in her car, hands on the wheel. 'Maybe.' she said to no one, 'Just maybe.' She started the engine and set off for Allerton.

Chapter Seventeen

Helen

12am, Saturday, June 25th, 2016

Helen switched on her laptop. Vinny was catching up with work. She despaired. He had spent his whole life running away. When she told him she was pregnant, he had run away from her and Speke, moving into town. The years they were apart were hard. Charlie didn't notice so much because his dad was back around by the time school started. Vinny had his precious university years, and he had a young girlfriend, Anne, from town. They took a big trip to Ireland, all while she was changing nappies. When the laptop fired up, she Googled 'suicide or overdose?' and began her research. Her mind drifted to the last visit with Sammo. It had not gone well.

When she arrived at Dymchurch, it looked like the dog had been taking him for a walk. It was full of energy bouncing about while he struggled to restrain it.

'Hey,' she said, winding down her window.

Sammo came to a stop next to the car. 'Hi.' She got out and locked the vehicle. 'Do you go far?'

'Far enough for it to have a shit.'

'Lovely,' said Anne.

'Well, you asked.'

'We go over to Speke Hall. He likes the woods.'

'Who's this little fella?'

'Icey.'

'Come here, Icey.' Helen leant to stroke the lively black puppy that was at Sammo's side. 'He's new, isn't he?'

'Yeah, turned up last week.' Sammo leaned down and ruffled the dog's short fur.

'What is he?'

'A pain in the arse. I don't know. Mongrel. I think he's got a bit of a terrier in him, little legs and fat body.'

'You look ok,' for an ex-addict she thought. His slim frame was lean, but muscular. His face had a sharpness, his eyes were bright.

'It's the exercise,' he said, slapping his chest.

'And eating well?'

'Yeah, all-vegan now. Would you believe it?'

'I would. But I couldn't imagine getting Vinny on that.'

'You're not looking bad yourself,' Sammo said as he indicated for her to follow him into the house. 'How's the little fella?' he asked.

'Not so little these days, and a bit of a handful.'

Sammo opened the door, and they went into the bare kitchen. The curtains were half drawn over grey nets.

'Have a seat. I'll put the kettle on.'

'Why Icey?' Helen remained standing. The pine table and benches looked like they could do with a wipe.

'Don't know...ice cream because he looked so cool, I guess. Silly, I know.'

Helen smiled. 'No, it's nice. Where did you get him?'

'He just turned up one day last week. Noticed him hanging around outside. Made the mistake of giving him a bit of food and letting him in, and can't get rid of him now,' he said, smiling.

Sammo spoke as he moved about sorting out the tea. 'Have you said anything to Vinny yet?'

'No, not yet. He's always been funny about you guys.'

'He was always the smartest.'

'And you can't tell me whatever it is?'

'I just want to talk to him. I think he would know what to do.'

'Okay, look, even if you don't tell me what it is, can you tell me anything?'

Sammo spun around. 'I told you I can't.' He spat the words out, and the dog cowered at his feet. His voice softened as he continued. 'Just ask him. He works for the University. People would listen to him. This stuff is dangerous.'

'Okay, I'll do what I can. I promise. Soon.'

They were interrupted by a banging, knuckles on wood. Sammo told her to wait and stay still. He lifted a corner of the curtain and the net. Then he moved slowly down the hallway.

The banging rang out a second time. 'It's me, Beep.'

Sammo opened the door and a man younger than Sammo entered the room. He wore a black Adidas track suit top, a green and yellow beanie. His chin and top lip were half covered in wispy growth.

Sammo made no introductions, and Helen never stayed for tea. She made her excuses and left. She never did get round to telling Vinny. Now Sammo was dead, and she hadn't kept her promise. Always waiting for the right time. Well, now there was no time. Of the three of them she knew as a teenager, Helen had a soft spot for Sammo. Macca was the good-looking one, and she made the mistake of falling for the look. She went out with him for a few months, but it was never more than kisses and fumbling. There wasn't much behind his tough-guy image.

By the time she dated Vinny, he was no longer hanging around with the others. He had become a bit of a loner, which was what attracted her. There was more about him; he had opinions and knew things. Sammo was the broken one. He thought he hid it, but most people could see it. All he wanted was approval and acceptance, a little love. Her tears flowed freely for Sammo, for the painful life he had, maybe even for the life he didn't have.

Before the Storm

The doorbell rang. Helen struggled to get up; she was in pain from the bruising. 'Hold on, I'm coming,' she shouted.

Using the furniture to support herself, she made it to the front door.

Helen opened the door and was surprised when she saw Claire, Sammo's daughter. 'Hi, Claire.'

'Are you busy?' Claire asked.

'No, come in.'

'Are you okay?'

Helen leaned against the wall. Claire moved forward quickly to help her stand, and Helen took the opportunity to give Claire a careful hug. 'I'm so sorry.'

'I know, love. Let's get you inside and sit down.' Claire supported Helen back into the living room, lowering her onto the sofa. 'What happened to you, then?'

'Car crash a couple of days ago.'

'Bloody hell. Shouldn't you be in hospital or bed, recovering?'

'It's not as bad as it looks, just bruising. I'm so sorry about Sam.'

Claire was pale and looked tired. Her usually vigorous blonde hair hung flat down to her shoulders. She wore a black skirt and a grey jumper under her black jacket.

'Please sit down.' Helen waved at an armchair. 'Do you want anything? Some tea? Coffee?'

'You're not in a condition to get something, even if I wanted it.' Claire smiled.

'No, you're right, sorry.'

'Don't be. So, who told you?' Claire asked.

'Vinny, he was at the house in Dymchurch the morning after.'

Claire's eyes widened in surprise.

'It's complicated,' Helen said with a wave of her hand.

'Okay. Why don't I make us something?' Claire offered.

'I can't ask you to do that.'

'You're not asking. I could do with a cup of tea,' she said, standing up. 'I'll be fine. Tea or coffee?'

'Coffee for me.'

Anne popped her head in. 'Hello, the front door was open,' Anne entered the room. 'Thought I would catch up. Sorry, I didn't know you had company."

'It's fine, come in. Actually, shut that front door first before anyone else wanders in.'

'Really, I can come back,' said Anne.

Helen smiled. 'I'm just joking with you. Come in. But really shut the door.'

Anne laughed. 'Ok, I've got it.' When she re-entered the room, Claire was carrying a tray of drinks in. 'I did an extra coffee, is that ok?'

'Perfect, here, let me give you a hand with those,' said Anne.

Anne dropped her coat and bag on an armchair and went to help Claire. Claire moved with care to put the drinks down. Helen indicated for Claire to sit on the sofa. Anne took the armchair.

'How are you?' Helen asked.

'Holding up. I don't know. What else do you say?' said Claire.

'Anne, this is Claire, Sammo's daughter. Claire, this is Anne.' Helen paused before adding, 'Vinny's ex.'

There was a moment's silence.

Claire smiled. 'Well, that's awkward.'

Helen and Anne both broke into smiles.

'I didn't know, Sam, but it can't be easy for you. I'm sorry for your loss,' said Anne.

'To be honest, I'm just trying to piece it all together.'

'Do you know what happened? Have the police said anything?' asked Helen.

'Is Vinny around?' asked Claire

'He's at work. I could call him,' Helen offered.

'I don't want to disturb him.'

'Oh, don't worry, he's not teaching today. I'll message him.' Helen swiped her phone.

'It's gone to the pathologist, then it'll go to the Coroner. I had to identify him in the Royal. The Police took me there. The Coroner decides what he thinks happened and once he has released the body, we can bury him.'

'It must have been horrible,' Helen suggested.

'Yeah, but you know, and I hate myself for saying this, at least it's over for him. Let's face it, he didn't have an easy time. Seeing him like that… it was the first time in God knows how long I wasn't worried about him. He looked peaceful. I wasn't worried about him being unhappy. Is that selfish?'

Helen reached out to hold Claire's hand. 'No, of course not.'

Claire shook herself. 'Anyway, the Coroner will decide the cause of death, but the police didn't seem that interested. As soon as they knew he had drug issues, it was an 'accidental overdose.' So that's what I expect the Coroner to say. The police aren't doing anything to find out any different, but to be fair, what can they do?'

Helen looked across at Anne. 'Well, Anne is a journalist. She's pretty good, actually. She's uncovered loads of stuff before.'

'Really? And you want to help us?'

'Vinny and your dad were friends as kids. Vinny asked me to see if I could find anything out. I hope you don't mind?'

'No, of course not. I've actually got something for Vinny. That's partly why I'm here.' Claire reached into her bag and pulled out a battered envelope. Sealed and resealed, covered in tape, with the original name and address scribbled out. A large 'VINNY' was written in black marker across the front.

Claire passed the envelope to Helen.

'We were probably both in the Royal at the same time,' said Helen.

'Oh, my God, weird, isn't it?'

'What do you think? Was it accidental?' asked Anne.

Claire spoke quietly but firmly. 'I don't think it was intentional, and I know, people can be in denial, but I have seen him a lot worse than this—did he shoot up? Fall off the wagon?—I guess we'll never know.' She looked straight at Helen. 'I wanted to come and say thank you. He told me you have been talking to him. I know he appreciated it.'

Helen squeezed Claire's hand.

The physical connection allowed Claire a release. She managed to talk through the tears. 'But... I'm also angry at him. I don't know... how, why. How could he do this? Why didn't he call me—' Claire's head dropped and she fought back the tears.

Claire lifted her head. 'It's not just my dad, though, is it? I mean, where did he get the stuff? I'll tell you something right. Everyone knows who's dealing, everyone. He's got a brand-new BMW, no job, but driving around in a big SUV — what's that about? I know, I could give you five names now, people who are running drugs. I've got a salon. We get them all, girls wanting three-hundred pound's worth of extensions, carrying handbags... it would take me a month to earn—' She stopped herself. 'Sorry, there's no point to this...'

'No, you're right,' Anne said. 'They've got kids shooting each other for this stuff. It's crazy.'

'I guess the police need evidence.' Helen offered.

'Evidence, my arse. It wouldn't take five minutes to round them up, get the guns and money from their houses. They just wait until they get a Mr. Big. Meanwhile, we have to put up with this. But as soon as they get one Mr. Big and it's all over the telly, there's another one next week, and the stuff is still on the streets,' said Claire.

'I think you're right, they don't care what it's doing to us,' said Anne.

The talking stopped as they heard the front door open. Vinny couldn't hide his surprise when he entered the living room. 'Anne. What are you..?'

'And this is Claire,' Sam's daughter Helen said.

Claire shifted her weight.

'No, don't get up,' said Vinny. 'I was sorry to find out about your dad.' he turned to Anne.

'I'm surprised to see you.'

'I've just come back from Speke police station.'

'Anything interesting?' Asked Vinny.

'I think so, said Anne, first of all. You'll never guess who I met?'

Vinny shrugged, 'Who?'

'Detective Inspector Dave Cooper.'

'Wow, really, that's interesting.'

'Ok, you're going to have to explain.' said Helen.

'Dave Cooper was the copper who tried to stop us from finding out the identity of a body under the bridge in Garston years ago. He was up to his neck in dodgy stuff.'

'What kind of stuff?' asked Claire.

'Drugs and Intelligence.' said Anne.

'You know who's behind the drugs in Speke?' Helen asked Claire.

'Of course, everyone knows. Gary Mac.'

'Is that Steve McNally's son?' asked Helen.

'Yeah, he's nasty. Into all this martial arts fighting. Has a gym that trains young kids. More like a little army.' Claire paused before adding, 'Someone should put a stop to it.'

'They should,' agreed Helen.

'This is for you.' Helen offered the envelope to Vinny.

'It's from my dad,' said Claire. 'He dropped it off in mine the day he died. I guess he wasn't expecting to see you, or he would have given it to you himself.'

Vinny turned the packet over in his hands. All eyes in the room were on him. He felt the envelope, checking to make sure there was nothing solid and round in it before opening it. He pulled at the tape and ripped the edge of the envelope.

'I'm not sure I wanna see whatever is in there.' said Claire.

Vinny stopped. 'Yeah, of course. Look, if you want, I'll open it later.'

'Am I being stupid?' Claire asked.

'No, if there's anything I think you should see, I'll let you know,' said Helen.

'Ok yeah, if you don't mind. I'd rather do it that way.' Claire collected her things. I'll let myself out.

Vinny waited till he heard the front door close. He opened the envelope. Anne moved the tray and cups, and Vinny spread the contents of the envelope over the coffee table.

Chapter Eighteen

Sammo

1.30pm, Friday, July 3rd, 1981

The policeman held on to Sammo's blazer, 'You can get in with him when the ambulance comes.'

'I want to go home,' Sammo could feel the stares of people gathered round. The copper frowned.

'Your mate will need you if he wakes up in the ambulance or at the hospital. Can't you stay with him till his family gets there?'

'Do I have to?' Even as he asked, he knew the answer.

'No, you don't, but is he your mate?' The words were thrown at him like a challenge.

'Yeah.' He looked down at Jaime. Was this another death? Like the old man? Another accident.

'It's up to you then, isn't it?' the copper said.

Sammo watched as Macca and Vinny backed away through the crowd. They were leaving him. What happened to 'All for one?' Vinny turned around and looked at Sammo. Sammo waved and shouted, 'Come here.'

Vinny shrugged, then disappeared into the crowd after Macca.

Sammo turned back to Jaime. The doctor turned him onto his side, and Jaime's face was bloody. Sammo wasn't sure where the blood was coming from. Jaime's eyes were closed, and Sammo hoped he wasn't dead. People leaned in, pushing. He didn't want to get closer, so he pushed back. The copper held onto his shoulder. Sammo pulled away from him but didn't run. He stood there, watching as people gathered round. He felt the treasure in his pocket, held it in his hand, and made a wish. He wished Jaime wouldn't die. They had talked about the old man dying, but that was a story. This was real. If you are not there, everything is a story, and nothing is real. When you can see the blood, it's real.

Sammo looked around. 'Where's his bag? Where's his school bag?' he asked. He had already saved the contents of the bag once today; he didn't want to lose it now.

The copper amplified his question. 'Can anyone see the kid's schoolbag?'

People began to look around.

Finally, an onlooker shouted, 'Here lad,' and handed the black Puma schoolbag with a leaping white cat to Sammo.

Sammo threw the strap over his shoulder, opened it, and looked inside. His books were mud-stained from the shore, but he could read his name: Jaime Jaware. They should have called him JJ. That would have been cool. Maybe his real mates did. He carried on looking. A plastic holder sewn onto the inside had his address, J Jaware. 5 Asbridge Street L8.

'What's his name?' asked the copper.

'Jaime, Jaime Jaware.' Sammo spelt it out for the copper who was writing it in his notebook. He showed him the address, too, and he wrote it down. 'His dad's a sailor,' Sammo said.

'Don't you worry, son, we'll find his family.'

Sammo wasn't worried about finding his family. He was worried about him dying. He looked up at the sun. It was a bright day, and the sky was blue. Do people die on warm sunny days? Shouldn't it be grey and rainy?

Other coppers had come over and were directing traffic around the car that hit Jaime. One of them talked to the driver.

The doctor was friendly. He was wearing jeans and even had

a t-shirt on, like the marchers. He turned to Sammo. 'Does he have any illnesses?'

Sammo shrugged. 'I don't know.'

'Don't worry. The ambulance will be here soon. I think he's gonna be okay.'

Sammo felt the air leave his body. Jaime was going to be okay. He wasn't going to die, because it was warm and sunny, he thought. I bet if it had been rainy, he would have died; people always died on rainy days.

Someone in the crowd said, 'We should take him to Garston Hospital. It's only round the corner.'

'What do you think, doc?' the copper asked.

'We should wait for the ambulance. They will take him to Broadgreen or the Royal, but they will know best.'

'Righto.' As the copper said this, the ambulance siren wailed as it came over the railway bridge from the direction of Speke.

The police sprang into action, clearing the way. Soon, there was just Sammo and the doctor next to the prone figure of Jaime. Sammo looked anywhere but at Jaime and the blood.

Then they were in the ambulance. The siren was on, and they were flying through the streets. The vehicle was swaying from side to side. The paramedic wiped the blood away from Jaime's head, then taped bandages in place. Sammo wished he could see outside, to see how fast they were going. They were swerving a lot, which meant they were going in and out of traffic, but there were no windows, so he couldn't see. It was really exciting.

'Your mate will be fine,' the paramedic said.

He had told Sammo to sit next to Jaime as he lay on the stretcher. Sammo watched while the ambulance man put a needle in his arm and attached a tube. The long thin needle went straight in. It broke his skin, then slipped inside a vein. Sammo was amazed he could see the thin blue line of his vein. The blood mixed with the medicine, a swirling mix of red and clear liquid. It looked like a mini lava lamp. Then he pushed, and the liquid was pumped inside Jaime. 'That'll do him good,' he said, wiping away a spot of blood that appeared when he pulled the needle out.

Sammo wondered how it would feel. The paramedic worked quickly as the ambulance sped through the streets. This would be a good job. Sammo wondered how you got to be an ambulance man. The radio crackled, the lights flashed, the siren blared, there were all kinds of beeps. It was crazy.

Then they pulled in at the hospital. The doors opened, and other people grabbed the stretcher. Sammo had to run to keep up with them. They went straight through the waiting room and wheeled Jaime into an empty space. The doctors wore green and face masks. They made Sammo wait outside.

A nurse came and asked him loads of questions. He didn't know most of the answers. He didn't want to tell them he only met Jaime that morning. It would look bad. He worried they knew he wasn't a real friend. He didn't know anything about Macca or Vinny, not as if they had any illnesses or were allergic. Who knew that stuff?

She was okay, though, and gave him a drink.

Sammo's head was nodding. It wasn't so late, around five o'clock, but he was tired. It had been a weird day. He slumped in the hard-plastic chair, legs splayed out in front of him. He had his blazer back on now. He closed his eyes and allowed himself to doze.

'Hey.' Someone was shaking his arm.

'What?' he jumped.

'Chill out.' A black guy, older than Sammo but not really old, stood in front of him. 'You all right, kidder?' his voice was warm and friendly.

'Yeah, good. What's going on?'

'I'm Jaime's brother Mikey. You're Sammo, right? Is that what they call you?'

'Yeah, that's right.'

'Come on then, kidder. Jaime wants to see you.'

'He's awake?' Sammo brightened up.

'Yeah, come on.'

Mikey led the way. Jaime wasn't in the room Sammo was outside. They had moved him to a different floor. Mikey knew the way, so Sammo followed closely behind. Doctors and nurses, visitors, and patients. The place was full of people, trolleys, and wheelchairs. It was the weirdest place. People in pyjamas and dressing gowns, slippers and flip-flops. He followed Mikey, dodging in and out. They got to the lifts and had to wait.

When the doors opened, and they got inside, Sammo was next to a man in a wheelchair. He had a plastic mask on his face, and a big red tank was attached to the back of the wheelchair. While the lift moved, Sammo could hear his breathing. It was a horrible sound, as if air was travelling through a tunnel and being bounced around, and then it was all crackling like radio interference. It nearly made him sick. He was glad when the doors opened and Mikey stepped out.

Mikey was tall, so Sammo followed his afro between the people. Mikey turned to him. 'Come on, kidder, nearly there.'

Mikey pushed through a double-door. The long room was full of beds. Jaime was near the end on the right. He was sitting up, and the white bandage stood out against his black hair and brown skin. He was leaning back against the pillows and didn't move much.

'Hey, mate.' Jaime smiled weakly.

'Hi.' Sammo gave a half-wave.

The woman sitting next to Jaime's bed stood. Sammo knew it was his mum. He could see the Chinese in her; she was slim and had straight dark hair and clear features. She stood when Sammo arrived. He was shocked when she reached out, pulled him in, and hugged him. He was embarrassed as she held him tightly, but it was nice. He didn't know what to do with his hands, so they stayed by his side.

'Thank you for looking after my son.' She sounded Liverpool to Sammo, no Chinese in it at all.

'You're all right.' Sammo grinned.

Jaime's mum sat back down. 'But your mum must be worried, too. How long have you been here?' she asked.

'I don't know. I didn't check the time. She'll be okay. She won't care till it gets dark. Then she'll just moan about me being late.'

'Has your mum got a phone?'

'No, but the Joneses have next door. We call them if we need to.'

'Do you know the number?'

'No, but they are in the directory, or you can get it from enquiries.'

'Michael can take you down to call. What's your name?'

'Sammo.'

'No, your real name. No mother gave you the name Sammo. What name did your mother give you?'

'Sam,' he replied. The name sounded strange.

'Sam, my Jaime here told me a big story about how he got to Speke. Did you see any of that?'

'Yeah, we saw him get thrown out of the police car.' Sammo lifted the bag from over his shoulder. 'Look, you can see how his books got muddy.'

'Those f—'

'Michael,' his mum snapped. 'I don't want any of that language.'

Sammo pulled out one of the books.

'Okay, son, I believe you,' she said, shaking her head.

'Here, let me take that off you.'

Sammo handed over the bag. 'It wasn't right.'

'No, son, it wasn't.' She turned to Michael. 'Right, take Samuel here—' She raised her eyebrows when she said, Samuel. '—to the phone. Speak to his mum and tell her you'll be taking him home.'

'What? To Speke?'

'Yes, to Speke. This boy looked after your brother today. That is, after you get him something to eat. You must be hungry, too, eh?' she reached out and caressed his hair.

'Starving,' Sammo said.

'Yeah, no sweat. Come on, kidder.'

Jaime tried to lean forward and grunted with the effort.

'You stay there, boy,' his mum scolded as she laid a hand on his chest, keeping him back against the pillows.

Jaime motioned Sammo to come closer. Sammo put his ear close to Jaime's face. 'Have you got it?' Jaime whispered.

'Right here, mate.' Sammo patted his pocket.

'Ask Mikey. He'll know where to take it,' Jaime said.

'Will do.'

'Come on, then. Let's see if there's a phone.' Mikey led the way again.

Sammo struggled again to keep up with him.

'God, you walk quickly. Can't you slow down?' Sammo asked.

'Places to be, people to see, no dawdling round me kidder.'

They made their way down to the hospital entrance. There were three public telephones in a row. There was no telephone box, just a funny arch thing to put your head under.

'Are we gonna call, then?' Mikey asked.

'Nah, not really.' Sammo shuffled his feet.

'What do you mean?'

'Me mam won't worry. It'll only cause a fuss if I call. It'll be okay if I just get home tonight. It'll be good.'

'Are you sure, kidder?' Mikey looked concerned.

'Yeah.'

'Why are we down here, then?'

'I didn't want your mum to worry. She looks like she would worry.'

'You're not wrong there, kidder.'

'Anyway, I've got this. Jaime said I should show you.' He looked around before carefully pulling out the chain first, and then the watch.

'Wow. What have you guys been up to?'

'It wasn't Jaime. It was me and my mate. Well, my mate, really. I just kept dixie.'

'Here, let me have a look.'

Sammo handed the watch over. Mikey raised it to his eye, carefully turning it over. He slid his fingernail inside the cover and opened it to reveal the face.

'It's our treasure.'

'What do you wanna do with it?'

'Get some money for it,' Sammo said expectantly.

Mikey raised the chain and examined the links. 'Are you sure?'

'Yeah, we tried in Garston, but the place was gone. Do you know anywhere?'

'Could do, kidder, could do. I'd have to run you over there, take you out to Speke after. You good with that?'

'Yeah, all good.'

'Okay, come on then. We'll tell my ma, then get on.'

Sammo stood with his hand out.

Mikey smiled. 'Sound kidder,' he handed the watch back.

Sammo slipped it back into his pocket. He liked Mikey, but he still had to protect the treasure for the other guys, even though they had left him in Garston with Jaime. They had broken the 'one for all and all for one.'

They were back up in the ward in minutes.

'Is your mother okay now? She knows where you are?' Jamie's mother asked.

'Yeah, all good,' Sammo lied.

'You take him right to his home now. None of your messing around, Michael. Do you hear me?'

'Yes, ma.'

'Well, go on then, it's late enough as it is.'

Jaime waved for Sammo to come closer. He moved his head in close. 'Good luck with the treasure.'

'Righto.' Sammo winked.

Jaime winked back. 'See ya, mate.'

'See ya.' Sammo turned and started walking down the ward to the exit. Near the end, he turned to look back. Jaime's mum was out of her chair and fussing over her son. Sammo felt a stab of pain. That must be love, he thought.

Chapter Nineteen

Vinny

11.30am, Saturday, 25th June, 2016

'Are you ready?'

Vinny ripped open the package and carefully emptied its contents onto the table, allowing the loose pages to spread out. 'Wow. What is it all?'

Anne sorted them out into different shapes and sizes. This was no journal. Maybe in this way, it reflected Sammo's life more accurately than he could have devised.

'It's all random,' Vinny said.

'It can't be. It's all collected in an envelope for you. Why would he leave it for you? Not give it to you?' asked Anne.

'I don't know. He was closer to Macca than me. They were both in the army.'

'Not recently, he wasn't,' Helen said.

'What do you mean?'

'Close to Macca. Okay, two piles to start. Handwritten and printed,' Anne added.

'How do you know?' Vinny checked the envelope to see if there was anything else inside.

'He mentioned they fell out, weren't speaking, had a row or something,' Helen answered.

'When was this? In your secret visits?'

Helen stopped sorting. 'He wanted me to speak to you, and I was going to, then all this happened.'

'Speak to me about what?' asked Vinny.

'He never said exactly. He said you were at the University and involved in anti-war stuff. I think he just meant you were respectable. People would take you seriously.'

'We should look for anything like a note,' said Anne.

'You mean suicide?' Helen asked.

'Yeah, or anything showing self-harm or whatever. We will have to take it to the police.'

'Shouldn't we take it all, anyway?'

'Maybe, but we need to work out what it is first.'

'Then dates,' Anne said. 'We should look for some kind of order.'

'What would me being in the anti-war movement have to do with anything?' asked Vinny.

'Maybe that was it? Something to do with the army? That's why he couldn't speak to Macca?'

'Or that's why he fell out with Macca? Maybe something happened?' said Anne.

'Who knows?' Vinny picked up one handwritten piece. It had childish writing, round where it should be round, and straight lines, not the interconnected slanted scrawl of most adults who have long past caring about legibility. As he laid them out, straightening them up, he could see a progression.

'Look for anything that dates a letter, see if we can find what connects it all,' said Anne.

Vinny could see some development. The writing became less clear and practiced, tighter and less self-conscious. One letter was different handwriting altogether.

He picked up an A4 lined sheet. It had been ripped from a school exercise book. He started reading. It was a school essay. It still bore the teacher's marks and corrections:

Jack Byrne

My perfect job.

I want to be a soldier. I saw the telly with the Falklands and the soldiers marching. It looked cold and hard, but they won. They beat Argentina who tried to take away the islands that are next to it but British because we found them years ago.

'There's all kinds of stuff here. I've got one from solicitors about divorce.' Helen started reading. 'Dear Mr. Maddows, We regret to inform you that we have filed the paperwork for divorce proceedings…'

'Should we be reading this?' Vinny asked.

He was ignored by Anne and Helen, who were each reading separate letters.

'This sounds familiar. Listen.' Vinny read the lines, pausing to achieve the rhythm.

I hurt myself today,
to see if I still feel.
I focus on the pain,
the only thing that's real.

'Do you recognise it?'

'Yeah. Johnny Cash. I think it was a cover of someone else,' Helen said.

'It was Nine Inch Nails. Really moving song. Is it suicidal?'

'I don't know. I don't think so. Aww, this is awful.' Helen held a page up.

'What is it?' asked Anne.

'It looks like a letter to Claire.'

'Do you think he sent it?'

'He can't have. It's here,' Helen said.

'No, maybe this is a copy, you know, trying to write it out. Then he sends the good one.'

Before the Storm

'Yeah, okay.'

'Okay, come on. What have we got? We need to make a list.' Said Anne.

My perfect job.

I want to be a soldier. I saw the telly with the Falklands and the soldiers marching. It looked cold and hard, but they won. They beat Argentina who tried to take away the islands that are next to it but British because we found them years ago.

I have to take some exams. The army fella I saw said I didn't need them, but it looks good. It's okay that I have a police caution but if I get any more record, they can't take me. You go abroad with the army and I want to do that. It means leaving Speke, which is good because here I just get in trouble. I don't want to get in bother or be back in court.

I would work in Fords, but you need exams and an apprenticeship. I am shit at Technical drawing. I'm good at art, but that won't do anything.

So my perfect job is in the army. But not in Ireland. They didn't talk to us about Ireland when they came to the school – but we watched a dead soldier go to the church for his funeral. He was from Speke.

———

Best Holiday Ever

We went to Talacre. We rented a caravan. My dad was there for two days and he didn't fight with my mum, so it was really good. Then he went back to work. It was before Dunlops shut, so he had a job. There was a beach, a really long beach with sand dunes. We mostly played on the beach. There were big jellyfish you could see right through them. The ones we saw on the beach were dead. We would poke them with sticks, but not touch the long lines that came out of them because they were stingy.

The caravan was crazy. Everything turned into a bed, the chairs, the sofa, there were beds everywhere. It was really scary at night, when mum and dad went to the club for a drink. The lights were out, and the caravan was shaking. It was the wind, but Marie told me it was ghosts shaking the van. I shit myself was scared, but it was a joke.

We went on the Crosville bus; it went from Speke all the way to there. One day we got the bus to Rhyl and had chips and walked on the beach. My mum had a fight with my brother, Ricki, cos he said he was bored so he got the bus home. But the rest of us thought it was great. It was our first holiday ever, so it was the best holiday ever.

So proud, my mam and sister were there for my passing out parade. We trained for weeks on how to do the marching in time. We did a lot of exercises, too, training. It was hard especially for me cos I wasn't the strongest – but they never gave up on me– shouting, hitting, kicking whatever it took to get me to finish exercises. I am glad they did now. Without it I would have been weak and a failure.

But in my uniform on the parade ground, I am a part of the company and regiment. We are comrades together. That is what it is all about, your comrades. To feel a part of something.

———

Dear Sir,

I served in 1991 operation Granby as a part of Desert Storm. In preparation for action, we were told we would get inoculated against anthrax and any chemical agents Saddam might use. We lined up and there were tables and we went from one to the next like a production line. I asked a medic what was in the shot. He said 'You don't want to know.'

After returning from my dismissal, I visited the doctor with a stomach rash. The doctor diagnosed and treated it as chicken pox, but other symptoms rapidly developed, chronic fatigue, headaches...

Before the Storm

At first, they treated every symptom individually. It was only after meeting with comrades who were suffering similar illnesses that we began to be aware of what is now called GWS Gulf War Syndrome.

All we want is for the MOD to be honest and release the information about the contents of the shots.

I have been unemployed and unable to work since returning from active service. My health worries and financial problems have placed severe stress on my marriage and family situation. When my daughter saw off her father to fight for his country, he was a fit and active man in the prime of life. Although I returned from active duty while some did not, the man who returned is not a shadow of the man that went to fight for his country.

I have been bounced between the MOD the DSS and the NHS like a bad smell everyone sends me somewhere else. This is my reward for risking my life for my country?

Sam Maddows

———

17th May 2016

You will lose some of your payment
This reduction will last 114 days

———

Dear Mr. Maddows,

On the 24th January 2016, you failed to attend a meeting with us at Garston Jobs Centre at 11.40am.

You attended an arranged interview on the 15th of May 2016

Because of this, you will lose some or all of your Universal credit for a time. We call this being sanctioned.

We have calculated the length of your sanction below.
What you will lose from your payment
Because of this sanction, you will lose £5.40 each day for 114 days.
107 days from the date of the missed meeting until 15th May 2016.

Plus 7 days — the basic number of sanction days for an offence of this kind.

You will lose the money either from your next or subsequent payments until the amount shown has been cleared.

Universal Credit is operated by The Department for Work and Pensions.

———

Meakins and Partners Solicitors

Dear Mr. Maddows,

I am writing to inform you that our office is now in possession of the decree nisi in your divorce proceedings from Mrs. Lynne Maddows nee Connor. The decree nisi (final declaration) was made on the 6th January 2016.

We will, of course, be happy to hold the document here in our files. Should you require access or prefer to keep it in your own custody, we will, of course, be happy to release it.

We look forward to your instructions.

Jeff Meakins

———

Hey Vinny

I guess Macca was right. You always were a prick and I shouldn't have gone to your work. All I wanted was to tell you something face to face, but you wouldn't listen. I'm leaving this in case anything happens. I can't leave the real stuff in case Macca or someone else finds it. You're gonna have to work it out, but you're smart you can do it.

Remember, we was kids together. All for one and all that me you and Macca times change though. Kids in the street mate, terrorise now. We was stray cats as kids these are street rats. Cos we gave them nothin they giving nothin back. They are what we were but I'm ex-army and they frighten me mate. I sent you this cos you were the clever one, always was.

I wanted to be something, thought The Army was it. I found my place. I had good mates. Yeah they would die for you-comrades. But it was no good. The road to basra highway to hell they called it mile upon mile burnt out black trucks and jeeps and carriers, all with the blackened bodies in like something from a horror movie they were running away. They were caught like rats in a trap and burnt bombed, blown to nothing. I drove along it, before it was buried in the sand mile after mile mate I'm not kidding. I would have come and told you, but Macca would go crazy.

Claire is my treasure now, but I couldn't help her, couldn't even see her. Most of the time, I don't blame her mum. My head was all over the place Gulf War syndrome feels like this shit. Is it payback for what we did? Macca knows. Macca knows I know. Some things just aren't right. They cut my money. They want my house I'm not going on the streets.

But hiding things don't work either didn't work when we was kids and don't work now. We done that as kids. I knew you were against it you always was. Funny how things work out.

I would have give it you, but you pushed me away. I know you will work it out cos your clever. I don't want the cop or Macca to get it. You will find the truth where Claire was.

Still your mate Sammo.

Helen looked up from the letter, 'Wait a minute. Listen to this.'

'What?'

'Just listen… *"Hey, Vinny. It's okay, I get it that you were busy. I shouldn't have gone to your work. I just wanted to tell you something face to face, but not sure if that will happen now."'* She paused. 'Did you see Sammo recently?'

Vinny sighed, and, a little deflated, said, 'Yeah, I was going to tell you.'

'When?' Anne and Helen were staring at Vinny. 'Last week. It didn't go well.' He closed his eyes. 'I didn't want to think about him. He's not my problem.' He corrected himself. 'He wasn't my problem.'

'So, what happened?'

Vinny closed his eyes and recalled his encounter with Sammo.

'I was going to work. Eleven o'clock. I was a bit late. I parked. I saw him as I got out of the car. I didn't know it was him. I just saw someone in black tracksuit bottoms and a grey hoodie. The figure was lurking in my peripheral vision, enough to set alarms off. I took the long way around the car to avoid him. I guess we all do these things to avoid the homeless and desperate people on the streets. I don't like doing it, but then, being honest, I don't like interacting with them either—'

Helen interrupted him. 'Can we have less of the speeches? Just tell us what happened?'

'I thought he was definitely coming over, making a beeline for me. I knew I didn't have any pound coins on me, no change at all. The smallest I had was a tenner.' Vinny broke the narrative. 'I'm telling you all this… I don't know, it seemed the least I can do.'

'Go on, then,' Helen said. 'I'm listening.'

Just twenty steps away from the entrance. I could see Roger, the security guy. Then I heard a shout, 'Hey.'

Whoever it was, they were behind me now, about five steps away. I still didn't know it was Sammo. I pretended not to hear.

'Hey, Vinny,' he shouted again. I was surprised. I looked over my shoulder. His face was thin and drawn, and yeah, you're right, he had greyish skin. He had his hood up, so his sharp features stood out, and when he called, 'Vinny' again, I noticed the misshapen teeth. I stopped. I still didn't recognise him, but there was something familiar about the face.

'All right, mate? Long time, eh?' he said. Then he pulled down his hood, saying, 'It's me, Sammo.'

He broke into a grin; I was shocked, but I recognised him. He looked terrible.

'Long time, man. I bet you didn't recognise me?' he said.

'No, you're right.' All I could do was stammer. 'You look... different.'

He looked down, not miserable, just tired. 'Yeah, man, a lot's happened,' he said. 'You know what I mean.' It wasn't a question.

I shook his hand. The handshake was firm, strong even. But I noticed his thin wrist.

Roger, the security guy, came up and asked if everything was okay. He probably thought a homeless guy was hassling me, and, to be fair, that's what I thought before I knew it was Sammo. Sammo reassured him. 'No worries, mate, we're old muckers.'

I wanted to get rid of him. Roger didn't look convinced. I kinda stumbled through. Saying, 'Wow. Yeah, a long time.'

'You know, one day at a time and all that.'

'I didn't know what to do, didn't want to take him into my office. I might never get rid of him. I just wanted to get rid of him.'

'Can you tell us exactly what he said?' asked Anne

'He said, "I need help. You should come round. I've got something to give you. It will blow everything up, if people know what was going on."'

The final part was the worst. He said he was back in his mam's. That she'd died. There were long pauses, and I was looking at my watch. Looking back, I think he was trying to tell me something. He ended with something like, 'I'll let you go. I just wanted to say, man, you should come round. I know you've been to Ireland.'

'Yeah, right.' And he said, 'Mad stuff. People should know.'

'Are you sure that's what he said?' Anne asked.

'Yeah, I think so. His last words were, "There's some stuff I need to say."'

'There was stuff he needed to say? He said that?' Helen pressed.

'Yeah, he said that.'

'And then what?'

Vinny pulled a face.

'What's up?'

'I gave him a tenner. He tried to turn it down, but I kind of insisted.'

'What did you do that for?'

'You know, to buy him a pint,' Vinny said weakly.

'Not actually go with him and buy him a pint, like a friend would. No, you gave him the money for a pint. There's a huge difference.' said Helen.

'I know.' Vinny's voice was heavy with regret. Helen shook her head. 'And did you go round and see him?'

'No.'

'Well, you've missed your chance. He's dead now.'

'Yeah, rub it in. Why not? Anyway, he walked off, and I carried on to my office.'

'I guess we both let him down. That much is clear.' She raised her voice a little. 'Something is going on, though. He's worried about Macca finding this. Something happened. What's "the real stuff?"'

Vinny shook his head. 'I don't know.'

'Well, he thinks you can work it out. You'd better start thinking.' Helen paused, looking at the papers spread out before her. She raised a hand to her face. 'This is terrible. This is his life here.'

Vinny, looking down at the letters, replied, 'No, it's even worse. His life is the stuff that is not written… the bits between the pages, between the words, is where he lived.' He paused for a second. 'This is his death.'

Chapter Twenty

Sammo

6pm, Friday, July 3rd, 1981

'Is that yours?' Sammo asked Mikey.

'Yeah, you like it?'

'Of course.' Sammo stroked the bonnet of the sky-blue Ford Capri as he walked round to the passenger side.

It was early evening, shops and streetlights competed with the fading sun. Mikey slipped behind the wheel and opened the passenger door.

Sammo eased into his seat. 'Wow. Love this.'

Mikey turned the ignition and revved the two-litre engine. Sammo grinned ear to ear as the engine roared and the car vibrated.

'Come on then, kidder, scran and dosh.'

'Yeah.'

Mikey pulled the car out of the car park and headed into the centre. They swung past St. George's Hall, with its imposing Corinthian colonnade and portico with classical frieze. Sammo felt great riding through Liverpool in a smart car. The acceleration of the Capri meant it could dodge and weave through the heavy traffic.

Buses dominated the city centre, serving the hundreds of thousands who lived in the estates on the outskirts. Sammo wound his window down to feel the rush of air as they made their way through town. He didn't mind the smoke or fumes — this was the smell of the city, as rich to him as candy floss in a fairground.

'What's this?' Sammo asked, pointing to the dashboard.

'Eight track stereo. Don't they teach you anything out there?'

'Never seen one.'

'Here, get a load of this.' Mikey pressed the cartridge in to play.

The opening bars of 'She's Not There,' filled the car. The sound bounced around, and Sammo couldn't resist nodding to the tune.

'Carlos Santana,' Mikey explained before laughing. 'Go for it, kidder.'

Jaime was okay. The music, the car, the city — Sammo was feeling good.

'Shit.' Mikey reached across and turned off the music.

'What's up?' The abrupt silence broke Sammo's reverie. He turned to Mikey when he saw a police car had pulled alongside them in the outside lane.

'Just look straight ahead,' Mikey said, his voice calm, his features immobile as he stared straight ahead.

Sammo froze. He knew what happened to Jaime and didn't want Mikey to get in trouble. Staring at the lights, willing them to change as a knot grew in his stomach. He used his last defence in extreme situations. Please, God, make them leave us alone.

The red seemed to last forever. Sammo looked out of the corner of his eye and saw Mikey was also looking straight ahead. Sammo could see the copper in the passenger seat staring at Mikey and looking the car over. The copper's face softened as he made eye contact with Sammo, and a half-smile appeared on his lips, and for the first time in his life, Sammo felt white. He slipped his hand into his pocket and gripped the watch. If they caught him with it, he'd definitely be in trouble. The smooth, round shape filled his palm.

The light changed to amber. They waited, and the light

turned green. The police car moved off, and Mikey turned left. He straightened the car as they climbed the hill.

Mikey exhaled, 'Bastards.'

'Did Jaime tell you what they did to him?' Sammo asked.

Mikey looked across. 'Yeah, no good, man. Those people,' he said, shaking his head.

'Why did they do that?'

'Power, kidder.'

Sammo wasn't sure exactly what Mikey meant, but the word hung in the air. Everything about the town differed from Speke. He caught sight of a kebab shop. In Speke, they had chippies or a Chinese chippy. No kebab shops or restaurants.

'I'm starving, though. We got a sarnie at dinner time, but my stomach's rumbling now,' Sammo said.

'Hold on. I'll feed you up.'

They had reached the top of Hardman Street. The shops had given way to the huge red brick Victorian hospital on one side and the more modern Philharmonic Hall on the other. Opposite the Philharmonic was Hope Street Police Station. A huge square fronted building, it stood like a fortress between the city centre's financial and retail spaces and the people of Toxteth. Swinging round to the right along Myrtle and Catherine streets, lined with Georgian terraces, they crossed the lights at Parliament Street to Princess Avenue. Everything was different — the houses, the buildings — everything was bigger, older, grander.

'Nearly home now, kidder.'

'Is this where you live?'

'This is home territory. We live round the corner.'

They took a left off Princess Avenue and made their way through the smaller terraced streets into Granby. This felt like Garston, and Sammo knew Garston: long rows of tiny terraced houses.

'This is home, kidder.' Mikey turned into the kerb and parked. 'Come on, some food?'

Before the Storm

Granby Street, early evening in June, the sun was disappearing somewhere out in Liverpool Bay. Mikey greeted a couple of guys on the street as they walked to the takeaway.

They sat on a small wall, eating chips and sausage from newspaper wrappers.

Mikey was finishing his chips. 'I think you should be careful.'

'Why?'

'The watch is gold, the chain as well. There is a hallmark on the watch.'

'What's a hallmark?'

'It's a stamp, to show if something is genuine, like real gold.'

'Oh, right? So it might be worth hundreds, then?'

'I doubt it, kidder. No one will give you anything near its real value, but let's see. A watch like that means someone will be looking for it.'

'I don't think Macca will be happy.'

'Who's Macca?'

'A mate.' Sammo scrunched up his papers and threw them in a concrete bin on the pavement.

'Good shot. Okay, are you ready? Let's see what we can sort out for you.'

Sammo followed Mikey. It wasn't far, just a couple of streets away. The tidy terraced streets ran off Granby Street from both sides into graffiti-covered terrace walls. Groups of young men and women stood on corners and around shop entrances. It was the same in Speke. There was still light enough for kids to be playing in the street when darkness descended, and the kids went inside, the streets changed.

Mikey stopped. They were outside a mid-terrace. Instead of knocking, Mikey gave a high-pitched whistle, two notes in quick succession. He leant forward and rapped on the door, whistling again as he did so. A curtain moved in the window, and a couple of seconds later, a youth with short, dark hair and freckled face opened the door.

'Is your old man there?'

The youth stepped aside and opened the door. Mikey led the way. Through the doorway, they stepped right into the living room. A sofa faced the telly in the corner, and a young boy and girl were watching TV. Across from them, in an armchair, was a woman. Sammo thought her to be their mum.

'In the back.' The youth nodded, pulling on his jacket to leave.

In the kitchen, an older man sat reading a newspaper. He shook it closed as they walked in.

'Hey, Johnny, I got something you might wanna have a look at,' Mikey said.

'Is that so,' the older man's glasses balanced on the end of his nose as he looked them over. 'And who's this young fella?'

'A mate of our Jaime's. He's got something you might like.'

'All right,' Sammo said in greeting.

'Let's see what you got, then.'

Sammo pulled out the watch and handed it over. Johnny weighed it carefully and polished it against his jumper. He changed glasses, putting on a rimless round pair. He raised the watch close to his eyes, flipped the cover. He turned it around, inspecting it from every angle, and then pulled out the winder while holding it to his ear. Then the chain, inspecting the clasp and the links. The sound from the TV drifted in. It was the theme tune for the news.

'The watch is gold, a good make. The chain is gold, twelve-carat, reasonable size, so there's value in that.'

'That's what I told him, but you're the specialist,' Mikey said.

'It's an expensive watch. Prolly' meant a lot to someone.' He looked over his glasses again at Sammo.

Sammo felt his face reddening. 'It's my granddad's. He just wanted to know how much it was worth.'

'Well, I could give you twenty, twenty-five quid at most, kid. I wouldn't make much on that myself trying to move it on. That's a fair amount for a nipper like you.'

Sammo had to think quickly. Macca would want the money, but would he believe that was all he got for it? What if Macca thought Sammo was cheating him? 'Nah, think I'll take it back to my grandad.'

He felt guilty saying the words; the old man was dead. He could never get the watch back.

'Thirty-five, but I can't go any higher,' the man said, lowering his glasses.

'Nah, sorry, I need to take it back.' Sammo had turned. The watch now, felt like a burden, not an opportunity.

The living room door to the street opened. Sammo could see through the kitchen doorway. The youth from earlier came in breathless. Sammo and Mikey heard the commotion and went to the doorway.

'What's up with you?'

'It's all kicking off, innit.' He was breathing hard.

'What is?'

'The police tried to arrest a kid at the corner of Selbourne and Granby Street. He was on a motorbike. They didn't get him. A group of lads let him get away. Then they started fighting. Police cars are everywhere now, and people are bricking them.'

Everyone in the room stared at him as he was trying to catch his breath. 'You can stay in here now then,' his mum said from the armchair.

'No, I want to see what's going on,' he protested.

'Get in here and sit down.'

'Mum... I'll be back soon, okay? I won't be late.' He left before his mum could say anything else.

'We better go, kidder. Thanks, Johnny. Later mate,' said Mikey.

Sammo held his hand out. Johnny placed the watch in his hand, and Sammo pocketed it and followed Mikey out the door.

Mikey walked quickly. Sammo had to trot behind him to keep up. The sound of sirens were rising and falling in the background. It provided a continuous backdrop of sound from different directions. It wasn't just Mikey; everyone on the street was moving rapidly. Doors opened as people stood on the steps, looking out along the street. Everyone turned to the noise and smell in the evening sky. Something was happening.

'What's going on?' Sammo asked.

'Come on, kidder, get a move on.'

They turned the corner into Granby Street. The groups that were chatting and relaxing earlier were now anxious and tense. A couple of youths came running into Granby from the direction of Princess Avenue. They were laughing and excited. 'We got em, man. Boom.'

The youth hit a fist into his open hand and bounced off in what Sammo took to be the acting out of a direct hit on a police car.

Mikey started running, and Sammo was right behind him. Mikey reached the Capri first, and he was in with the engine on when Sammo caught up and threw himself into the passenger seat.

'Things are kicking off big time,' said Mikey.

He drove the car slowly down Granby, looking down each side street. Near the end, he took a left onto Kingsley Road and then to the roundabout at the bottom of the Avenue. 'We gotta get away from here quick.'

Mikey took the route towards Aigburth. As they drove out of Toxteth, police cars were coming in the opposite direction. They were out of Liverpool 8 now, but sirens were still sounding as reinforcements streamed out of the surrounding areas towards town.

'Gonna be a crazy night,' Mikey said.

'What will happen?' Sammo asked.

'I don't know, kidder, but them police are gonna taste some, for sure tonight. As my man Sam Cooke says, "It's been a long time coming."' He paused, before adding, 'And a price is gonna be paid.'

'Who's Sam?' Sammo asked.

Mikey smiled. He leaned over and ruffled Sammo's hair. 'You's okay, kidder. Let's get you back to your people.'

They drove in silence along Aigburth Road. Sammo had the chance to sell it, but the watch was still with him. Whose watch is it now? The old man died when the watch left him. His time was over. Whose time is it measuring now?

Ten minutes later, Mikey was turning off Speke Boulevard into Rycroft Road.

'You can drop me here. I just walk down to get to mine. It'll be easier for you to turn round.'

'You sure, kidder?'

'Yeah, thanks for getting me home.'

'No problem. Look after yourself.'

Sammo climbed out of the car. He stood while Mikey turned the car around.

Mikey pulled up next to him and wound down his window. 'Look after yourself, brother, and if you need us, you know where we are.'

They clasped hands through the open window. Sammo watched as Mikey moved off and rejoined the Boulevard. It had been a crazy day. There was something about the way Mikey had said "brother" that made him feel warm and good. He walked down Rycroft along Dymchurch. The night had darkened now, and the streetlights threw out an orange glow, illuminating little. The street was quiet. He was glad. He had enough of sirens and noise, and he began to feel the weight of the day. All he wanted now was his bed.

They lived right at the bottom of Dymchurch Road. As he neared his house, he saw the light was on in the kitchen. A figure emerged from the darkness.

'Where have you been?'

It was Vinny.

'Hey,' Sammo said tiredly.

'I've been waiting here for you for hours,' said Vinny.

They sat on the short wall that fronted the small patch of grass that passed as a garden.

'What have you been waiting for?'

'We wondered what happened to you. Macca was going crazy when you went off with the treasure.'

'It's not treasure. It's a watch.' Sammo stared out into the darkness. He was home. The house behind him had his bed, but he didn't move. 'I didn't go off with it. Don't you remember what happened?'

'Yeah, of course. Jaime got hit by a car.'

'Yeah, and he could've died.'

'Did he?'

'No, he didn't. But you didn't care anyway, right?'

'What do you mean?'

'You didn't even ask what happened to him? You left me there on my own.'

'Well, I guess if something bad happened, you would have said. There was no point, all of us going in the ambulance.'

'Yeah, right?' Sammo was too tired to argue.

Vinny put his hand on Sammo's shoulder. 'I'm sorry. I was thinking about it all day, honest. That's why I waited for you.'

'He was a good lad, and I met his mum and brother. His mum was Chinese, just like he said. What happened to you and Macca?'

'We walked back with the marchers. We were collecting money in buckets from people in the street as we walked. Macca got nearly three quid out of it.'

'For himself, you mean? He took it out of the bucket?' Sammo asked.

'Yeah. I didn't. I gave all mine to the marchers. Macca was going crazy about you, but don't worry about it. Have you still got it, then?' asked Vinny.

'Yeah.' Sammo slid it out of his pocket. 'Here, you can have it.'

Vinny stood. 'No, I don't want it. It's Macca's now.'

'What happened with the dead feller?'

'I don't know, but the bizzies have been round there.'

'Here.' Sammo offered Vinny the watch again.

'Can you hide it?' Vinny asked. 'I will owe you big time if you can. Anytime you need anything, you just ask me.'

'I guess so.' Sammo stood and walked to the outbuilding that held the family bin. Inside, just above the door opening, was a shelf with a loose brick. Sammo showed Vinny and placed the watch there.

'Thanks, mate. I really owe you,' Vinny said as he backed away.

'A price is gonna be paid,' said Sammo into the darkness.

He stood for a minute and wiped his hand across his face. He remembered how Jaime's mum had fussed over him in the hospital and how Mikey said "brother." A tear slid out of Sammo's eye. He was crying for the love and friendship he didn't have.

He heard the front door open behind him.

'Sammo, is that you out there?' his mother yelled.

'Yes, mam,' he shouted back.

'You'd better get your arse in here. Look at the telly — they've all gone mad in Liverpool, burning the place down.'

Chapter Twenty-One

Vinny

7pm, Saturday, 25th June, 2016

Vinny was kneeling, pointing at the letters in front of him. 'This is a lot to deal with.' He stood and paced the room. Every time he thought of Sammo now, he thought of the watch and Helen's grandfather.

The presence of the letters in front of them was shocking. It was like ten-pin bowling. The pins were the elements of Sammo's life and along came this ball, smashing through them, knocking down pin after pin, until...

'Did you ever see anyone else at Sammo's?'

'Yeah, the last time I was there. Why?'

'Something's been bugging me.' Anne sat back in the armchair.

'What?' asked Vinny.

'Who called the ambulance?' Anne posed the question.

'Good point. If Sammo took the drugs in his living room, how would anyone know there was a problem?'

'Unless they were in the room with him?' said Anne.

'What did the police say?' asked Helen.

'Something about a neighbour, but the call was anonymous?' It sounded weird at the time. If it was anonymous, how did they know it was a neighbour? Or how would a neighbour know what was happening inside his house?'

'I met someone the last time I went round there,' said Helen.

'Did you get a name?' Anne leaned forward.

'Just Beep, Sammo called him Beep.'

'Beep. Shit, I think I heard that when we were kids.' said Vinny.

'So, real name?'

'I don't know, but I'll find out,' Vinny went to the kitchen. Anne followed him and spoke quietly. 'It's time you told Helen.'

Helen raised her voice. 'What's going on out there?'

Vinny shouted back. 'Do you want a drink?'

'Yeah, go on. A white.' Anne collected her things from the living room. 'I've got things to sort out.'

'Thank you.' Helen offered her hand. Anne accepted it. Less a handshake, more a squeeze. 'I understand now just how good you are.'

'Aww shush, you'll embarrass me.' Anne smiled.

'Keep me updated,' said Helen.

'Of course,' Anne called through to Vinny in the Kitchen. 'Look after her.'

Vinny shook his head. Typical, now Anne and Helen were a team.

Vinny heard the front door close. He knew he had to deliver his news and wasn't looking forward to it. He selected a bottle of white from the fridge. He reached for glasses, carried the bottle and glasses into the living room. He edged a letter aside and put the glasses down.

'Not on there,' Helen said, rolling her eyes.

Vinny shrugged and moved the glasses to the dinner table that was between the living room and the kitchen. He unscrewed the cap, poured the wine, and passed a glass to Helen. She took a drink and placed it on a side table next to the sofa.

'This Macca stuff is weird.'

'You really hate him, don't you?' Helen asked.

'Yeah, I guess I do. I don't hate many people, but yeah, he's up there. You know he's all for Brexit, a councillor now. Going on about immigrants. Speke is as white as a… I don't know, as a… polar bear party in Iceland.'

'They don't have polar bears in Iceland, and it's not just about colour these days. Now they argue for putting British people first or protecting our Christian culture.'

'You know what I mean,' Vinny continued. 'He's a bully, pure and simple, always looking to blame someone else, even as a kid. I never knew what you saw in him.'

'I didn't go out with him for that long. It was before we got together, and I've told you we didn't do anything.'

'Yeah, I know,' Vinny said.

'You're not exactly in a position to criticise my fidelity or loyalty.'

'Okay, I know.' Vinny knew where this was going and regretted his comment.

'You were the one who left me, remember? Left me with a baby while you went off to finish your studies, do your masters, and go gallivanting around Ireland with Anne.'

'Okay. I'm sorry I said anything. I was messed up then. All that stuff with my dad freaked me out.'

Helen raised her hands, palms up, and lowered them in a calming motion. 'This isn't helping either of us.' She took a drink. 'Okay, so we agree. There's something between Sammo and Macca. What else?'

'The black car, the overdose. Where do you want to start?' said Vinny, frustrated. 'The car, okay… it looked like it was coming straight at me, but loads of men drive like that.'

'Well, I know someone was following me, and they weren't hiding it, either. Whoever it was wanted me to know. It was a big black BMW. I saw the driver briefly through a windscreen, but I think I would recognise him. The problem is, Liverpool is full of thirty to fifty-year-olds, close-cropped, sharp-featured, muscled men.' said Vinny. 'There must be a factory somewhere knocking out cheap copies. Maybe I'm getting paranoid,' said Helen.

'You're not paranoid. Something is going on. We can assume it was the same black car. There's something else as well,' Vinny said.

'What?' Helen asked.

'I mean, why didn't Sammo give you the envelope? Or why didn't he give it to me the week before?' asked Vinny.

'Yeah, you're right. He could have given it to me in person.' She looked at Vinny. 'Something happened between him seeing me and you and him leaving the package. But what?'

'Who knows?' Vinny said.

'Whatever it was, it must have been serious for him to think he couldn't wait? He might not have had time?' Helen wondered aloud. 'That's weird.'

'Should you be having that with the medication?' Vinny asked. He was building up to it.

'You're the one who poured it for me,' she answered.

'I know. Anyway, I will go and see Macca.'

'Really? Are you okay with that?'

'Yeah, we've got to sort this out.'

'Have you met Macca's son, Gary?' Helen asked.

'No, but I've heard he's a bit of a scally,' said Vinny.

'Scally isn't the half of it. According to Claire, he terrorises Speke now. People are frightened. You should be careful. You know their first instinct is violence.'

'And you think I can't handle him? Is that it? I'm not man enough?'

'Vinny, no, you're my husband. I love you. I don't see things in those terms. That's ridiculous.' Helen paused. 'What about Sammo's letter to you? He seems to think you will work everything out.'

'Yeah. I've got no idea what it means. I get that he had a bad time in the army. The thing with Macca again, and they both knew I was actively against the war. So he would think I'd be sympathetic to his horror stories. I don't know what else to think.' He wondered if Sammo was on about the watch. He threw the question back at her. 'You?'

'No, the same, but there has to be a reason. It's in here somewhere.'

'What does he mean when he talks about keeping schtum? Where is it?' Helen rifled through the letters. 'We know this is his last letter because he mentions speaking to you.'

She read it out loud:

'Then keeping schtum don't work either, didn't work when we was kids and don't work now. We done that as kids. I knew you were against it, you always was. Funny how things work out.'

'I know what that is.' Vinny took a drink from his glass.

'Really? Do you want to tell me? What was that about a jigsaw and all the pieces?'

'Yeah,' Vinny said reluctantly. 'There's something we did when we were kids. We promised to keep quiet about it. That's what he means. He says I was against it, and he is right.'

'But you're not kids now.' Helen's tone was sharper. 'Are you going to tell me?'

Vinny stood. He reached for the letter and read the section as if to check the words. 'The thing is when we were kids, Macca robbed a house. A house in Speke.'

'Yeah, come on. I knew you weren't angels. There must be more to it than that.'

Helen sat up. Vinny paced.

'The thing is… the guy in the house died by accident the same night. It was nothing to do with Macca. He was the one who went in… but… the guy was your grandfather—'

'Wait…' Helen interrupted. 'My grandad?'

Helen went quiet for a minute.

Vinny sat opposite her. 'Obviously, I didn't know that at the time. None of us did. I mean, it was just a random burglary. You know, for meters.'

Helen raised a hand to her face. For a second, it covered her eyes, and then she drew it down, stretching out her features. Her eyes narrowed, and she tilted her head.

'There was no point in telling you before—' Vinny tried to explain.

Helen had her hand up to stop him. 'Wait... wait a minute.' Her voice was cold and hard. 'You're telling me that you were part of robbing my grandfather's house the night he died?' she paused. 'The night he died... and you have known for all these years. I'm just speechless, really. What the hell am I supposed to say to that?'

Vinny panicked. He knew he had hurt her. 'I don't know. It wasn't intentional, none of it was. It just sort of happened. It just grew. I didn't even know he was anything to do with you. It was only later I realised that Joe Doyle was your cousin. Even then, it didn't really come up.' He spoke quickly, trying to get all his arguments out at once. 'We didn't start going out for a long time after that. You know, I haven't seen Macca or Sammo for years. Even back then, we stopped knocking round together.'

'They went off to the army,' Helen said. 'You were here. You knew what happened, you knew me.'

'I know. I know... It's not enough, I know, but honestly, I buried it. I haven't thought of it, or them, until all this. It was a kid's thing.'

'Don't lie to me. Don't tell me you haven't thought of it. How could you not think of it? Every time I mentioned my grandfather? Every time you met my family? What a mess.'

'Here.' Vinny offered to top up Helen's wine.

'That's not going to fix this.'

'I know that.' He topped up his own. Then he sat next to her on the sofa.

He reached out to hug her.

She leaned in cautiously. 'It still hurts.'

'The bruises?' he asked.

'Both,' she said.

The hug was brief and uncommitted. Vinny withdrew a little, but at least she wasn't screaming at him.

'Then you had the watch?' Helen looked quizzically.

'Yeah,' Vinny answered.

'What happened to it?'

'Long story. We tried to sell it, but couldn't, then eventually, I think Macca kept it. What he did then, I have no idea. My guess is that he sold it. Why would he keep it?'

'Joe was pretty cut up about it. I think if he found you then, you would have been in trouble.'

'Yeah, we knew that.'

'I can't believe you all knew. Even Sammo, these last few weeks, he never said anything.'

'It was a long time ago. No doubt, he has had bigger things on his mind since then.'

'But, Macca.' Helen's face hardened. 'That bastard was my boyfriend. He knew whose house it was. He must have known. How could he do that? It makes my skin crawl just thinking about it. Even if he didn't tell you, he knew it was my grandad's.'

'Here.' Vinny handed Helen her drink.

'What are you doing?'

'I want to make a toast,' said Vinny. 'To justice.' He held his glass up.

Helen raised hers. 'For what?' she asked.

'It might be a bit late for your grandad, but let's get to the bottom of this thing between Macca and Sammo.'

'No,' said Helen, lowering her arm. 'I don't think I'm ready to clink glasses with you. You do realise that you have just admitted to lying to me for years? I'm mad at Sammo and Macca, but you're my husband. You lied, have been lying...'

Vinny's stomach sank. 'I don't think that's fair. It's not like it's been continuously discussed, and I didn't know at the time. Or not till much later.'

'Okay, I'm not sure how much that helps.'

Before the Storm

Vinny got up and paced the room. 'Just think about it… even back then, Macca was lying. He lied to us about not knowing your grandad, he lied to you about the robbery. He has been playing everyone.'

'That's nice and convenient for you, isn't it? Macca gets all the blame. We don't know what happened to Sammo, we don't know who was driving those cars,' said Helen.

'He's guilty all right. The only question is how much,' said Vinny.

'He's not the only guilty one here. I need to sleep. I'm going up.'

'I'll put this stuff away and join you,' said Vinny.

'No, don't bother,' said Helen.

'I should put it away. I don't want Charlie to see it in the morning.'

'I mean, don't bother coming up. I don't want you near me tonight.'

Vinny's shoulders dropped.

'And I don't want Charlie finding you on the sofa. Make yourself other arrangements.'

'Really? You're kicking me out?'

'I just don't want you here tonight. You usually don't mind spending time in your office.'

'I've had a drink.'

'You can afford a taxi, can't you? I'm going up. Lock up before you leave.'

Helen stood and walked slowly towards the stairs, leaning on the furniture as she moved.

Vinny put all the letters back in the envelope. Fuck.

Chapter Twenty-Two

Anne

10,00am, Sunday, June 26th, 2016

Karen opened her office door to let Anne and Helen in. A thin woman in her late twenties, she was never rushed. Her movements and speech were purposeful and determined. The Addiction Treatment Centre was attached to the doctor's surgery. 'Come in, ladies.'

'Thanks for seeing us on a Sunday,' Helen lowered herself into a chair.

'No problem. I am not usually here on Sundays. Of course, I heard about Sam, so anything I can do. Are you okay?' Karen asked Helen.

'Yeah, fine, just a few bruises.'

Anne sat next to Helen.

'How can I help you?' Karen asked.

The room was basic, with a table and four chairs. The walls were full of posters with words like Understand, Heal. Grow. Lots of pictures of desperate looking people, enlarged syringes, and capital letter warnings.

Karen noticed Helen looking at the posters. 'They're mainly for relatives. No one believes for a minute they have any effect on those using.'

'Yeah, right,' Helen agreed. 'It's like I said on the phone.

About Sam Maddows.'

'Let me say, I am sorry for your loss.'

Helen replied. 'Thanks, I'm not family, but yeah, I knew him from when we were kids. You knew him, didn't you?'

'Yeah, on and off. I met Sammo a few times over the years. I was really pleased to see him recovering. He seemed to be doing really well. I didn't know him as well as Joe Doyle, you know, over at the Venny.'

'Joe Doyle from Harefield Road?' Helen asked.

'Yeah, that's right. Do you know him?'

'Yeah, he's my cousin.'

'Oh, right, nice guy? Does a lot of Welly rights.' Karen clarified, 'Welfare advice, benefits, and payments. Universal Credit is going crazy. But yeah, I met Sammo.'

'We both thought he was off the drugs, so it was a shock when we heard that he had overdosed.'

'That's why we're here, really. What I want to ask is, how easy is it to overdose... accidentally?' Helen asked.

'Well, absent any evidence of intention, it is the easiest conclusion,' said Karen.

'You don't sound too comfortable with that?' said Helen.

Karen leaned back in her chair. 'No, don't get me wrong; it's the most likely. But as long as this stuff is unregulated, no one knows what's in it. The dealers and the authorities know this, so they are both taking risks with the lives of users. The dealers for profit, the authorities for politics. And with the introduction of fentanyl, odds go up massively. So the idea of accidents in this situation is a bit strange. It's like someone selling dodgy petrol. The government knows about it, and every time someone's car blows up, they call it an accident.'

'So, the idea of an overdose is not a surprise for you?' asked Helen.

'No. I'm afraid not. There are two problems. The first is that having successfully come off and had a period where his body begins to recover, his tolerance for heroin would go down. What would have given him a high a few months ago, could kill him. Like I said, the second problem is that no one, and I mean no one, knows what is in the drugs that are on the streets.' Karen paused. 'Dealers have been cutting up heroin with fentanyl, and this has devastating effects. It is even more addictive and is more potent than heroin, but some users just can't take it. Instead of getting high, the body shuts down completely, the brain function stops, the brain literally stops telling the body what to do. People go into a coma and die.'

'Jesus, why do people take the risk?' asked Helen.

'The high from fentanyl is a super high. That's what it is all about. The brain craves that rush. It's relatively new here. We heard about it from America, but it has started to appear.'

The two women listened silently as Karen continued.

'It also depends on what Sammo was taking. To be honest, I was surprised when I heard, but you can never rule it out. He was a heroin user. Once someone has become addicted to that, they live with it. It's managed, controlled, but never disappears. The bottom line is, if they are using, they are at risk.' Karen paused again. 'I know it's probably not what you want to hear.'

Helen was the first to respond. 'No, I would rather you were honest.'

'But he can't overdose if he doesn't take it in the first place,' said Helen.

'Of course,' Karen replied. 'But it's really hard to second guess a user. I've been there... you can be feeling strong, and something happens. It could be something small that just hits you, that and the opportunity, if you get the opportunity to use.'

'What about suicide?' Anne asked.

'When drug addicts die, there are no notes.' Karen paused. 'That doesn't mean there aren't suicides. In a sense, every time someone injects is a mini suicide. They know every time there is a chance they won't be coming back from it. They might not admit it, but they know. The high is more important to them than coming back — that's their reality. So, you don't find notes. It just goes down as another accidental overdose.'

Anne had her notebook open. 'Where does the fentanyl come from?'

'It's a synthetic opioid. Man-made, it can be up to fifty or a hundred times more potent than heroin. There's a black market in the prescription drugs, but a lot are IMF Illicitly Manufactured Fentanyl dealers cut it into heroin.'

'Could you commit murder by overdose? Or would it be obvious in a post mortem?'

Karen's eyebrows raised. 'You know I've never considered it. It's not really an area I'm familiar with. You would need a toxicology specialist.'

Anne folded her notepad up and slipped it into her bag. 'Yeah, of course. Thanks for your time. Actually, there is one thing, if you don't mind, was Sammo associated with anyone? You know, like a partner in crime, a mate, maybe even another addict?'

'No, not that I'm aware of.' Karen looked at her watch. 'I'm sorry but… I just wish I had something more positive to say.'

'You've been a big help. Thank you.'

* * *

Back in the car, Anne turned the ignition.

'Murder by overdose?' asked Helen.

'We've got to ask the question: accident, suicide or?'

'But why? Why would anyone?'

'Kill him?' Anne finished Helen's question. 'That depends on what he knew, and what he was going to say? Can you call Claire, ask her if she can arrange to see the pathologist, ask her if I can tag along?'

'Jesus, this is getting scary.' Helen said.

'Are you ok? I can run you home,' said Anne.

'No, in the letters, Sammo was on about the street kids.'

'Yeah?' asked Anne

'Start your engine and follow my directions.'

Anne put the car in gear, reversed, and made her way out of Morrisons' car park. Helen was on the phone with Claire while giving directions. When she finished her call she explained. 'We're going to Dymchurch. I know people down there. Let's see what we can find out?'

Helen's phone beeped. She swiped to see the message.

Vinny: Collected Charlie, going to see Macca.

'Important?' Anne asked.

'Vinny's on his way here to see Macca.'

'Are you two okay?'

'He's in the doghouse.' She swiped his message to clear it. 'He got up to some stuff with Macca and Sammo he's only just told me about.'

'I know they weren't angels,' said Anne.

'They robbed my grandad's house the night he died. It's not even the robbery. Vinny didn't do it. But he knew about it for years and didn't tell me. I just can't get my head around it.'

They were driving along Central Avenue.

'It was just up there.' Helen nodded as they passed Harefield Road.

'It's easy to forget the things that hurt — we bury them,' said Anne.

'Including things we're responsible for?' Helen asked.

'Especially those,' said Anne.

'You might be right.'

They had turned onto Western Avenue and then left into Rycroft Road. The Dymchurch estate was a later addition to Speke. Completed in the late seventies, the houses were small, red-brick boxes, tagged on to the end of the estate, which was largely built after the Second World War. It comprised Dymchurch Road, which ran in a long curve about half a mile, and small cul-de-sacs off the main road on either side. In the early days of the estate, the place was a nightmare for the police. Car thieves would head for the estate, abandon a car, and escape on foot, leaving the police stumped. Anne pulled to the kerb in front of a house that opened directly onto the road. The front door was pillar-box red in high gloss, so the surface was smooth and shiny. It had a brass knocker, which Helen used to rap sharply twice.

There was no response from inside, so she knocked again. 'Okay, I'm coming,' a voice called before the door opened. 'Helen. Long-time no see. What can I do for you?'

'Hi, Sharon, sorry to bother you, love. I was on my way to Sammo's.'

Sharon's tone changed immediately. 'I heard. Terrible thing.' She threw the door open wider. 'Are you coming in? I'll put the kettle on.'

'I don't want to trouble you.'

'No, of course not. Come in.'

'I've got Anne with me, an old friend.'

'Come in, both of you.'

Sharon stood back, holding the door open. 'Go straight through to the kitchen.'

Anne led the way. Helen followed her. They sat on a bench seat on one side of a pine table. Sharon moved effortlessly around the room, sorting out the tea things. Dressed in a red velour tracksuit. 'Milk and sugar?' she asked.

'Yeah.'

'Just milk for me,' Helen was getting tired. The pain from the bruising was wearing her out.

Sharon arranged everything on a tray and brought the tea over to the table. 'Here we are. I was sorry to hear about Sammo. It was an OD, wasn't it?'

'Looks that way,' said Helen.

'Awful. You know everyone is worried,' said Sharon.

'Worried about what?' Anne asked.

'The stuff going round. If Sammo OD'd, who's next?'

'Did you see much of him?' Anne asked.

'Not really. Saw him a bit more after he got the dog. Cute little thing.'

Sharon took a drink of her tea. 'The thing is, it's everywhere now. If the kids aren't using, they're dealing. There's a whole industry. Drivers, runners, people hiding it, moving, guarding it.'

'How's your Chris doing?' asked Helen.

'My Chris. Well, he's not using, that's got to be a bonus.'

'Is he in school?'

'What school? The two schools we had growing up are both gone now. They shut All Hallows and Speke Comp. Kids had Parklands for a while. Big new building cost millions, but they shut that after ten years. Now kids have to get a bus to Garston or Widnes.

'The authorities don't care. That's the truth of it — we know it, and the kids know it. You can talk to them about drugs and the dangers 'til you're blue in the face. When it comes down to it. I know, and the kids know, the people with the best cars on this estate are people involved in drugs. How can we compete?'

Chris came wandering into the kitchen, rubbing his head and eyes. Chris was wearing a white t-shirt and blue checked boxer shorts. 'Who's doing all the yapping?'

'Some friends of mine. Don't be cheeky, and go and put some clothes on,' Sharon told him. 'Do us a tea then, mam.' He sat opposite Helen and Anne.

'Did you know Sammo?' Anne asked him.

'At the bottom of the street? Yeah, he died, right?'

'Right,' Anne replied.

'Messed up, man. This whole place. Telling you, it's crazy.'

'He had a hard time with some of the kids?' Helen asked.

'Yeah, the youngers. I don't mess with them, you know what I mean. He pissed them off. How? I don't know, but it don't need a reason sometimes. They get word, and they mess with people,' Chris said.

'What word… who from?' Anne asked.

'You know, him, Mam. Hey, where's my tea?'

Sharon brought a mug over.

'Oh, I need that,' he said, taking a gulp.

'Who?' Sharon asked.

'You know, him. They call him G-mac. Big guy, drives a nice motor. Into all the MMA and stuff.'

'What about him?' asked Anne.

Helen's phone rang. She nodded to Anne, 'I should take this.' she walked toward the front door.

'He's the one who gives the kids the word. If not him, one of his boys like Beep.'

'How do you know?' Anne asked.

'Seen him,' Chris spoke in fragments.

'You saw him talk to the boys?' Anne continued the questioning.

'Yeah, but seen him go to Sammo.'

'You saw him go in?'

'Yeah, other night, wasn't it? He went in, see his black mark five parked up. He got out, goes in. The kids see it, too.'

'Who went in? Gary Mac or Beep.'

'Beep, then the BM pulls away like.'

'Has anyone told the police?' Anne asked.

'You're kidding, aren't you? They fit you up. Even if you're a villain, it doesn't matter. They fit guilty people up all the time.'

'When did you see him going in?' Anne tried to clarify.

'Wasn't last night, so yeah, night before, or one before that?'

'That would make it Thursday night?' Anne asked. 'Do you know Beep? His full name? Where he lives?'

'Nah, down the east side somewhere, but I don't know. Just know him as Beep. Saw him go in. But he was in before that as well. I seen him.'

A look of realisation was shared between Anne and Helen. They needed to find this Beep character.

Chapter Twenty-Three

Vinny

11am, Sunday, June 26th, 2016

Vinny shivered and shifted uncomfortably, pulling the blanket tighter around his body. Stretched between two chairs, his sleep was broken, fitful, and now impossible. The morning light and his dry throat forced him into consciousness. It was time for breakfast, or at least a cup of tea. Luckily, he didn't have far to go. The Uni was surrounded by cafes. There was a Starbucks on the corner of Myrtle and Hardman Street. It was a while since he'd slept in his office.

Helen, Sammo, and Macca came to mind, and more than these, Charlie. He hadn't moved yet, uncomfortable and awkward wasn't just a description of his physical position. He had ended the relationship with Helen when she found out she was pregnant. They decided not to get back together because of the pregnancy. This was sensible, logical. It was also convenient for Vinny. He had just started university. In fact, they were apart for the first four years of Charlie's life.

Vinny's relationship with fatherhood was difficult. His dad had abandoned him as a kid, and Vinny had repeated the trick with Charlie. It seemed fathers leaving sons was becoming a family tradition. After the trip to Ireland, he wanted to break the cycle, so he moved back into the husband and dad-shaped hole in Helen and Charlie's life.

Fuck. His legs responded stiffly. He stood, folded the blanket, and placed the chair back in its place. He moved his fingers through his hair and rubbed his face. Breakfast, he had to look after Charlie this morning, but he was also determined to face Macca.

On his way out of his office, he waved at Roger without making eye contact; he didn't stop to chat.

* * *

'Where's your mum?' asked Vinny.

'She went out.' Charlie was concentrating on the screen in front of him.

'Where?'

'How am I supposed to know?'

'Maybe she told you?'

'You're kidding, aren't you? No one tells me anything.'

'Alright, well, any info?'

'Someone called Anne collected her. They went off together.'

'Ok, well, you're with me this morning.'

'Why?'

'Because your mum doesn't want you on this all day. Come on, sort yourself out. We've got somewhere to be.'

Ten minutes later, the vibe in the car was kidnapper and hostage. Vinny steeled himself. What was he supposed to say to Macca? He knew he had to do this, but wasn't looking forward to it.

'Are you okay?' Charlie asked.

'Yeah.' Vinny was concentrating on the road.

'Where are we going?'

'To Speke.'

'What for?'

'I have to see a man about a dog.'

'Really?' Charlie asked, looking brighter.

'No, that's just an expression.'

'Stupid expression,' said Charlie.

'Yeah, you're probably right, kidder.'

'Kidder? Okay, don't tell me another saying from "back in the day."' He made air quotes with his fingers and rolled his eyes.

Vinny smiled. Charlie's disdain was a daily reminder of how useless and unimportant he was.

'Are you and Mum okay?'

'Yeah, sure. Why?'

'You didn't stay at the house last night?'

'I know I had some work to do and ended up kipping in the office.'

'You mean you got drunk and didn't want to face Mum?'

Vinny smiled and looked across at him. 'All right, smart arse.'

He drove through Allerton Road, quieter than usual on this Sunday morning. It was normally bustling with shoppers and students. That was how society should be: lively and vibrant. The population of the city centre, like the tide in the Mersey Estuary, swept in and out, but instead of a timescale of hours like the ebb and flow of the river, the population changes were over a century. In Liverpool, everything started in seven streets around the river and castle. When the docks, workshops, warehouses, and chandlers opened, the wealthy began to leave. The arrival of the Irish during the famine accelerated the process. The wealthy built houses in Toxteth Park and Aigburth. When the unwashed masses spilled out from the centre, the wealthy deserted these areas, too.

After the Second World War, slum clearances swept tens of thousands to new estates, ringing the city. The centre was cleared of slums and workers and rebuilt. It became habitable by the up and coming… Vinny's family, like so many others, had been swept out to Speke. A good salary and job meant he moved back on the ebb tide into Allerton.

Before the Storm

Vinny didn't know what he would say to McNally. The letters had shown this wasn't so much about Sammo's death as his life. Something went wrong between Macca and Sammo. They had always been close. Something must have happened.

He was on his way to Parklands, the new centre for all things official in Speke. Macca had his councillors' surgery there. Vinny had his leaflet on the seat next to him: 'Steve McNally Spekes for you.' He could imagine Macca and his cronies coming up with that slogan and thinking they were so clever.

This would be his second time in Speke in as many days, probably as many times as he had been in the last ten years. The place had everything he left behind: poverty, uniformity, depression, lack of ambition.

'Can you show me where you lived?' Charlie asked.

'What for?' Vinny said.

'When you were a kid. I want to see where you lived.'

'There's nothing there, just a house.'

'But it's where you grew up,' Charlie insisted.

'Okay, maybe.'

'You never show me anything.'

'That's not true. We do things together.'

'Like what?'

'I don't know, watch TV?'

'You don't go to football like other dads.'

'You don't play it.'

'I know, but I like watching it.'

Vinny drove down Western Avenue, a broad dual carriageway with robust semis on either side of the road. With large front and back gardens, these ex-council houses were highly prized, and in any other location, would be highly valued.

'Down there. Look, can you see? That's where we lived.'

'Yeah, I guess,' said Charlie, disappointed as they sped past Linner Road. 'Who are we going to see?'

'When we get there, I will go inside and see him. You can

wait for me outside, okay?'

'Really? You bring me all this way, then leave me outside?'

'I will get you something on the way home. We can stop at a shop, okay?'

Charlie crossed his arms. Vinny pulled into the car park of Parklands. It was meant to be a new administrative and social space for Speke, so naturally, it featured a Morrisons and on Sunday Morrisons was busier than the local churches. The complex housed one of Liverpool's few remaining public libraries. The library was on the ground floor, and the various housing, welfare, probation, community, and care services were housed in the rest of the building. 'Come on, let's go.' Vinny masked his nerves by hustling Charlie along. They assigned local councillors an office, and Sunday morning was "surgery time."

The door opened, and an old couple was leaving. Macca led them out towards the main entrance. 'You leave that with me. I'll do what I can.'

He held the door open as they left. When they were gone, he turned to face Vinny.

'Mr. Connolly and son, I believe. Come in.'

Macca held out his hand. 'And what's your name?'

Charlie reluctantly accepted his hand. 'Charlie.'

'Charlie: a good strong name. Like your dad, are you Charlie? Yeah, you look like a big strong lad.'

Macca moved across to a side table and returned with a flyer. 'Here, this is just what you need: martial arts training.'

Charlie looked at his dad. Vinny led him to a chair. 'Okay, you sit here. I'll be out in a few minutes.'

Macca didn't offer his hand and moved aside, allowing Vinny to enter the small office. 'He's a good-looking lad. Wonder where he gets that from?' Macca said.

'Must be his mum,' Vinny replied, using sarcasm to deflect the barb.

'Must say, I'm surprised to see you. What can I do for you?'

Before the Storm

Macca stood in front of a large Union Jack that covered the wall behind his desk. Beside it were photos of Macca, shaking hands with various people. None of whom Vinny recognised.

'Shall we sit?' Vinny asked. He would feel better with the desk between them.

'Of course. What am I thinking, please?'

Macca took his seat. 'So, Mr Connolly. I don't believe you are one of my constituents. Haven't you fled the nest, as it were, for leafy Allerton? Moved up in the world, as they say. What drags you back to lowly Speke?'

Vinny sat back in his chair. 'Okay, you can drop the sarcasm. I want to know what's going on here. What's the story between you and Sammo?'

'All right.' Macca moved forward and placed his elbows on the desk. 'No messing about.'

'Why did you call Helen?'

'A warning.' Macca leaned back in his chair. 'Look, I don't like you, never have really, even when we were kids. But I have got nothing against Helen, or your boy out there. I know Sammo. Sorry, I should say I knew Sammo. He was weak, he always was. I looked after him for years, kept him on the straight and narrow. The message was about Sammo, but I think you know that now. What I wouldn't expect you to know is that our friend had a rough time over the years. You could say civvy street wasn't kind to him.'

'You wanted Helen to stay away,' said Vinny.

'Don't be so dramatic. You want me to be honest? Okay. It was advice. Sound advice, for your missus' and for Sammo's benefit. He didn't need charity from guilty middle-class do-gooders. What he needed were real friends and comrades.'

'You know I grew up here, so did Helen. So don't give me that *middle-class* crap.'

'Not anymore, though, Vincent? Semi in Allerton, two-car family. What are you, professor at the university? You might be just a couple of miles up the road, but you are a long way from home, and you know it. I bet you feel it now, don't you? Nervous when you come back to Speke. In your guts, you know, and I know, you don't belong here.'

'Where I live has got nothing to do with this. You sent Helen a warning — the next minute, she was driven off the road. Crashed her car, ended up in hospital. Hours later, we learned Sammo was dead. There's something going on here.'

'You've been reading too much Agatha Christie. Sammo was a junkie. It's not nice to say it, but once a smack head, always a smack head. So you think there's some dark conspiracy... to what? Get rid of Sammo? Why? And... You think I did it? That's pretty sick.' Macca pushed his chair back and stood.

'You might be a professor, but you're not the brightest, are you?' he tapped his finger against the side of his head. 'Me, his closest comrade? And why? What the hell would I get out of Sammo's death?' he paused and reached out to a group of framed photos. He raised one, showing uniformed men posing in front of a military vehicle. They were wearing fatigues. Vinny raised his hand to his face, as if wiping away the anxiety he felt.

'Here, you know what this is?'

Vinny glanced at the picture. 'Yes, I know what it is. You and Sammo...'

'Bingo,' Macca said. 'Look around you. Where are we? I am an elected councillor for Speke. Do you know that? I care about this community. That's why I'm on the council and sat here on a Sunday morning. These are my people.' He thumped his chest. 'My people, and this is my country.'

'The message... and the crash,' Vinny objected.

'Think about it: when did Helen get the message?'

'Friday morning,' said Vinny.

'When did Sammo die?'

'Sometime Thursday evening or night.'

'So if I knew about his death, why would I be texting Helen

Before the Storm

Friday morning?'

It was weird, but Vinny hadn't thought about this. 'I don't know... there is a lot we don't know yet, but I'll find out.'

'Whatever.' Macca dismissed him with a wave of the hand. 'You and your liberal bollocks. You are part of what has ruined this country. What this country needs is leadership, strength.'

'Oh, give me a break.' Vinny felt he was on safer ground. 'People like you with your bigoted views. That is what I'm getting away from — not the place, not Speke.'

'See, that's where you liberals get it wrong, because I'm not a racist. I don't care. I like a chicken vindaloo, or biryani as much as the next man. Honestly, I don't care... Muslims, Hindus, Pakistanis, Africans. They've all got good and bad things about them. I don't care. This isn't about race or colour. It is about our culture and our ideals.' He pointed to the flag on the wall. 'This nationality and culture, you can even get rid of the monarchy, a bunch of whinging snobs. This is about the kind of society we live in. Order, discipline, values... British,' Macca said.

Vinny smiled. 'You're right, it's not about race, not even about Europe. It's about having free rein to do what you want without obstacles, hindrance, laws, liberals, parliament, unions, or workers getting in the way. You're missing something, though?'

Macca sat down again. 'Okay, smart arse, what am I missing?'

'You think you're part of this? This British thing? This order? You think that when they achieve this new society, you'll be one of the chosen who are liberated, freed?' Vinny laughed. 'The people who run things will piss all over you. They need people like you to keep places like this in order. You can risk your life for them, fight for them, but if you get in their way, you get out of line, you might as well be black, Asian, or a Muslim because they will throw you away like a dirty rag.'

Macca leaned back in his chair. 'I am an elected member of Liverpool Council. Who the fuck are you?'

There was a knock on the door behind Vinny, and it opened

immediately. Vinny turned to see a young man enter. Behind him, he could see Charlie reading a magazine. He waved, but Charlie didn't look up. The man who came in was solidly built, muscled, not pumped up like a bodybuilder, but defined and solid. His jawline was firm, and his features sharp.

'Gary. Here, let me introduce you to an old friend of mine, Vincent Connolly. University professor no less.' Macca was playing at bonhomie.

Vinny stood and held out his hand.

Macca continued. 'My son, Gary.'

'Nice to meet you,' Vinny said, and felt stupid as soon as he said it.

Gary shook his hand firmly, but with no malice. He met Vinny's eyes and gave a quick nod.

'Gary here is one of my best community assets. Organises an MMA class for local kids… very popular it is. Helps keep order, keeps the scallies under control. Eh, Gary?'

Gary didn't reply. The door was still open, and Macca called out to Charlie. 'Hey Charlie, do you want to do martial arts training?'

Charlie stood and moved towards the office.

Vinny called out, 'Charlie, wait out there, sit down. I won't be long.'

'You see Vincent. There's another difference. Close the door, Gary. I trust my son.' Macca stood to leave. 'My son is in here, not outside. Is there anything else I can do for you?'

Vinny stood. 'Yes. You can tell me why you and Sammo fell out?'

'None of your business.' Macca bristled. 'But it doesn't take a genius to work out. Sammo lost the plot, drugs, and God knows what else—'

Vinny interrupted. 'And of course, you wouldn't have anything to do with breaking the law, would you?'

'You're right, I wouldn't. I'm here to make sure the law is

followed, not broken.'

'You're such a hypocrite.'

Macca laughed.

Vinny pointed at him. 'Remember. I know you. I know who you are and what you have done.' Gary moved forward and grabbed Vinny's arm. The grip was powerful and painful.

'Hey…' Vinny protested.

'Do you want him out, Dad?'

Macca smiled. 'You think you can frighten me with your kid's stories from decades ago? Grow up. Even if you could prove something, no one would give a shit.' Then, speaking to Gary, he said, 'You can let go of him. He's harmless. He hasn't got the balls he was born with.'

Vinny pulled his arm away and turned to the door. He felt a push and was thrust out of the door.

'Come on, Charlie. We're going.'

He could hear laughter behind him. He went back to the car park, fuming. What a bastard. Ignorant loudmouth bastard. He noticed a poster for a public meeting with McNally. 'Let's leave the car. Come on, let's walk.' Vinny said. In one sense, Macca was right. The area had changed. The whole Parklands development itself was new. They walked down Stapleton Avenue.

'Where are we going?' asked Charlie.

'You wanted to know where I lived? I'm showing you.'

'Okay, cool. Who was that guy?'

'Someone no good, a bully and a bastard.'

'Why were you there?'

'It's complicated.'

'Yeah, right?' Charlie's tone shifted.

'What's wrong with you?' Vinny asked.

'It's complicated, means, "I can't be bothered telling you."'

'Okay, sorry, I didn't mean that.' He knew Charlie was right. They walked on in silence. Vinny fuming at his treatment.

'See here.' Vinny pointed to their right. 'There used to be a huge church, Saint Christopher's, but they knocked it down in the nineties, I think. It made your gran furious. They built that little thing.'

'Why?'

'Because ever since she moved here from Garston, they were collecting to build and then to pay for the church. Every couple of weeks, the priest would come round the house, collecting money.'

'Was Nan rich then?'

'No, they did it with everyone. Well, all the Catholics anyway. Didn't matter how much you had, they collected. So when they knocked it down, she was angry. The people of Speke paid for it, but got no say in what happened, and didn't get anything back. Behind it up that road, there was the school I went to. Let me show you something.' Vinny stopped and pulled up his sleeve. He held out his wrist. 'Can you see that?' his finger was following a faint line etched into his skin.

'Yeah, I think so,' said Charlie.

'You can't see the shape now, but can you guess what it is?'

'Let me see again.' Charlie stared at the faded blue lines. 'Nah.'

'This sounds stupid, but it was an anchor.'

'Like on a ship?'

'Yeah, I don't know how old I was. Maybe younger than you are now. Me and a mate stole a bottle of Indian ink from the teacher's storeroom, climbed up on that roof there, and gave ourselves tattoos with a needle. It was supposed to be like Popeye or a sailor. You know, an anchor.'

'Wow, that's so stupid.'

Vinny laughed. 'I know.' He ruffled Charlie's hair.

'You wouldn't get me doing anything that stupid,' Charlie said.

'Imagine what your mum would do if she saw you had a tattoo?'

Charlie made a sign like his head exploding. They both laughed.

'What did your mate do?' Charlie asked.

'I don't know, can't remember,' Vinny said.

'You should ask him,' Charlie said.

'Can't do that now,' Vinny said. 'He died last week. Heroin overdose.'

'Wow, the guy you went up on that roof with?'

'Yeah.'

'I guess things were pretty different then.'

'I guess. But we moved. If we stayed here, things would be the same. Or worse.'

'That's kinda shit,' said Charlie.

'You know, you're right, it is,' said Vinny.

'What happened? To your mate? Why was he doing smack?' Charlie looked at Vinny, then answered his own question. 'I know, it's complicated.' He turned away and began walking. The disappointment in Charlie's voice was obvious.

'Wait,' Vinny said. Charlie stopped and turned.

'Come on. I want to show you something.'

'Where are we going?'

Chapter Twenty-Four

Vinny

12am Sunday June 26th, 2016

They were back in the car. Vinny wasn't ready to face Helen. 'Oggy,' Vinny turned the ignition and drove towards the exit.

'What's Oggy?'

'Oglet shore, The Yonk,' said Vinny.

'Can you speak English?' Charlie asked.

'I am… it's old English; Oglet means oak by the water.'

'Am I supposed to be impressed?' Charlie had his hands open, palms up in exasperation.

'Never mind. You'll soon find out.' Vinny drove through the estate and onto Eastern Avenue. He turned right by what used to be The Dove and Olive and was now a vacant lot. The pub had been demolished. Nothing remained of the huge purpose-built structure except a pillar. It had a brick base and then a metal structure. It used to stand in front of the pub. At its top, it had a large rectangular metal frame for the pub sign. The sign, like the pub and the spirit of the estate, had gone, and the frame swung empty in the breeze.

'Shit, The Dove and Olive has gone,' said Vinny.

He took a left and turned into Dungeon Lane. He was able to go a hundred yards in before a metal fence blocked the lane.

'They've closed it off. I can't believe they've closed it.'

'It's no big deal. Let's go home,' said Charlie.

'I wanted to go down to the river. I wanted to show you Oggy shore.'

'Well, it's closed. It's the airport now.'

Vinny did a three-point turn, mumbling the entire time.

'Are we going home?' Charlie asked.

'No. I can't believe they closed it. It's the only way for people in Speke to get to the river.'

'Is it important?'

Vinny sighed. 'I'm going to try.'

He turned right and drove a few minutes out of Speke and into Hale Village. The housing changed immediately, from red brick terraces to large detached bungalows set in gardens behind high walls and hedges.

'There must be a way down here.' He turned right down Bailey's Lane, and they rolled on beyond the housing. The road slimmed down to one lane and then a track on through scrubland. On the right, banks of runway lights were visible through a sturdy steel fence. A layered sky opened up before them — the bottom half grey and the top blue. The lane came to an end. Concrete bollards blocked the path. 'Come on, let's go,' said Vinny.

They got out of the car and followed the overgrown path down. On either side, weeds and bushes fought to retake the pathway. The bottom opened up into a view over the river: to the left, the ICI complex at Runcorn with newly placed wind turbines in the foreground. Across the river, the chimneys and towers of Stanlow Oil Refinery were visible.

The path continued down the grassy bank, waterlogged with recent rain and turned to mud. Before them was a clearing. The remains of a stone wall ran along the river's edge. A clear, flat area was visible. To the left concrete pyramid structures bunched together like abandoned kids' building blocks.

'It's getting cleaned up now. When we were kids, there was all kinds of shite down here… well, not here, along there.' Vinny pointed off to the right. 'In the eighties, it was a favourite place for burning out robbed cars.'

'Did you do that?'

'No, by that time, I had settled down a bit. That's Ellesmere Port over there,' said Vinny, pointing.

'What were you like as a kid?' asked Charlie.

'That's a strange question.'

'Not really. You're my dad. I should know something about you.'

'I wasn't as clever as you. You are much smarter than I was.'

'You're a professor. How much smarter can you get?'

'That's a different kind of clever. I was always good at talking. You know, I could find the words for things. But I wasn't good at deciding what to do, working things out. In fact, I made two big mistakes. No, that's not true. It was one mistake, but it had two outcomes, and both were bad. It was deciding to keep quiet about something.'

'Let's go down.' Charlie went ahead and skidded down the incline towards the riverbank.

Vinny followed him gingerly down the slope.

'Be careful, Charlie, it's muddy there, soft mud.'

'I'll be okay. Don't worry.'

They stood in the clearing. The river was full, and the grey-brown water lapped and slapped the stones at the edge. They stared out across the river.

'The thing I regret most in life is not being there for you when you were young,' said Vinny.

'It's okay, Dad. Don't feel bad. I don't even remember it.'

'You will, though, and it's not what you remember now. We don't know where it will come out, but you should be aware of it.'

'How do you mean?' asked Charlie.

They walked along the riverbank.

'I never knew my dad. I asked my mum, and she said he died in the war. It was stupid. The dates didn't work out. I think everyone knew it was stupid, but I went on saying it. My dad was Irish, so he wouldn't even have fought in the Second World War. I was living a lie. My mum was living a lie. I didn't argue or question it, even as I got older. I started studying history but didn't know my own. Eventually, I guessed that my dad had run off. He didn't die in the war. He must have left us. For another woman, whatever.'

'So, what happened? Did you find out?'

'Yeah, I did eventually, but I want to explain this thing first. I guess I knew it was a lie, but the reality was not having a dad. I didn't know what a dad did. I didn't talk to, play with, or do anything with him. I had a few vague, dreamlike memories of him polishing his shoes. Stupid, but it was all I had.'

'What I am trying to say is I could see what a dad should be from TV and movies, but I didn't feel what it was to have a son or be a dad.'

'It's okay, you don't need to do this.'

'I do though, Charlie. Not just for me, but for you, too. Things we don't know in our childhood come up and bite us on the arse in later life, and they can drag us down. I want you to be aware of it, ready for it.

'My mate, Sammo, who died, died with regrets, with secrets. He wanted me to try to clear them up, and I will, but I also have to deal with my own. Put my house in order, and it isn't easy.' Vinny stopped. It was just yards from here that the whole story began. He remembered how Macca had bullied Sammo and told Jaime to fuck off. Sammo had stood up to Macca all those years ago. Sammo had joined with Jaime to stand up to Macca. Maybe Jaime was the missing link.

They followed the path in a single file along the bank; the wind whipping around them. Vinny stopped. 'Our parents look after us the way they were looked after. They try to improve on it, but the only model they have is what they saw around them. The Irish in us would never talk about pain. The secrets and lies were everywhere, partly because they couldn't deal with them, partly because they would be judged for them.'

'All right, Dad, I know you're a lecturer and stuff, but this is heavy and complicated. Did you find out what happened to your dad?'

'Yeah, he did a bunk because he was in trouble. He beat someone up, and the man died, and your grandfather went back to Ireland.'

'Wow, no shit.'

'Yeah, shit.'

'Did you go after him, try to find him later?'

'Eventually, but he was already dead.' Vinny looked into the distance.

'The thing is, I spent my life kind of in the dark, knowing nothing, and in Ireland, he was going crazy because he missed me. That's kinda what I found out.'

'That's sad.'

'But in a weird way, losing him and then finding him in Ireland led me back to you.'

'How far are we going?' asked Charlie.

'Do you want to go to the lighthouse? You can see it at the end there.' Vinny pointed.

'No, I'm good,' Charlie said. 'It's all right down here, but it's fucking freezing.'

'Hey, language.' Vinny gave Charlie a gentle push. 'Come on, then, let's turn back.'

They walked along, side by side.

'I guess what I want to say is, if you do something wrong, don't let it eat away at you. We've all done stuff we shouldn't.'

'Speak for yourself. My hands are clean,' said Charlie.

'Well, if you do, own it, don't run away from it,' said Vinny.

'Like you?'

'You're one cheeky bastard. Did I tell you that?' said Vinny, laughing. He stopped walking. 'But you know what, you're right. That's exactly what we did, from here to Garston. That's when we met Jaime.'

Charlie stopped walking and turned. 'Who's Jaime?'

'Back then, he was a young kid from Liverpool Eight.'

'And now?'

'You know what? I think I should find out.'

Back in the warmth of the car and out of the wind, Vinny looked up. In the short time they had been down the shore, the layered sky had gone, blue had replaced the grey.

'Come on, then, home.'

Chapter Twenty-Five

Anne

Anne had dropped Helen at home. Propped up on the sofa, Helen felt better — not comfortable, but at least able to moan and wince instead of keeping it in. There was something about vocalising pain that helped deal with it.

She was scrolling through YouTube videos, not really looking. What she wanted was something she could watch while thinking. Helen had a theory that the mind worked better when it wasn't focused on the problem, allowing the brain to do its thing in the background. So she looked for something moving and happening without requiring the engagement of her conscious mind. Perfect, 'The Blue Planet.' She had downloaded the entire series, so could watch it whenever she needed. The gorgeous photography was enough, but then throw in the warm, comforting tones of Attenborough's concerned, curious, and slightly surprised narration, and she had the perfect vehicle for mental relaxation and recovery.

She had come a long way. When she realised she was pregnant with Charlie, she had just finished with Vinny. He was starting university and mixing with all kinds of new people. He was also a bit of a dick — thought he was smarter than everyone else, started looking down on people. It was a natural break when Vinny went to university. Then she found out she was pregnant. Not telling him went through her mind, but in the end, she told him. He was relieved she didn't want to get married. He visited the baby once or twice in the first few months, but then he lost interest. Charlie was her world, and she was happy in it. Vinny started showing up again a few years later, wanting to be a dad again.

Helen heard the front door open. 'You look happy,' she said to Charlie as he bounced into the room.

Vinny was a minute behind him.

'Okay, I'm going up.' Charlie stopped near the stairs, turned, and said, 'I'll see you later, Popeye.'

'What's that about?' asked Helen.

'Boys talk,' said Vinny, smiling.

Charlie bounded up the stairs. Vinny's smile disappeared, and he started to speak. 'Look, I'm really—'

'Sorry. I know,' she interrupted. 'Come over here.' She patted the sofa.

Vinny flopped down next to her.

'How did you get on with Macca?' she asked.

'Nothing I didn't know before, although I need to try to find Jaime, the kid from Oglet shore. How about you?'

'It was useful. I can see what you mean about Anne. She doesn't let go, does she?'

'Like a pit bull.' Vinny laughed.

'Although far more attractive,' smiled Helen.

'Oh really? I hadn't noticed.'

'She's going with Claire to see the pathologist on Tuesday morning, and all jokes aside, there is someone you need to go and see.'

'I know.' Vinny nodded. 'I'm not looking forward to that one.'

'Joe Doyle. You owe him an explanation, but I found out this morning that Joe had also been helping Sammo. Do you remember someone called Beep? He was the guy I met at Sammo's. He was seen going into his house on the night of the overdose.'

'Wait, Beep, it does sound familiar. I think there was a guy who would spray his name on walls. No idea of his real name, though.'

'Joe might.' suggested Helen.

'Do you think Joe knows about the watch? Do you think Sammo told him?' asked Vinny.

'No, he can't have. I'm sure he would have told me.'

'You're right, though. I owe him an explanation and an apology.'

'No time like the present. Shall I call him?' Helen lifted her phone.

'Alright. Yeah, go for it,' Vinny said. His stomach turned at the thought of the conversation.

Chapter Twenty-Six

Vinny

1.30pm, Sunday, 26th June, 2016

'You know he was ill?' asked Joe.

Joe Doyle walked around the perimeter of the Venny. The Venny was short for "Adventure Playground." High chain-link fences separated it from the housing opposite and the school next door.

'What was it then?'

'They're still not sure... a form of PTSD or a group of physical symptoms.'

Vinny walked beside Joe, enjoying the sounds of the kids playing. Some boys were kicking a ball around on the tarmac. In a separate corner, a group of girls had a skipping rope and were singing a skipping song. The girls' song rang out in the early afternoon air.

On a mountain stands a lady,
Who she is, I do not know,
All she wears is Gold and Silver,
All she needs is a fine young man.

'I think I remember that myself. I heard it so many times as a kid. This place is pretty impressive,' said Vinny.

Before the Storm

'We do what we can. We used to have full-time workers. Now we are lucky if we can pay part-time hours. It's staffed by volunteers now.'

'I wish we had this when I was a kid.'

The activity centre was impressive. The outdoor play area had a tarmac section they were in now, and a grass area with half-sized goals for five-a-side football.

'Twenty years too late, if you ask me,' Joe said.

Joe was a tall, slim man in his sixties. His hair was solidly grey at the temples, with patches on top. He moved so well that Vinny walked faster to keep up.

'How's that?' Vinny asked.

'We're competing with PlayStation and Xbox's. It doesn't stand a chance. There are kids out there earning more money than their teachers. Fourteen and fifteen years old, can earn tens, hundreds of pounds a day. It's crazy. We can't compete, nor can the schools or parents.'

'Are things that bad?'

'We get kids all the time, talking about guns and machetes and Samurai swords. They know the brands: Uzi, Glock, Mac-10. Half of it is off YouTube, but there are guns out there in the hands of kids.'

'Frightening.' Vinny

He knew he had to get back to Sammo and make his apology.

'It is. They'll give a kid three-ton to have a pop at someone. The kid gets kudos and scares the shit out of a competitor, or actually gets someone killed.'

'How did we get to this?'

'She won, and we're paying the price for that now,' Joe said.

'Who's she?' asked Vinny.

'Thatcher. She knew what she was doing. She saw Heath beaten by the miners, and she set out to break them. After the miners, everyone else fell in line. "There's no such thing as society." Remember that?'

'Yeah, vaguely.'

'That was her. She had everyone waving the flag during the Falklands. Used the union jack to gut the opposition.'

'Things haven't changed much,' said Vinny.

'Shall we go in?'

'If you want?'

'These kids are fine.' Joe nodded towards those playing and led the way inside.

The brightly lit main area included table tennis and table football. The pat-pat of the table tennis cut into the murmur of voices that occasionally rose to the level of shouts but were good-humoured and playful. A snack bar at one end served soda and crisps. A couple of kids were playing chess on one of the sets of tables and chairs near the food counter.

'A cup of tea?'

'Yeah, sure. Don't you ever close?'

'Two teas, please, Marge. When the schools are closed, we're open.' said Joe.

A woman in her thirties began pouring from a large pot into two mugs. 'Help yourself to sugar.'

'How much?' Vinny asked, getting his wallet out.

'On the house.'

'No, really,' Vinny insisted.

'Fifty pence for both,' Marge said.

Vinny pulled a ten-pound note and handed it over. 'Keep the change.'

'You don't have to do that,' said Joe.

'No, you don't have to, but we appreciate the contribution,' said Marge, putting the tenner in her cash drawer.

'We do meals three days a week now, free for kids and parents. It's not much, but it's a basic meal. I know without it, those families would go hungry. You asked how we got to this?' Joe led Vinny to a spare table, and they sat on either side.

'Getting back to Sammo,' Vinny said.

'Okay, I know you want to ask about him, and I will tell you. But this is part of the same story.'

'You mean Blair and the whole mess in Iraq?'

'Yeah, but before that, what replaced the idea of solidarity among working people? When they destroyed the union culture in working-class communities, what replaced it?'

'Dog eat dog,' Vinny ventured.

'No, selfishness on its own never had strong appeal. I mean, it obviously works with some people, but it can't become a moral centre, a vision.'

'I don't know.' The impromptu history lecture was getting tedious.

'Nationalism, that's what. British this and British that. The Falklands War, the war in Ireland. Then the war in Iraq. Until people here break from the Union Jack, any rogue can run the flag up and get people to salute. Those that don't salute, or wear a poppy, or are foreign, become the enemy. Doesn't matter what else they have to say.'

'Yeah, I guess so,' said Vinny.

Joe took a drink from his tea. 'Okay, I can take a hint. So Sammo. What do you want to know?'

'I heard that you helped him out quite a bit?'

'With his paperwork. He struggled for a long time with the army and with the Social. After the army, he couldn't settle, couldn't find work. Then he started getting ill. Rashes on his stomach, nausea, tiredness… the Social thought he was trying it on. The army was in full denial mode. He just got worse, physically and mentally. He split up with Lynne, went back to his mum's. He kinda went into free fall, and then it was drugs. So for a whole period, I didn't see him. No one did. He was off the map,' Joe said.

'He sorted himself out, though, recently?' Vinny inquired.

'Yeah, that's when I saw him again. He had a mate who was helping out. He mentioned him a few times.'

'Did he mention any names? Beep for example?'

'I know Beep.'

'You do?'

'Yeah, Brian Palmer.'

'BP, that makes sense,' said Vinny.

'Bit of a scally. He was Sammo's partner when he was on the gear, his mate.'

'Do you have an address for him?'

'No, I could probably find out, though.'

'Did he talk to you about Ireland?' Vinny didn't want to bring Macca's name up directly, not yet anyway.

'In general terms, but nothing specific. You know, we talked about his illness and trying to get compensation from the army. It was that side of things.'

Vinny was disappointed. 'He didn't try to speak with you in the last week or so?'

'No, nothing. The last time I saw him was about ten days, maybe two weeks ago. He got a letter from the council. They wanted the house back, wanted to move him to a single bedroom flat somewhere.'

'Bastards.'

'Heroes, eh.'

'They call them that, so you can't criticise what we ask them to do. You say anything negative, and it's all, "we have to defend our brave heroes." Until they end up ill or homeless or traumatised, and then it's someone else's problem.'

'Fuck, makes me angry.'

'Like the kids out there.' Joe waved his hand.

Vinny was confused. 'What?'

'Angry. At each other, society. And people like our own McNally are pointing the finger at anyone but those responsible. Foreigners, immigrants, the EU, the flags are out again,' Joe said.

'That's the main difference between now and when you were a kid. It's a harsher, crueller world, and politics have been driven to the extreme. We are running out of time and excuses. Things are going back to basics, more open class struggle. But remember, these kids have guns. This is the quiet before the storm. Here, let me show you something.'

Joe stood and walked to one of the side rooms off the main hall. Vinny followed him. The room was a small library.

'Nice,' Vinny said.

'No, not this… here.' Joe pointed left to a section entitled "Our History."

Vinny scanned the titles: The Ragged Trousered Philanthropist, The Iron Heel, Spartacus.

There were books on Trade Union struggles, The Cuban Revolution, South Africa. 'This is my contribution, building our history, one book at a time.'

Vinny cut through Joe's speech. 'I have a confession to make.' He paused. 'I'm really sorry about this. I came today to ask you about Sammo, but also to tell you something.'

'Confession to me?' Joe's eyes widened in surprise.

'Yeah. You and Helen.'

'Okay, you'd better come in.'

Joe ushered Vinny into the mini library. 'Here,' he said. 'Sit down.'

Vinny sat. Joe drummed his fingers on the desk. 'Is this about Sammo?'

'Partly.'

'Come on then, spit it out,' Joe said impatiently.

'Okay. When we were kids, I used to knock around with Sammo and Macca. McNally, the guy who's standing in the election.'

'Yeah, I know who he is.'

'Macca stole your grandad's watch.'

Joe's eyes narrowed as he struggled to understand what Vinny said.

'What? Are you fucking kidding me?'

Vinny shifted uncomfortably in his chair. 'No, do you think I would joke over something like that?'

Joe stood and walked to close the office door. Vinny felt Joe's presence standing over him. 'I fucking hope not,' Joe said. 'Because I'm telling you, I am seriously pissed off right now.' He paused for a few seconds. 'I don't get it. You come in here with all these questions about Sammo, then you tell me this? What the fuck is going on?' Joe moved back to the other side of the desk.

Vinny felt a little relieved.

'Macca burgled your Grandad's house. The night he died.' Vinny carried on, not wanting to dwell on the horror of his words. 'Sammo was keeping a lookout for him. They brought the watch to me after, and the three of us tried to sell it. But we couldn't.'

'So, you have known me all these years...' Joe trailed off.

'I didn't know what happened to the watch. I lost touch with Macca and Sammo. I moved away.'

'Fucking hell. That's some story. To be honest, I'm having trouble getting my head round it.'

Joe put his head in his hands. 'You know, I wondered for years whether the heart attack was connected to the burglary. We just didn't know. He was in bed, so there was no struggle, we know that. But did he hear something? Did he get a fright? A shock? He was ill, so he could have gone at any time.' Joe's voice started to break as something that had been held down for so long neared the surface. 'But thinking that his last moments might have been in fear, that's just fucking sick.'

He stood and paced back and forward. Vinny sat nervously, not knowing what to do or say.

'I know you were kids. But for fuck's sake... you know what makes my blood boil?'

'Go on.'

'That you do this to your own kind. My grandad brought that watch from Ireland. And you lot, like parasites, cannibals, couldn't wait to get your hands on it.'

'What can I say? It's no excuse to say we were kids. I'm sorry. I'm sorry I didn't come to you sooner.' Vinny knew the watch's real history since his trip to Ireland. He could never tell anyone because of what they did.

'And does Helen know about this?'

'I told her last night. She wasn't too impressed either.' Vinny took a deep breath.

'And you came here to tell me today? Or would you have just got what you wanted on Sammo and left?' Joe asked.

'Both. I wanted to tell you, but I'm sure there was something going on between Macca and Sammo. I thought he might have said something to you.'

'No, he didn't tell me. Maybe he told a friend.'

'I think he was going to tell me, but I never gave him the chance,' said Vinny

'I didn't mean you. I meant a real friend,' said Joe.

'I guess I deserve that,' said Vinny. He dropped his eyes to the floor.

'Yeah, you do. Sammo mentioned Jaime, a guy he knew from town.'

Vinny nodded. 'Yeah, Jaime, we knew him as kids. I wouldn't know where he is these days, though.'

'The church on the avenue, with the statue. The black Jesus, do you know it?'

'Yeah, I know it,' said Vinny.

Chapter Twenty-Seven

Helen

5pm, Sunday, 26th June, 2016

'You're late.'

'I know, sorry, it took longer than I thought.'

Helen walked to the bottom of the stairs and shouted, 'Charlie, come on, we're leaving!'

'How did it go?'

'Not easy, but useful. He thinks he can find Beep.'

'I spoke to Anne.'

'Any news?'

'She knows Jaime. She's set up a meeting for you in the morning.'

Vinny shrugged 'Ok. At the Methodist church?'

'Yeah.'

Charlie came bounding down the stairs. 'Where are we going?'

Vinny looked at Helen.

'Pub in the Park?' she answered.

'Let's go.'

Charlie grabbed his coat and was out of the door. Helen moved toward Vinny. She reached out for him; he squeezed her hand; she moved in to hug him.

'This is taking its toll on you. I can see it.'

Vinny held the contact for a minute, then moved back. 'It's serious stuff. I don't know where it will end.'

'Come on, let's get some food in you. Give me the keys, you can have a pint.'

He handed over his keys. 'You know, I think I need one.'

They walked out holding hands. Helen stopped to lock the front door.

Charlie stood beside the passenger door. 'What's all this? Lovey-dovey.'

Vinny clipped Charlie round the head. 'In the back.'

The warm sun had brought people out. Clarke's gardens were full of kids and couples, and couples with kids.

After they had cleared their plates. Helen smiled, 'So Mr History, tell me something about this,' she spread her hands.

They sat at one of the ten garden tables outside the pub. The grand red sandstone Mansion now hosted a carvery and family pub.

'The first Palladian style house in Liverpool,' said Vinny.

'Can you tell us something interesting?' asked Charlie.

The imposing building had been extended over the years, but the original building stood three storeys high, a solid rectangular building all straight lines and square angles.

'How about its role in two civil wars?'

'What? That doesn't make sense.' Charlie pulled a face.

'Someone on the losing side in the English civil war lost the house.'

'Who lost?' asked Charlie.

'The King,' Vinny smiled. 'Ok, so that's one. I bet you didn't know that the Confederate Flag flew above this building?'

'Really?' said Helen.

'Yeah, a lot of the merchants supported the South because they made their money through the cotton trade, and the last Confederate ship surrendered here in Liverpool. The Shenandoah. So that's your second civil war.'

'What was that thing you used to say? You turn over a stone…'

'You look under any rock in Liverpool, you'll find two things, the Irish and Slavery.'

'Ice cream?' asked Charlie.

'Yeah, why not?'

'Come on, I'll go in with you.' Helen stood.

Vinny watched his wife and son cross the grass in the warm sun. He knew he was lucky and pushed back the thought of Sammo's pain.

* * *

'Why did we go out for dinner?' asked Charlie.

'Because your mum didn't want to stand in the kitchen all afternoon,' replied Vinny.

'Then why didn't you cook?'

'Let's just say your dad's chips are okay, but I wouldn't trust him with a Sunday roast,' Helen said.

'I don't know. I'm not sure if that's fair,' said Vinny.

'Yeah, that's fair,' Charlie laughed.

'Oh, well, thank you for the support. Anyway, I don't know if you noticed, but I had other things to do.'

'Your chips are good, though,' Charlie agreed.

'Right, we should do this more often,' Vinny said.

'Can I be on the Xbox when we get home?'

Vinny looked at Helen, who nodded.

'Yeah, on two conditions, your bag is ready for school tomorrow, and you have no homework.'

'Deal,' said Charlie.

'Pinky promise,' Vinny laughed, offering his hand over his shoulder to the backseat.

'Don't be daft, I'm not a baby.'

Vinny turned the car into Ensworth Road. It was Sunday, so the street was pretty busy with cars. He found a space and pulled up to the kerb. The front door of their house opened onto a paved area in which Helen had placed planters. Her various flowers and bushes broke up the otherwise hard surface. A brick wall and gate closed the area off. Vinny was out of the car first and went to open the gate. As he reached it, he saw something black on the ground behind it. He pushed the gate gently. For a second, he thought it was a cat sleeping until he realised it was a dog, not a cat, and that it was dead. Oh, fuck, what next?

'Wait,' he called back to Helen.

Charlie was out of the car.

'Charlie, stay there with your mum.'

'Can you take Charlie round the back way?' Vinny said in a monotone voice, staring directly at Helen.

She got the message. 'Charlie, come on.'

'Why? I want to go in the front.'

Vinny looked back down. The dog had been dropped over the gate, so he had to push the body with the gate to get inside. Its head was at a funny angle to its body. Its neck had been broken. Poor thing, what a sick bastard.

Vinny snapped at Charlie, 'For once, can you do what you're told?'

The dog's tongue hung out between its jaws, and glassy eyes stared blindly.

Charlie had reached the gate. 'Eww, what's that?'

'Jesus, I told you to go round the back.'

'It's too late now,' Charlie said.

Vinny stepped over the body and unlocked the front door. Helen was now at the gate.

'Oh, my god. It's Icey.'

'Who's Icey?' Charlie asked.

Vinny went into the kitchen, found a roll of black bin bags, and tore one off. He went back out through the door and covered the dog. Charlie stepped over the dog and walked towards the house while Helen made her way carefully past the body.

'What is that about?' Charlie asked, coming through the

front door.

'Never mind. Go on. You wanted your game. Make sure your bag is done for tomorrow,' said Vinny.

'No way,' Charlie said.

Helen was now in the living room, too. 'What's going on?' she asked.

'Dad is trying to send me upstairs.'

'I thought you wanted to play on your computer?' said Vinny.

'Not now, now I want to know what's going on,' Charlie insisted.

Vinny shrugged.

Helen put her bag down. 'Okay, look, let's all calm down. Work out what we have to do.'

'Am I right in thinking it was Sammo's dog?' asked Vinny.

'Yeah, I'm pretty sure,' said Helen. 'Who was it? Do you know?' she asked.

'It's another warning,' said Vinny.

'Looks like,' said Helen.

'Okay, I get it now,' Charlie said.

'Do you think it was Macca? Surely, he's not that sick, is he?' asked Helen.

'This is all to do with the guy who had an overdose? And the guy in Speke, Macca,' said Charlie.

'Okay, well, this is intimidation. It's got to be. What do we do? Call the police?' Helen asked.

'I think we have to. They have brought this to our house,' said Vinny.

'Do you think Macca killed your friend, Dad?' Charlie asked.

'No. Probably not, but to be honest, we don't know.'

'And you're not scared?' asked Charlie.

'Yeah, I am. I'm worried that you or your mum will get hurt. Your mum was already in a crash.'

'And you had that guy, that black car you called a bastard,' said Charlie.

'Yeah, that's right. I'm calling DC Crowley. We have to get this on the record.'

'I'm calling Anne.' said Helen. 'We need to work out what to do.'

Chapter Twenty-Eight

Vinny

6pm, Sunday, 26th June, 2016

Anne arrived before the police. Vinny had managed to bribe Charlie into his room.

'This… the dog is a warning,' said Anne.

'We have to find Beep. We need to know what went on the night Sammo died,' said Vinny.

'There is something very dodgy going on. Why did DI Cooper meet me in Speke? He's always been connected to intelligence.'

'What do we do now?' asked Helen.

'I've called the police. DC Cowley.' said Vinny.

Anne looked surprised. 'What for?'

'We need this on the record. God knows what else we can expect.'

'Ok, fair enough. You should go with Joe, see if you can find this guy, Beep. I'm going with Claire Tuesday, to see the pathologist.'

'I didn't know you knew Jaime,' said Vinny.

'L8's a small place for those from there.'

'And what do I do?' asked Helen.

Anne smiled. 'You keep everyone sane.'

The doorbell rang out and Vinny opened the door to DC Cowley and two uniformed officers. The three of them filled the front room. Vinny led them out the back to where the bin bag was. They checked the contents of the bin bag before the two uniformed officers carried it out.

'I'll be out in a couple minutes.' DC Crowley followed Vinny back into the house. 'We finally get to meet,' said Anne.

DC Crowley raised his eyebrows.

'I made an appointment with you, but when I got there, I was met by DI Cooper?'

'Yeah, he told me you were old friends.' he shrugged.

'This is pretty horrible,' DC Crowley said.

'The thing is, can you do anything?' asked Helen.

'I would recommend you speak to your neighbours, see if they saw anything today with the dog.' He spread his hands, palms up, in a gesture of openness. 'I'm not sure what else I can say. I will fill out a crime report, give you the number.'

Vinny showed him to a seat at the table.

Anne stood. 'I should get going. There's stuff I wanna check out before tomorrow.'

'Macca is having a meeting later in the week. A public meeting,' said Vinny.

Helen stood. 'I know, I've seen the flyers.' she paused. 'I can't tell you not to go, but I wouldn't advise it. He will be on home turf with his supporters.'

'Why do you want to go?' asked Anne.

'I don't know. Stand up to him?' Vinny said. Helen shook her head. 'Men.'

Anne smiled. 'I really have to go.' She let herself out.

Vinny waited till Crowley had finished writing out the crime sheet and promised to call if anything else happened.

When he returned to the living room, Helen asked, 'Why do you want to go to the meeting?'

'Someone should call him out for what he's done.' Vinny knew he had to respond. The question was, how? How do you take on a couple of bullies?

'We can't prove he's done it, any of it,' said Helen.

'Dad's right, you can't let this guy get away with it,' Charlie was coming down the stairs.

'Let me and your mum talk about this.'

'Okay, but remember what you told me, Dad. "You've got to face up to things."'

Vinny winked at Charlie.

'Up.' Helen pointed at the stairs.

Charlie climbed back up two at a time.

'So, you're going to face up to Macca?' Helen asked.

Vinny was tired, and he needed to think. 'Why not? You don't think I'm up to it?'

'No, it's not that. It's not your job. You don't have to. And if you do, you will be asking for more trouble.' Helen paused. 'If you want my advice, don't go. I don't want you to go.' She reached forward and picked up his hand. 'Please.'

Vinny stood. 'I'll think about it.' He walked into the kitchen. 'Do you want a drink?'

Helen nodded.

Vinny returned with two glasses of wine.

He took a drink. 'Let's face it,' he paused. 'I have been running away for years, hiding for years. It's not just the watch. It's the way we kept quiet about it. Like it didn't exist, it wasn't us. You can't do that without it eating away at you. Sammo understood that. We have to accept who we are, the good and the bad.'

'Are you talking about yourself or the country?' asked Helen.

'Both. We cling to a false identity, or not just false, but partial, skewed.'

'Okay, I get it. It's a difficult time, and you are facing things that have been buried for years. But you have to be careful this doesn't overpower you, throw you off track,' said Helen.

'It changes us. It's not throwing me off track — it's getting me back on it. You know, the whole "Popeye" thing with Charlie was because I told him about Speke. Not so much the place, but what made me, and who I am. It only happened because I was forced to accept that I am not just a history professor in a nice house with two cars and a pension. But I am the scally, who stole, lied, was racist, abandoned his friends, and most of all, was a coward. Not just physically, though that was true, but morally. I have never fought for anything.'

'I think you are being too hard on yourself,' said Helen.

'I don't think so. I'm not saying I am crap, no good. It's the difference between having done bad things and being bad. We need to accept that until we recognise and move away from what limits us. Then we will be stuck with crappy outcomes.' Vinny paused before declaring, 'I'm going to the meeting. But first I have to face Jaime.'

Chapter Twenty-Nine

Vinny

10am Monday 27th June 2016

Vinny knew the Black Christ. Most people who travelled to South Liverpool by bus did. As a kid, he passed the statue on the wall of the Methodist church on Princess Avenue often and was drawn to its dark beauty.

The Methodist church, a nondescript modern brick building, was set back slightly from the road. The figure that leaned forward and out into the roadway was the most notable thing about the building. It was much more active and dynamic than the normal, painfully resting or restricted depiction of the crucified Christ. This black metal structure was bursting from its constraints, leaping forward, arms outstretched. It was more walking dead than the Lamb of God. It was a portrayal of Christ resurrected, his limbs stretched and taut, muscles and tendons visible in this portrait of pain and suffering brought back to life in shocking realism.

Vinny parked his car and walked towards the battered blue door of the church. He was nervous. He wasn't sure how Jaime would react after all these years. Before he got to the door, it opened, and in front of him stood a tall, well-built man in his mid-forties with a bald head and a smiling face.

The man extended his hand. 'You must be Vinny.'

Vinny smiled in relief. 'Yeah. Jaime?'

'That's me. Come on, let's walk. Do you mind walking? I could do with some exercise.'

'No, it's fine. Do you work there?' Vinny nodded towards the church.

'Yeah, but it's not what you think. We organise community outreach from the church. I'm not a pastor or vicar.'

'You had me worried for a minute.' Vinny smiled.

'It's as much community centre as church these days.'

Jaime was a powerful man, and Vinny had to move quickly to keep up. 'Wow, it's weird to see you. To be honest, I wouldn't have recognised you.' It was true, Vinny remembered the slim athletic boy, olive skin, and closely cropped black hair.

Jaime ran his hand over his head. 'Easy come easy go. What can you do? I was surprised to hear from Anne and sorry to hear about Sammo.'

'I didn't realise you knew Anne?'

'Yeah, we go way back, from round here. She's working on something for me.'

Vinny's eyebrows rose. 'Oh, right?' he changed the subject. 'Joe Doyle told me you and Sammo were in touch?' said Vinny.

'Yeah, off 'n on, you know how it is, but yeah, Sammo dropped by now and then. Ever since that day as kids, we had a connection.'

They walked along Beaconsfield Street towards the heart of Liverpool 8, where the bay fronted terraces were squat and solid.

'That was a strange day,' said Jaime, turning sideways to make eye contact with Vinny.

'Yeah, including you getting run over.' Embarrassed, Vinny remembered leaving Jaime lying in the road.

'You don't have to remind me.'

'You know, I waited for Sammo to get back that day. It was the first day of the riots, wasn't it?' Was he trying to justify himself, change the subject? He wasn't sure.

'The uprising, yeah, mate. I was still in hospital. They let me out the next day. Everything here was wild.'

They had reached the junction of Beaconsfield and Granby Street. As they walked, the number of boarded-up houses increased on both sides of the road. The squat Victorian brick-built terraces had metal covers over the windows and doors. Some enterprising locals had painted curtains and even flowerpots on some shutters.

'What's going on here?' Vinny pointed at the houses.

'Renovation, rejuvenation, or clearing — depends who you speak to,' said Jaime.

Jaime led the way across Granby Street, a once busy intersection at the heart of the community. It now looked deserted and half-empty, full of shuttered shops and empty pavements.

'Okay, enough fresh air. Do you want a cup of tea?'

'Yeah, whatever, that'd be great.'

'Okay, my mum's is just up here. I want to pop my head in, and then we can go on to Lodge Lane. Is that all right?'

'Yeah, sure.'

They continued up Beaconsfield, crossed over the larger Kingsley Road, and then entered Asbridge Street. Jaime popped into one of the few occupied houses.

'Seriously, what's with the houses?' he asked when Jaime came out.

'The Council and the Housing Association are supposed to be redeveloping the area, but in order to do it, they have to move everyone out. Then they say they have run out of money or are waiting for grants. It's been going on for years now. Eventually they'll demolish or sell on to private developers.'

They reached the end of the Street and were on Lodge Lane. Kebab shops and cafes, signs for restaurants and money transfer offices, all jostled together. The street was busy with cars and buses.

'Come on.' Jaime led the way into a cafe.

'What do you want? Ali here does a good coffee.'

'Tea for me,' Vinny said.

Vinny got a table near the window. He watched as mothers with prams and kids went back and forth. It was a lively high street, except the shops and restaurants looked locally owned, and unlike Allerton Road, there were no national brands or chain stores here. There was much more of a racial mix.

'This place is buzzing.'

'Yeah, this is Yemeni. Up the road there's a new Somali cafe, a whole new generation of people, new communities. You've just walked through the last forty years,' Jaime said.

'What do you mean?' Vinny looked confused.

Ali brought a tray over with Vinny's tea, milk, and sugar. 'Princess Avenue and the Methodist, then Granby, were the centre of Liverpool 8, back in 81'. Over the last forty years, that community has gone or is going. They've displaced the families and networks that existed there all over Liverpool. What you see here is what's left of that: the African, Caribbean, famous Liverpool Born Black, mixed in with the new arrivals — refugees from Syria, Somalia, Yemen, Afghanistan. If there was a war fought over it, some casualties will be here. But you're not here to get a history lesson. What can I do for you?'

This wasn't news to Vinny. Theoretically, he understood how Liverpool was changing, but here he could see the faces of change.

'A history lesson might not be too far off the mark. Sammo's death has just brought everything back up, you know, from when we were kids. As far as people could tell, he was trying to sort himself out. It just doesn't seem right for him to overdose like that. When Joe said Sammo had been seeing you, I thought he might have told you something,' Vinny explained.

'He had a hard time. I guess he always did. Macca and you both had a big influence on him. Funny really, he looked up to both of you for different things.'

It hurt every time someone said Sammo looked up to him.

It was like a knife sliding into his side, reminding him of his selfishness. 'I hadn't seen him in years. I think you probably knew him better than I did,' said Vinny. He paused, then added, 'And I'm not very proud saying that.'

'Yeah, no doubt, but he knew what you were up to: history professor at the University, not bad for a lad from Speke. He was proud of you.'

'Life takes us in different directions, I guess.' His justification was wearing thin.

'It does, indeed. Sammo admired you, and then, of course, Macca.'

'Did Sammo tell you why they fell out?' Vinny asked.

'In a way, he did, but not the details. Like I said, he looked up to you 'cos of the whole Uni thing. With Macca, it was leadership, you know, being decisive and willing to go for things. I think Macca had dominated him since they were kids. He felt betrayed in Ireland. Something definitely went wrong for Sammo. He just wasn't the same guy when he came back.'

'Nothing specific?' Vinny asked.

'No, not that I can think of, sorry.'

'I'm surprised he kept in touch,' Vinny said.

'Why?' Jaime asked. He took a sip of his coffee and leaned back in his chair.

Vinny felt suddenly exposed. Why did he say that?

'I don't know. We only met that one day.' Vinny wondered if he had said the wrong thing.

Jaime took another drink. The silence weighed heavily between them.

'It was a big day. As it turned out, bigger than any of us knew,' said Jaime.

'Yeah, the whole riots thing, sure, I understand. Don't know why I didn't think of it.'

'The uprising,' Jaime corrected him for the second time since they'd met.

'Yeah, sorry, just not used to calling it that.'

'I can see,' said Jaime. 'You remember how we met that day?' Jaime asked.

'Yeah, of course. The police threw you out at Oggy shore.'

'For us, that was the daily experience, that harassment, bullying, racism. So when people fought back, it wasn't "a riot" — it was a community saying "enough."'

'I didn't mean anything by it,' Vinny apologised.

'You do remember that day?'

'Yeah, I just said.' Vinny was feeling stressed, not sure if he was being tested.

'So I got picked up by the bizzies, took to the arse end of nowhere out in Speke, got racially abused by these two fully grown coppers. I got slung out, and what happened next?'

'That's when we met,' said Vinny.

'Funny how memory works, isn't it?' said Jaime.

'What do you mean?' asked Vinny.

'That's how you remember it?'

'Yeah, I remember the coppers throwing you out, and then you came along with us.'

'See, how I remember it is you called me a slur, and Macca told me to fuck off. If it wasn't for Sammo, you would have left me there.'

Vinny sighed and nodded. 'Okay. You're right. I was stupid, prejudiced. But I was a kid—'

'So was Sammo,' Jaime interrupted. 'But he had humanity. You know, empathy for another individual, even solidarity.'

'At that time, I wasn't able to stand up to Macca, and yeah, Sammo did.'

'And in Garston? Sammo stayed with me while you and Macca legged it. I told Sammo when he came here telling me about his two mates: the clever one, the University professor, and the hard one, his mate Macca. I told him then and would tell him now: he was better than the both of you put together.

He stood up to both of you that day by the river. He could see the world clearer than you and knew what was right and wasn't scared to do it.' Jaime wiped a hand across his face. 'He was all right. Then the army fucked him up.'

'You're right. I owe you an apology.' Vinny held out his hand.

Jaime took it. 'Nah, mate, it's all a long time ago. I guess what Sammo did that day, and the few days after, meant something to me, always has. I'm sorry he went out the way he did.'

'The days of our lives,' said Vinny.

'That's why we're here today.'

'What do you mean?' Vinny asked.

'I mean, that's why we are in this café. After the uprising, our community was slowly but surely replaced. Look at the Georgian quarter. Lovely houses, top prices, no locals, not anymore. The pubs up there, Peter Kavanagh's, The Caledonian, The Blackburne. Now, if you're local, you'll be told you're too loud, scaring the other punters. This is it now, Lodge Lane.'

'Do you remember the march in Garston?' Vinny asked.

'Yeah, an unemployment thing.'

'Looking back, though, there was a lot going on that day.'

'Wasn't there just..?' Vinny stared out the window. 'Hang on, you might have something.'

'What do you mean?'

'What was the most important thing that day? To us, I mean, it wasn't the uprising, and it wasn't the demonstration. It was the—'

'The treasure,' said Jaime, smiling.

'Exactly, the treasure. If Sammo wanted to tell me something, the treasure… I think I know what it is.'

'You've lost me now.'

'I think I know what Sammo meant. He talked about the treasure and truth. He left some letters for me. I have just worked it out. I should get back. I have to check something out.' Vinny drained his tea and stood.

'No problem. I'll walk you back to your car.'

This time, Vinny led the way.

Vinny clicked to open his car. 'Thanks for meeting me, and for helping me understand what's going on.'

'I'm not sure I did anything, but you're welcome.' Jaime held his hand out.

Vinny pointed up. 'I used to see that statue on the way home from town. It's weird how something can be both so frightening and so beautiful. He's the Black Christ?'

They shook hands.

'He's supposed to be the resurrected Christ, but you know the guy who made it?' asked Jaime.

'No, no idea.' said Vinny.

'Arthur Dooley. Whenever I see the statue, I don't see resurrection, but death. To me, he looks more like a famine victim from Ireland than a resurrected Christ.'

'Wow, maybe you're right.' Vinny looked at the statue, arms outstretched. Black or Irish, who was the figure appealing to? 'I'll see you next week. I guess.'

'Yeah, Sammo's cremation.'

'See you there.'

Vinny waved as he pulled away from the kerb. He had to wait for a set of lights on Aigburth Road before he could swipe his phone. He tapped on Joe Doyle's number.

'Joe, it's Vinny. Can you do me a favour?'

Chapter Thirty

Vinny

1pm, Monday, 27th June, 2016

'What's this about?' Joe Doyle wasn't pleased to be disturbed.

'I need a favour,' Vinny said. He knew it was a big ask from Joe after what had happened.

'Yeah, I heard that bit on the phone.'

'I don't expect you to do it for me, but for Sammo. I think Sammo told me something in a letter he sent before he died. I need to check it out, but I need a witness. If I'm right, I can't think of a better witness than you.'

Ten minutes later, Vinny was driving Joe along Dymchurch Road. 'What are we looking for?' asked Joe.

'I'd rather not say. I just want to see if it's there.' If it was, it would be worth it. If not, more apologies, but he didn't think he could sink much lower in Joe's eyes. A black SUV headed towards them. Vinny had a moment of déjà vu. That was the car, the car that had followed him. He was sure of it. As they passed, the driver turned to look at Vinny. Yeah, that was him. Gary Mac, chiselled and pissed off. Vinny didn't feel fear this time, but anger.

It was a Monday, and Dymchurch Road was quiet. The road ended in a cul-de-sac. A few older kids circled each other on bikes. Vinny swung left at the end of the street and pulled up outside Sammo's house.

'How are you going to get in?' Joe asked.

'If I'm right, we won't have to.' Vinny led the way up the path. Instead of facing the front door, he faced left to the opened the half door to where the bin was kept. He felt above the door opening on the inside and he moved his hand from side to side. The kids on bikes were now at the bottom of the path, watching them.

Vinny's hand followed the brickwork. 'Here! There's something wedged in a gap between the bricks.'

Vinny pulled it out. A manila envelope like the one he received from Claire, but this one was smaller, folded over twice into a compact square and sealed with tape. 'Come on, we should get out of here.'

Vinny moved quickly down the path. As he did so, the black SUV they passed a few minutes ago came round the corner. Vinny opened the car door. The SUV parked behind them, and Gary Mac got out. He was wearing a black Adidas tracksuit covering a white T-shirt.

'What are you doing here?' Gary asked.

'Not sure what it's got to do with you, Gary,' Joe answered. 'Get in the car, Vinny,' Joe ordered.

'I don't think you want to do this, Joe. You know how much support my dad has given the Venny over the years,' said Gary.

Joe didn't respond.

'Just tell me what you were doing here,' said Gary.

One of the kids on the bike called out, 'They got something out of the bin shed.'

'Is that right? Is it?' Gary said.

'Yeah, I saw it meself,' the boy said.

Gary moved towards Vinny.

Joe stood directly between them and ordered Vinny, 'Get in the car. Now.' Turning to Gary, he said, 'Think about it. Do you really want to be in the papers for hitting a pensioner? Because

I'm not moving.'

Vinny got in, locked the door, and started the engine.

Joe edged past Gary and moved to the passenger side. Vinny released the lock.

Climbing in, Joe said, 'Come on, let's get the hell out of here.'

As they pulled away, Vinny saw Gary making a call on his mobile and was relieved. 'He's not following us. How did he know we were there?'

'He's not following because he doesn't need to. He knows where we both live. The kids report anything that happens. So, you found what you wanted then?' Joe asked.

'I've got something. Not sure what it is till I get it open. Where should we go?'

'To the Venny. Gary won't try anything there.'

'Do you want to open it?' Vinny handed the package to Joe.

'Why me?' Joe asked.

'Let's just say I've got a feeling that there might be something in there for you.'

'Let's wait,' said Joe.

Vinny checked the mirror. 'I'm pretty sure it was Gary following me,' he said.

'One of the kids would have called him,' said Joe.

'I don't mean now. A couple of days ago. I think it was him that made Helen crash as well.'

'I wouldn't put it past him,' said Joe. 'From what I've heard, he's capable of that and more.'

'Does Macca know what his son is up to?'

'I don't know. Maybe he does, maybe he doesn't. We all like to think the best of family.'

Vinny accepted the rebuke. Did Macca know what Gary was up to? Vinny wasn't sure. Surely, it would be stupid for a councillor. He remembered the text Macca sent the morning after Sammo died telling Helen to stay away. Was that an alibi? Covering himself. Or did he really not know Sammo was dead?

Before the Storm

* * *

Back at the Venny, and behind closed doors, Joe ripped away the tape and cautiously emptied the contents onto his desk. Vinny and Joe stood on either side. Joe put his hand in and pulled out a paper napkin, opening it up. He saw for the first time in decades his grandfather's watch and a pen drive.

'Well… I'll be…' He picked up the watch. He held it, feeling the smooth, solid surface, letting his fingers run over its curves. He slid a fingernail under its cover and snapped it open. 'God, it's weird.' He then held it up to his ear to listen to the mechanism. Joe brought the watch down and flipped open the cover. On the inside, the inscription was still clearly visible.

'We thought it was Latin,' said Vinny.

'*Faugh A Ballagh*,' read Joe.

'Do you know what it means?' Vinny asked.

'No, I know it's Gaelic. I know because we told the police back in the day about the inscription being Gaelic, but no one could remember what it said. It feels like it should be profound, but I don't know what it means,' said Joe.

'I think I do,' said Vinny.

'You know what it means?' Joe was surprised.

'It's "Clear the Way." It was the motto of the Royal Irish Rangers,' Vinny said.

'Wow, I thought he got the watch off the railway. Why would he have an Irish Army watch?'

'British Army. The Irish Rangers were recruited locally in Ireland, but they were a regiment in the British Army,' Vinny said.

'How do you know this?' Joe asked.

'A few years ago, I went to Ireland to see what I could find out about my dad. Let's just say I found out more than I wanted. It involved an officer from that regiment, so I know the motto.'

'How did you know it would be there?' asked Joe.

Vinny pulled up a chair.

'I didn't.' Vinny paused. 'It was the connection between time, truth, and treasure. When we were kids, that's what we called the watch. So, when Sammo used the word "treasure" for Claire, I got a feeling. He said in a letter he left for me, "Claire is the treasure." Then something about it's where Claire was. It didn't make sense, but it wasn't meant to.'

'I needed time for it to sink in. You said something, then I went to see Jaime, and it kinda clicked into place. If Claire is the treasure and the treasure knows the truth, then maybe if I could find the treasure, we would find the truth. That was the logic of it, if there was any. Sammo showed me the hiding place when we were kids. But after all this time. God knows where it has been since those days.'

Joe checked the time.

'How is it?'

'Bang on.' He smiled. 'It means a lot to me.' Joe polished the cover with his jumper.

'I'm glad I could be part of bringing it back, since I was part of taking it in the first place.' Vinny picked up the pen drive. 'And this. What the hell is on here?'

'Here.' Joe held out his hand.

He fired up the laptop that sat on his desk. 'Do you have any idea what's on it?' Joe asked.

'No, nothing.'

Joe clicked away. 'It's a sound file. Are you ready? Do you want me to play it?'

Vinny leaned forward, elbows on his knees. 'Yeah, go for it.'

There was a click and shuffling sound for a few seconds, and then Sammo's voice came clear but nervous.

Hello… Vinny. If you're listening to this, then you got my letters, and you worked it out. If it's anyone else, this is meant for Vincent Connolly.

Before the Storm

So I'm gonna hope you're listening, Vinny. First, well done. I knew you'd get it. You always were the clever one. Macca was the hard one. Not sure what I was… what I'm supposed to be. The one in the middle, maybe. So, why am I doing this? Gary Mac is giving me the creeps. He's been calling round. I told Macca that I can't live with the shit anymore. Macca must've told Gary cos he's doing my head in.

I wanted to tell you, but you fucked me off. I thought Helen might get you to talk to me, anyway I need to sort this stuff out. I need to tell someone. This has been eating away at me.

I'm doing this for me, no-one else. Some secrets aren't meant to be kept. Although we did a good job with the treasure, remember that? All these years, no one said anything. It's kinda connected as well. Back then, you said I could tell you anything. So I am.

There was a pause in the recording. The Venny was silent, no kids' sounds. Joe had stood and was looking out of the window, staring off into the distance.

Sammo came back, stronger voiced.

Macca gave me the watch and the longer I had it, the more I knew it was a sign of what he could do. Of his power… if he could hide this for all these years, the watch and the old feller dying, then he could get away with anything, and we did.

As kids, we signed up for the first Armoured division in Yorkshire. At that time, Macca wanted to avoid serving in Ireland. Funny, as it turned out, 'cos later he couldn't wait to get over there.

Joe had sat back down. He leaned forward and paused the recording. 'Are you sure you want to listen to this now? I mean, with me here.'

'Yeah. I need to have someone else listening,' Vinny said.

'Okay.' Joe clicked to continue, and Sammo's voice filled the office again.

We went to Iraq and I guess that was the start of it. Have you heard of the Highway to Hell? Well, we saw it.

Another pause. This time, his voice was weaker, the words stretched and halting.

What can I say… mile after mile? Cars, vans, trucks, minibuses, and some military vehicles. Not like in a line, but in places like car parks, as if some nasty kid had taken a flamethrower to his car collection. Burnt out, wrecked shells, metal skeletons. There were thousands of 'em. God knows how many people…

Turned out the Americans blocked the top and the bottom of the road, then bombed and strafed the shit out of everything in between, miles and miles of it. They spent hours to bomb, burn, and shoot everything. Everyone trying to get away from Kuwait City got caught up in it — civilians, foreign workers, Palestinians, women, kids, anyone who didn't want to be around when the Americans arrived. They were retreating, running away. Carbonised bodies. People turned to cinder, sat hands on steering wheels, arms extended, heads on shoulders. They weren't blasted to bits — they were incinerated. Bodies burnt everywhere, half-burned, shot or blown to bits by cluster bombs. There were clothes and suitcases, hairdryers and dolls, crayons and… everything… Does it sound like hell? Sound terrible?

Static crackled between Sammo's audible pacing.

This isn't the worst. I know it's bad enough — you know what so-called Stormin Norman, the American general, said, "Anyone on that road deserved what they got. They were murderers, rapists, and criminals." What a twat.

Anyway, something changed because when we got back, Macca got right into the intelligence corps. As usual, I went along with it. We went and did some courses and training and eventually transferred.

We trained to kill enemies and ended up helping to kill our own. War in the desert is one thing, but war in village pubs is another. At first, the Adrenalin rush kept you going. The IRA was having it away with snipers and bombings. They'd raised their game, and we had to raise ours. So we did. They got guns from Libya, so we turned a blind eye while Loyalists got gear from South Africa. There was so much of it. Two cars were stopped near our base, a farm in the middle of nowhere. When the local cops opened the boot, they nearly shat themselves. There were so many Czech VZ58s rifles.

Those guns killed dozens of people. We kidded ourselves the killers were taking out IRA operatives, but we all knew they were making Catholics pay a price for the IRA's war, trying to make them stop. The thing is, when you're in the middle of it, when soldiers and police around you are getting killed and blown to bits, and bombs are going off in London and Manchester, then anything seems better than doing nothing.

I can give times and dates, names and places. The thing that got me was what they called The World Cup Massacre. That was the end for me. We had watched and helped these guys, including serving members of the army and police. We helped them, look up the Force Research Unit, the Joint Support Group. We were hand in glove with the Glenanne gang. The Murder Triangle was ours, and we played it like a fucking instrument.

Joe stopped the recording. 'This is devastating stuff. Did you know about it?'

'I've heard some of the names, the FRU but not the details, and I had no idea Sammo and Macca were involved.'

'Fucking hell, if Sammo was going to go public with this.'

'Enough to have him killed?'

'Not half mate, not half.'

'Come on then, let's get through it.'

Joe pressed play;

I got out after that. For years, there was silence. But those families just wouldn't give up. Six men were shot dead and more injured while watching the football. The morning after I went to the bar, the devastation, broken glass, blood. We did that; we were responsible for that. The three men, balaclavas, overalls, and automatic rifles who sprayed that bar did it because we let them. Ireland had just scored against Italy. They were Catholics watching fucking football.

There was a pause.

Everything screamed at me that this was too much. The informants and touts we used against the terrorists were now using us. The tail wagging the dog. Everyone, right up the chain of command and government, knew if this got out, we would be finished. The local Special branch covered it up. I got out of the military, but I couldn't get the military out of me. Macca stayed on for a while, but the peace process came soon after. We thought it was over, finished. But the families wouldn't let it go. Year after year, they probed and asked. Now the shit is hitting the fan; a couple of weeks ago, a new report said there was collusion between the security forces and the killers at Loughinisland. They didn't name names, but I can.

I told Macca I'd had enough. I wanted to tell people I needed to get it out of my head, or at least stop hiding it, lying about it. He wasn't happy. Told me no one would believe a junkie. He might be right, but I don't give a shit anymore.

Joe spoke over the recording. 'This should go to the police. It might be evidence.'

'Evidence of what?' Vinny asked.

'War crimes. State-sponsored killing, I don't know,' Joe replied.

'What do you think they'll do with it? No, we have to use this ourselves.'

Joe checked the file. 'Not that much. We are near the end.'

'Okay, let's see what else is there.'

Before the Storm

Things have been getting pretty crazy. I don't know if Gary Mac has said anything, but the kids are being a pain in the arse. I think they all look up to him. Banging on the door all hours of day and night. Throwing rubbish in the garden. One of them on a bike lifted his shirt so I could see he had a gun stuck in his waistband. Can you fucking believe it? I think he's letting me know what life will be like if I do say something. All you need is one person to call you a grass. To be honest, the council wants the house back anyway, so fuck 'em. I don't know what you can do. I just think people should know… Maybe they do know and don't care. But I need to stop hiding shit. You know what I worked out? When we hide stuff, it's not hiding it from the world. We are hiding from it. I need to come out of hiding. If I am going to sort myself out, I need to face things I have done. Being around Claire is the hardest thing you can't love and ignore the pain. We can only hide it if we don't feel it. But you know that. What the fuck, eh Vinny? Will anyone even care? If something happens to me, at least you will know why.

The recording ended with some shuffling noises, then a click.

Neither man spoke. Each letting the consequences of the recording sink in, not just for Sammo, who was now dead, but the families and survivors of the atrocities he described.

The last few sentences hit Vinny hard. It was the honesty, the clarity. For so long, Vinny had accepted the fiction that he was 'the clever one.' He had got out of Speke, had a good job, a nice house.

'Fuck.' Vinny wiped away a tear.

'Are you okay, mate?' Joe asked.

'Yeah.' Vinny struggled to say it. The tears began rolling. 'I'm sorry.'

'Don't be.' Joe was calm. 'I think you need it.'

'He knew, Sammo fucking knew…'

Vinny leaned forward, his head in his hands. He let the sobs out, and they came. He couldn't stop them and didn't fight them. His shoulders heaved as he cried. He didn't know if he was crying for Sammo, for Sammo's pain, or for his own. But for the first time, he knew the day the old man died, something died in them, too. They knew about it and buried it. That death had lived within them all. Denying death was denying humanity, not just the old man's, but their own.

He straightened up and coughed. He wiped away the tears.

'I still think it should go to the police. I think you should tell them the whole story.'

'DI Cooper in Speke? Anne met him the other day.'

'There's no Detective Inspector based in Speke.'

'Are you sure? Anne met him.'

'Whoever she met, he wasn't based in Speke.'

Joe unplugged the pen drive from his laptop. 'Here, this is yours.' He handed it over to Vinny. 'It's your decision what you do with it.'

'Did you know about this stuff in Ireland?' Vinny asked.

'I'm guessing it never made the front pages.' said Joe.

'True enough.'

Vinny thought for a moment. 'We really need to find this Beep character.'

'Come back in the morning, I'll have an address.' said Joe.

Vinny shook hands and left the small library. He walked through the main room of the Venny with the pen drive safely in his pocket.

Driving out of Speke, Vinny checked his mirror every few seconds. No one was following him. The confusion was settling. He was beginning to see a clear path. Sammo was threatening to talk about his experience in Ireland. The recording was clear. It was also clear Macca and his son Gary knew about it. Gary had been getting heavy with Sammo. Sammo had been clean and looked to be rebuilding his life, but suddenly overdosed. Problem disappears. Could it be so simple? Would Macca be so desperate? So stupid?

Driving along the boulevard, Vinny looked left to the Dymchurch Estate. He remembered an old joke: 'You can take the man out of Speke, but you can't take Speke out of the man.' It was said about many places. Vinny also remembered his student's example from Chekov. The student touched both ends of history at the same time. It was the answer to the question, 'How did we get here?'

The watch, a treasure, a curse, or a link in the chain between that day and this, that time and this.

Chapter Thirty-One

Anne

Tuesday, 28th June, 2016

The Mortuary, as you would expect, was on the ground floor round the back of the hospital.

'Your second time here?' asked Anne

'Yeah. Not a pleasant place. Though, to be honest, they were very good.'

'Were the police here when you identified your dad?'

'Yeah, DC...'

'Crowley?' said Anne.

'Yeah, that's right, young feller.'

'Who are we seeing now?'

'APT David Mercer.'

'APT?' asked Anne.

'Anatomical Pathology Technologist, a bit of a mouth full.' Claire smiled.

The entrance door opened onto a narrow corridor. At the end, there was a window next to a set of double doors. Claire tapped lightly on the window. It was swished aside.

'I'm here to see APT Mercer. I have an appointment.'

The young woman checked her screen, fingers tapping away at the keyboard. Her response was appropriately clinical. 'Through the doors and take a seat in the waiting area.'

Before the Storm

The doors opened onto a wide area. Blue plastic chairs were fixed to the walls. The only other person present was a large, heavily built lady. Anne and Claire took seats near a door marked "visitors." The large lady was writing notes in an open file.

A minute later, a door opposite them opened and a man in his early thirties with messy brown hair and wearing a white coat over green scrubs entered the area. He walked with a file open in front of him.

'Mr Samuel Maddows?' Claire and the lady opposite both stood.

'Yes.'

'Actually, I'm here for the same case. Can I assume you are family? The lady opposite asked.'

'Yes,' Claire responded.

'That's very good. I was just about to check in with APT Mercer here, but more than happy to have a quick chat if you are up for it?'

Claire looked from one to the other, not knowing what to do or say.

Anne stood. 'Excuse me, Anne McCarthy family friend. Can I ask who you are?'

'Oh, of course, excuse me. How silly of me. Pamela Jones, Investigation Officer for the Coroner's Court.' She flipped open her warrant card.

'Oh, right.' Anne was surprised.

'You wanted to see me, Ms Maddows?' APT Mercer asked.

'Yes.'

Mrs Jones spoke up. 'That's why I'm here love, the Coroner has to be aware of all the circumstances of the deceased and if you have questions, we would also like to know what they are.'

'Oh right. You told the police my father died from a drug overdose?' Claire asked APT Mercer.

'Shall we use the room?' Mrs Jones led the way into the visitor's room, which had a table and chairs and was decorated like a living room, flowered wallpaper and sofa, a polished table and upholstered chairs. When everyone was seated, Claire repeated, 'You said my father died of a heroin overdose?'

APT Mercer flicked through his file. 'Yes, that's right. Body fluids and tissue samples were analysed for morphine and 6-monoacetylmorphine, utilising a capillary gas chromatography procedure. The concentration of free morphine in the blood was 0.01-mg/1.' He looked up from the report. 'Heroin is first metabolised into 6-monoacetylmorphine, then into morphine. So, heroin abuse can be confirmed with certainty by the identification of 6-monoacetylmorphine. In this case, the toxicology report shows 6-monoacetylmorphine was identified and quantified. Its presence clearly demonstrated heroin abuse.'

'Oh, right?'

'We can tell from the puncture marks and from the level of toxin in the blood that the heroin was delivered intravenously.'

'Is there something you're not sure about?' asked Mrs Jones.

'Was fentanyl detected in the blood?' asked Anne.

'No, we wouldn't normally test for that. Morphine and fentanyl have different molecular structures. We would have to test specifically for it.'

'Is there a reason you think fentanyl may have been present?' Mrs Jones asked.

Anne replied. 'We are not sure. You see, Claire's father had been a user, and while we know in that case, accidental overdose is always a possibility, we just want to check. Nothing else was going on.'

'Let me explain. The Coroner's Court has to establish the cause of death. My job is to assist the Coroner with that task, by establishing as far as possible the facts surrounding the death. Possible outcomes of the inquest include natural causes; accident; suicide; unlawful or lawful killing; industrial disease and open verdicts. If you have any information that would help us determine that outcome, we would be grateful to hear it.'

Before the Storm

'When will the inquest take place?' Asked Anne.

'That is down to us. When I think we have enough evidence to present a case to the Coroner, or there is no more evidence to be obtained, then I will advise the Coroner and she will set a date for the hearing.'

'As it stands we have the toxicology report indicating the use of heroin and a police report advising that there were no suspicious circumstances to the death, given the deceased's prior history of substance abuse, and after an examination of the scene, in the absence of evidence of intent then the most likely determination as to the cause of death would be accident.'

'Can you test for fentanyl?' asked Anne.

'Yes, we can…' said APT Mercer.

Mrs Jones interrupted. 'But they would need authorisation from the Coroner's office or a request from the police.'

'Exactly,' said APT Mercer.

'Unless you have any further questions, I think Mr Mercer can leave us. If we determine further toxicology is required, I will let him know.'

APT nodded to Anne and Claire, stood and left the room. Mrs Jones leaned back in her seat. 'I am curious. Why do you want this test?'

Anne leaned forward. 'I know it sounds crazy, but we have reason to believe someone might have wanted to harm Mr Maddows.'

'I'm listening,' said Mrs Jones.

'Someone was present with Mr Maddows just before or at the time of his overdose. We have a witness who saw someone entering Mr Maddows' house on the same night as the overdose.'

'OK, and…'

'The police said a neighbour called an ambulance but that the call was anonymous. The question is, how could a neighbour know that an overdose had happened inside the house?' Mrs

Jones had a legal pad on the table and was taking notes. 'Anything else?'

Anne looked at Claire.

Mrs Jones put her pen down. 'Look, let me explain something. If the Coroner determines accidental death, that's it. There will be no further investigation, the file will be closed. If the Coroner decides it was a case of unlawful death, the police will be obliged to open a criminal investigation. Now, I can't determine the result of any criminal proceedings. But if there are doubts about the circumstances of this death, it is in your interest to tell me everything you know.'

Claire nodded to Anne. 'We have a voice file of Mr Maddows, recorded in case anything happened to him. In it he expresses fears for his safety.'

'Does he say why he feared for his safety?'

'He was a soldier in Ireland and he said he had names and dates of collusion. He also names the people he is afraid of.'

Mrs Jones had picked up her pen and was scribbling again. 'I will need to hear that recording and have it validated. Although, I will authorise further tests for the presence of fentanyl, and I will recover the 999 call from the ambulance service.'

'Thank you,' said Claire.

'Have you passed this evidence to the police?'

'Not yet,' said Anne.

'Have you found the potential witness?'

'Again, not yet,' said Anne.

'I want to make this clear so you both understand the situation. My investigation is independent of the police. Of course, I will cooperate with them and supply information should they request it. But I am not reliant on them. My job is to collect information for the Coroner. She handed her card to Anne. That is my direct number. To prepare for the inquest, I will need to speak to any witness to the circumstances of Mr Maddows' death. Am I making myself clear?'

'Yes, absolutely,' said Anne. 'Witnesses may also be called before the Coroner to help make her determination.'

'Can we make the arrangements for my dad?' asked Claire.

'Yes, I will order a full forensic toxicology report. Once completed, we can authorise the release of the body.'

Claire's hands were intertwined on the table. 'Right, thank you.'

Mrs Jones stood and led them to the double doors. She held the door open as Claire and Anne walked through.

Outside the sun was shining on Liverpool, and all the cars and buses, the noise and fumes, couldn't stop Anne appreciating the summer morning.

She swiped her phone.

Chapter Thirty-Two

Vinny

Tuesday, 28th June, 2016

'Morning.' Vinny pulled up in Harefield Road. Joe Doyle lived in the same house his grandfather occupied all those years before.

Joe opened the door and climbed in.

'Have you got any news for me?' Vinny asked.

Joe fastened his seat belt. 'Brian Palmer's family are in East Damwood Road.'

Vinny started the car and drove to the end of the street.

'You remember the way?'

'Of course.' Vinny swung left and followed the road around the estate. The houses were large terraces with front and back gardens, most were built from the 1930s. Speke had a combination of housing, individual houses and tenements, as the years since the slum clearance of the bombed-out centre of Liverpool past, the tenements were slowly replaced with street-level housing. The streets of older houses were not designed for traffic, and now cars had to mount the pavement to park.

'What number?' asked Vinny.

'254 up ahead on the right, but hold on. There's someone at the door.' Vinny pulled the car over and mounted the kerb. They were around thirty feet away.

'For fuck's sake,' Vinny said, as the man at the door turned.

'You know him?'

'Yeah, I do. That's Detective Inspector Dave Cooper.'

'What's he doing here?'

'My guess is the same as us.'

Vinny's phone beeped. He swiped to accept Anne's call and pressed to put it on speaker. 'Hey, I've got Joe with me here. You're on speaker.'

'Ok. Hi Joe.'

'Hi,' said Joe.

'How did you get on?' Vinny asked.

'Good news. We met an investigator for the Coroner.'

'I didn't know that was a thing,' said Vinny.

'Yeah, I know, but it turns out she's pretty good. She's ordered a new forensic toxicology report that will look for fentanyl, and she's getting the recording of the 999 call.'

'That sounds great.'

'How are things there?'

'You'll never guess who I'm looking at?'

'Go on, surprise me.'

'DI Cooper.'

'Where?'

'Believe it or not, he is at the door of the Palmer family. Looks like we are not the only ones interested in Beep.'

'Let's hope we find him first or God knows what'll happen to him.'

'Ok, he's on the move. I'll speak to you later.' Vinny closed the call and slipped the phone back into his pocket.

DI Cooper walked down the path and opened the passenger door of a waiting car.

'What shall we do?' asked Vinny.

'Follow him,' said Joe.

Vinny looked across at Joe and smiled.

'What are you smiling at?'

'Watching the detectives?'

'Get on with it, then. He's moving off. '

Vinny slipped the car into gear and pulled out. He tried to stay back, but it was difficult to remain hidden, as there were very few cars on the road.

'I hope he doesn't see us,' said Joe.

'Nah, they won't expect this. You didn't get it, did you?'

'Get what?'

'Watching the Detectives, the Elvis Costello song.'

'I did get it. It was stupid.'

The blue car they were following turned onto Stapleton Avenue, one of the larger roads that ran through the estate; they followed them all the way down toward Western Avenue. The junction with Western Avenue was blocked by the blue BMW saloon pulled up at the kerb just beyond the junction with Linner Road. Vinny turned left. 'Try to see what number he's at. I'll get to the bottom and turn round.'

He drove down to the bottom. The roadway was too narrow to do a U turn. He had to get to the other end before he could turn round and come back up. When they reached the top, the blue car was just pulling away.

'What shall I do?'

'Get after him.'

They followed the car left and right, but stayed within the estate.

The DI Cooper passed Speke Post Office and took a sharp right, the road was no wider than an alley, on the left were the back fences of houses, and the right the brick wall of the post office compound, 'I can't follow him down here, he'll see me.'

'Never mind. I think I know where he's going. Go straight on.'

They went on, then doubled back with three right turns. They were on Conleach, houses on the left and fenced off buildings on the right. 'Go up a bit.'

Vinny moved slowly up the road.

'OK, pull up here.'

They were across from a path of untended ground at the back was a one story brick building. They were looking at the back of it, and could see the blue BMW parked at the side. The front entrance was on the other side.

'What is it?' asked Vinny.

'What was it back in the day, you mean? The Honkey, Honkey Tonk, The Ponderosa.'

'I remember a drinking hole, used to be, at one point it was, Speke Labour Club.'

'And now?'

'Derelict, as far as I know.' Joe paused. The back of the building had a double window covered with a rusty metal grill. 'Though I wouldn't be surprised if it was being used as a crack or smack house, they take over empty spaces pretty quickly. That's why council "tin up" the buildings.'

'So we could be getting close to Beep?'

'Who knows? Hold on, look.' Joe nodded toward the building.

The window, the metal grill, was moving. It was being lifted from inside, a body squeezed out from the window pushed the grill out. The person fell to the floor, and the grill snapped back in place. Whoever it was got to their feet quickly and began a shuffling run toward Damwood Road.

'After him?'

'Absolutely,' said Joe.

Vinny turned in the road, leaving the police and the Honkey behind. They kept the shuffling figure in sight as he made his way along Damwood.

'What now?'

'I don't know. Do you know what Beep looks like?'

'No.'

'So much for watching the fucking detectives, then?'

'Do you? I'm not sure. I think I would recognise him.'

'Ok let's have a chat with this guy.'

Vinny accelerated. They pulled in a hundred yards ahead of

the figure and got out. They waited and timed it to reach the pavement just ahead of him.

'Hey, wait up. We want to talk to you,' Vinny said.

In front of them was a young woman, in trainers, jeans and a black anorak pulled tight, despite the warm weather.

'We're not police, I'm from the Venny,' said Joe

The woman stopped.

'What do you want?'

'The police are after Brian Palmer, Beep. It's better if we get to him first.' said Vinny.

'I don't know what you are on about.'

'Look, he could be in big trouble. Did you hear about Sammo?' said Joe.

'Yeah man, heard a guy took a big hit.'

Joe spoke softly. 'Well, we need to find Beep to make sure the same thing doesn't happen.'

'That musta' been good shit, no kidding.'

'We need to find Beep before anyone else does.' Vinny repeated.

'Is he in trouble?' she looked around her as if speaking trouble's name would bring it to her.

'He's in danger if we don't get to him first,' said Joe.

'He got out.'

'Do you know where?' asked Vinny.

'In the village, Garston, a flat above the Cash Converters.'

'Thanks,' said Joe.

They turned back toward the car. Vinny stopped, got his wallet out, pulled out a twenty-pound note, and handed it to the woman. 'Cheers,' she muttered, before shuffling off.

Back in the car, Joe asked. 'What did you do that for?'

'I dunno, reward,' answered Vinny.

'It'll go straight for smack.' said Joe.

Vinny shrugged. 'It is what it is.'

Chapter Thirty-Three

Vinny

7pm, Wednesday, June 30th, 2016

Vinny pulled into the car park. Morrisons was still open, and shoppers were rolling trolleys through. It was the last gasp at 7pm on a Monday. Even Morrisons must shut sometime. He looked over to the library entrance. A few people milled around outside, among them smokers desperate for the last drag. He locked his car and walked over to the building.

On the drive in from Allerton, he was conscious every minute of getting closer to the past. He knew what he was doing, but didn't know what would happen. Relieved, he saw Joe Doyle standing off to one side. He approached him. 'Hey, Joe.'

'Good line for a song.' Joe smiled.

'What?' Vinny was genuinely perplexed.

'Hendrix,' Joe explained.

'Yeah, right?'

'Other things on your mind?'

'Just a bit,' said Vinny. His anxiety was growing.

'You'll be fine.' Joe offered his hand. 'Helen not coming?'

Vinny shook it. 'No, she thinks I'm stupid even being here.'

'Maybe she's right?'

'I guess we'll see,' Vinny said, shrugging to deflect his concern. 'Are there many in there?'

'A few.'

'Any news of our friend, Beep?'

'Not yet, but fingers crossed.'

'Are you going to say anything?' It would be nice to have some backup, he thought.

'I don't know. It depends what happens. Let's see what Councillor Steve McNally has to say,' Joe replied.

'Speak of the devil,' said Vinny.

Steve McNally came out of the main door to the library. Vinny made eye contact. McNally came over. 'Hi, I didn't realise you two guys were friendly?'

'Yeah, Joe is Helen's cousin,' Vinny said. He launched a pre-emptive strike. 'Didn't you know?' Vinny paused for a second. 'Actually, I think you knew all along, didn't you, Macca? Even back in the day?' he was pushing things, referring directly to the past.

'Nah, whatever,' Macca dismissed him and moved on.

'Is there any press here?' Vinny asked.

Joe looked around. 'Yeah, Lynne there is on the Chronicle.'

Macca was in conversation with a young woman.

Vinny moved across and offered his hand. 'Hi Lynne, isn't it?'

Macca gave Vinny a quizzical look. 'I didn't know you knew Lynne?'

'I don't,' Vinny replied. 'Joe, this is Lynne.'

Lynne smiled at Joe, a little confused.

'Councillor.' She nodded towards Macca. They obviously knew each other.

'All publicity is good publicity. Isn't that what they say?' Macca grinned.

'That is what they say, isn't it?' Vinny smiled. He felt like a cat playing with a mouse. Macca's eyes darted around. He walked away from the group and began greeting others.

Vinny turned away from the reporter to Joe. 'Did you bring it?'

Joe slipped the watch into Vinny's hand.

'I hope you know what you're doing,' Joe half-whispered.

'Me, too. Shall we?' Vinny led the way in, while Joe greeted people. Vinny didn't recognise anyone except DC Crowley, who was sitting near the front.

The meeting room was just inside the main library on the right. The library had a closed sign on a stand. The meeting, "Time for change" as the poster on the door announced, was the only activity that evening. The chairs were arranged in rows, facing double tables at the front. The only decoration in the room was a Union Jack behind the speaker's table. Vinny thought this type of public event had ended in the '80s. Wasn't everything supposed to be YouTube and memes now?

Macca was at the front of the room, every inch the ambitious politician. A smart suit, ready smile, and handshake.

Vinny made his way along the sidewall and found a seat near the back and Joe sat beside him. Lynne, the reporter, sat next to DC Crowley.

'Been a while since I've been in a public meeting,' said Joe.

'Was thinking that myself. Not something you see much of anymore,' said Vinny.

Joe nudged Vinny. 'There's your mate, Gary Mac.'

Vinny nodded. 'Yeah. He looks like trouble.' Vinny was sure Gary was behind all the intimidation.

The room filled and settled down. People found their chairs. The murmuring eventually ceased, and the chairman called the meeting to order. Macca made eye contact with Vinny. Vinny held his gaze. Fuck you. Fuck you.

Macca was staring, his face immobile for what seemed like an age. Eventually, it broke into a sneering smile. The confidence remained, but Vinny sensed some doubt as Macca looked away and scanned the audience.

The chairman opened the meeting. 'I guess you have all heard the news? The good news, I should add. Not only have we voted to leave the EU, but the Prime Minister, David Cameron, has resigned.'

As he said this, he led a round of applause with a few people cheering. Macca joined in, raising his hands to produce an overhead clap that looked to Vinny more suited to the terraces than the meeting room.

The chairman continued, 'Anyway, our one and only speaker tonight will be our good friend and councillor, Steve McNally.'

The clapping was more subdued for this. Neither Joe nor Vinny moved a muscle as Macca stood and began speaking. Vinny found himself critiquing his style and method as much as his words. He was practised, Vinny could see that, with the relaxed posture and tone as if he were speaking to a friend rather than a roomful of people. His hand gestures were mobile and flowing — okay, for the introduction. Vinny had seen it all before.

'We have a long and proud history of standing up to tyrants and bullies in this country through hundreds of years of history and two world wars. The freedoms we gained in war, we are in danger of losing in peace.'

Macca's eyes passed over Vinny as they scanned the audience. He seemed to prefer to make eye contact with supporters, people who would nod approval.

'But no more. The historic decision of the British people to leave the European Union opens a new door to the world. Don't believe those who would present this as "little Englanders." Nothing could be further from the truth. In fact, once we are out of the EU, we will be able to trade freely with the rest of the world.

'I am not going to go on too long tonight because we are here for a celebration. I just want to remind you that the politicians and elites in Westminster and Brussels don't know or care about your lives. They are liars and thieves.'

There was an outburst of applause at this line. Vinny almost spoke out: "Liars and thieves" couldn't be a better description of Macca.

'Traitors willing to sell this country down the river for their careers.'

Vinny could tell Macca was getting into his stride. Gone was the warm, relaxed tone of speaking to a friend. Now, his voice was sharper, faster, the sentences shorter, his arm movements more decisive, banging an imaginary table with each new accusation.

'They have forgotten the real people of Britain.'

Vinny pulled out the watch and opened it. He raised his hands high enough for Macca to see. He studied Macca carefully. He saw the question in his eyes and heard the hesitation in his voice as he, too, saw the watch.

'We need to get rid of these traitors and cowards…'

Macca looked directly at Vinny. There was a new chain on the watch, and he swung it from side to side like a hypnotist. Macca became more and more agitated.

'They are destroying our country — thieves, lazy, dirty scum.' He almost spat the words as his venom built.

Vinny could see Macca coming apart.

The chairman looked quizzically at McNally. Macca's eyes travelled around the room, searching for refuge, but drew back time and time again to the swinging watch.

'Some of us have fought for our country, seen comrades die on the battlefield. I have seen the blood and guts of battle. We didn't risk our lives for the scroungers and migrants… the lazy… dirty…' Flecks of spittle flew from Macca's mouth.

The Chairman interrupted. 'I think we should thank Mr. McNally for—'

'Excuse me, Mr. Chair. I have a question for the councillor.' Vinny stood.

'I'm not sure…' The Chairman hesitated.

'That's okay, that's okay,' Macca said, appearing to calm himself down. 'Our professor friend here from Allerton no doubt has some trick question he thinks he can trap me with.'

Vinny had bet on Macca's arrogance.

'I do as it happens. Did you kill Sam Maddows' dog and put it outside my house yesterday?'

'Don't be stupid. That's a completely outrageous claim. This man, like all remainers, will say anything to blacken our name and character. He is a liar and a coward.' Macca's denial was firm.

'So, you are not responsible for the dog?' Vinny calmly asked.

'No, absolutely not,' Macca said.

'Did you rob a house and steal this watch when we were kids? The watch that belonged to Joe's grandfather?'

'Don't be ridiculous.' Flustered, Macca saw the trap closing. 'Chair, can someone shut—'

'Not only did you do it, but you have been lying about it for forty years,' Vinny interrupted Macca.

Not giving Macca a chance to say anything else, Vinny said, 'Sam Maddows died of a heroin overdose. Do you or your son know anything about that?'

Joe stood and pointed at Macca. 'This man is a liar and a fraud.'

The chair banged the table, trying to restore order.

Then a sound broke through the pandemonium, and for a minute, everyone stopped.

Sammo's voice rang out loud and clear. Vinny was holding his phone aloft.

'You've got the watch, our treasure. Such a stupid name, but then I guess we were kids. I gave it back to Macca. He kept it all those years. Never tried to sell it. Not sure why... guess it came to mean something to him. Or he was just scared someone would find out where he got it.'

'You've got the watch, our treasure...'

Gary Mac was the first to spring into action, and he rushed towards Vinny. 'You bastard.'

Macca was trapped behind the table at the front. 'Shut that off.'

DC Crowley placed himself between Gary Mac and the back of the room. He put a restraining hand on Gary's chest and raised a warrant card in his other hand. 'I don't think so, Gary. Get back.'

The chair announced, 'This meeting is adjourned. Meeting adjourned.'

Vinny watched the chaos unfold. He breathed deeply, getting the anxiety and nerves out of his system.

'Well, you fucked that up good and proper,' said Joe.

'Yeah, I know.' Vinny grinned.

Two uniformed police officers entered the room and spoke with DC Crowley. They helped to clear the room.

Vinny raised his mobile phone. 'The wonders of new technology.'

'And the police and The Chronicle to be here?' Joe asked.

'Like the man said, all publicity is good publicity. Let's see how that works out for him.' Vinny was on a high, adrenaline pumping through his veins. He got the bastard.

'You're gonna have to watch your back with that lot.' Joe nodded to the front of the room.

Gary Mac was now guiding his father out of the meeting, pushing people aside to get him out quickly.

'DC Crowley told me he will warn them off,' Vinny said.

'Here, I think this belongs to you.' He handed the watch to Joe.

Joe walked Vinny to his car. They left the library in time to see Macca hustled into Gary Mac's black BMW SUV.

'See you tomorrow,' Vinny said. It was Sammo's service and cremation. Then asked, 'Are you going to the crematorium?'

'No, I think I'll just go to the pub,' said Joe.

'We can come and collect you if you want a lift?'

'Are you sure?'

'Yeah, no problem. Family,' Vinny said.

'Don't push it.' Joe smiled.

Chapter Thirty-Four

Vinny

11am, Thursday, June 30th, 2016

Vinny pulled up to the kerb in Harefield Road. The brown brick terrace had an entry that ran down between every second house, allowing access to the rear. The front door opened as the car drew to a halt. Joe Doyle stepped out of his front door.

'This is the house,' Helen said.

'Yeah, I know.' Steven McNally had crept down this entry thirty-five years earlier. All entries looked dark and sinister to Vinny, even in daylight. 'Morning,' said Vinny. He appreciated Joe's understated, no-nonsense approach to life. He contributed more to the surrounding community than Vinny ever had — his little library of "Working-class truth, building the future one book at a time."

'Thanks for picking me up.' Joe climbed into the backseat. 'Hey, Charlie.'

'Hi,' Charlie replied.

'No luck finding Beep?' Helen spoke over her shoulder.

'No, he's gone to ground. No one has seen him.'

'The place in Garston?' asked Vinny.

'No, nothing. If he was there, he's not now.'

'Are Macca and Gary going to be there today?' Joe asked.

'I don't know. Macca was Sammo's friend for a long time,'

said Vinny.

'You know the audio is all over the internet?' said Joe.

'No, really. You mean Sammo's? The full thing?' asked Vinny.

'Yeah, I've had three or four people send me links,' Joe said.

'Wow, that's got to blow things open.'

'Was that you?' Helen asked.

'No. The only person I gave it to was DC Crowley,' said Vinny.

'Well, it's out now, and people are not happy,' said Joe.

'What do you mean?' asked Vinny.

'Both ways. Some angry at Macca, others with Sammo,' Joe replied.

'Why would DC Cowley or anyone leak the audio?' asked Helen.

'Maybe they think it will diminish the effect. Sammo makes a lot of claims, but he doesn't provide any evidence,' said Joe.

'Well, he can't now, can he?'

'Exactly,' Joe replied.

'So everything just goes back to normal?' Asked Helen.

'Anne is still working on stuff. It's not over yet.' Vinny drove through the estate. 'Gonna be an interesting day,' said Helen.

Family and friends collected in the first two rows of Myrtle chapel, one of the two at the busy crematorium. The other eight rows were empty. McNally, father and son were already present when Vinny arrived. The largely empty rows were depressing. All eyes turned towards their group as Vinny, Joe, Charlie, and Helen took their places. Helen led them into a row behind Claire, Sammo's daughter. The coffin draped in the union flag was on the catafalque, with a framed photograph of Sammo at his passing out parade, smiling, young and healthy.

Jaime and Anne made their entrance shortly after Vinny's group. They took a position in the row behind. Vinny turned and shook hands with Jaime. Claire and her mother, as the immediate family, were in the front row.

Fortunately, there was no requiem mass to drag things

out. The celebrant officiating reflected the emptiness of the chapel with anodyne words that lacked knowledge, empathy, or relevance to Sammo's life. Empty homilies and reflections were spun out into the thin, damp air. Sadness, in all its forms, was real and filled the void. The celebrant asked if anyone had anything to say. Claire turned to look at Vinny, he looked down at the floor. There was silence… and then movement behind.

Jaime shuffled along the row. He went to Claire, everyone heard him ask. 'Is it OK?'

She nodded her approval.

Jaime ascended the steps.

He pulled out a piece of paper and unfolded it. He gathered himself before speaking. 'None of us know how, where or when this day will arrive for us, or what will be said or thought of our lives.

'There is one thing we can say about Sam, Sammo… he was taken too early. The tragedy of his death is that he had so much to live for, not yet an old man. He spent the years of his youth in the armed forces, fighting for the flag that now drapes his coffin.

'For Sammo, that fight never ended, and in the end, the flag took his life, because the years of service left him scarred and disabled. The scars weren't visible. He had no wheelchair or crutch, and yet his disability was obvious to those who knew and loved him.

'Death takes away life, but we shouldn't let it take away the spirit or meaning of life. Anyone that knew Sammo as a kid knew a smiling, happy, generous soul. He was no angel, but in this place in those times, none of us were.

'One of the things that stood out then, and at the end, was how Sammo would stand up to bullies. I remember the teenage Sammo standing up for me. His courage was evident, even as others stood silently by.' Jaime's eyes flicked to Vinny.

'He stood up, against the group, and against others bigger than himself. He stood by me when I needed it… even as others denied me.' Jaime paused and raised a handkerchief to his eye.

Before the Storm

'So I was happy to stand by him in later years as he struggled with addiction. I didn't see him often, but never turned him away. Even in his pain and even through his addiction, he was trying to do what was right. He fought for what he thought was right, until it felt wrong, and despite the battle that raged within himself, he spoke the truth.

'I think most of us have heard those words, and no doubt we will hear them again. Claire, you can be proud that your dad never stopped fighting. In the end, he lost. As we all will, but he won victories along the way and who knows his greatest victory may yet be in the truth he left us.'

Jaime lowered his head. 'Now you can rest in peace, Sammo.' Jaime made his way back to his seat. In a preordained sequence, the music began, and the coffin was lowered. As the coffin disappeared, Simon and Garfunkel's "Bridge Over Troubled Water" played out, the melodies and lyrics filling the chapel.

Once the casket was lowered, the women in Sammo's life, his ex-wife and daughter, led mourners out of the crematorium and into the fresh morning air.

The dozen or so mourners, including McNally and son milled about, a few cigarettes were lit to fight the freshness of the air. Vinny approached Jaime, hand outstretched. 'Fine words, really, excellent.'

Jaime nodded, 'Thanks,'

'Are you coming to the pub for a drink?'

'Not sure. Where is it?' said Jaime.

'Tell Anne to follow us.'

Anne had been speaking to Claire and approached them.

'Any news?' asked Vinny.

'Yeah, but not here, eh? Maybe in the pub,' she said, looking around.

Vinny waited for the hearse to lead the way on its final leg of the journey, from the crematorium to the pub. .

'It's been a strange week. I'm glad it's coming to an end, and we can get back to normal,' said Helen.

'Somehow, I think that will be harder than it sounds. Some steps, once taken, are hard to retrace.'

'Jesus, is this how you are with your students?' asked Helen.

'What do you mean?' Vinny's outrage was only partly feigned.

'Speaking in metaphors and allegories? Why do I feel everything you say is meant to be taken as some kind of profound historical comment on society? Like there's someone running round behind you writing everything you say down for posterity.'

'Maybe because I have realised how intimately tied we are to the events through which we live.'

'Yeah, I'm with you, Mum,' said Charlie. 'Talks like he swallowed a dictionary.'

'Hey, come on, are you two ganging up on me?'

'I've never heard as much waffle or bollocks,' said Joe.

Everyone laughed except Vinny, who grumbled under his breath as he followed the hearse out of the cemetery grounds and back on the road to Speke. Helen reached across and stroked his hair.

The drive was slow, but traffic was courteous and accommodating to the hearse. Death and its pain were universal. It was a well-worn track and a familiar route for Vinny towards Speke as they passed the ASDA, but instead of taking a left as he expected, the hearse went straight through the lights. This upgraded road led to the new John Lennon Airport terminal. Before reaching the airport, the hearse took a left. The only part of Speke that could lay claim to the picturesque was All Saints Church. The red stone construction, one of the few surviving buildings of the original farming village, was built in the 1780s. It had witnessed the growth and decline of this overspill estate. Now huddled among the ex-council houses, it was a link from the pre-industrial farmland to post-industrial society. Fifty yards beyond the church, "The Dunnies" made the same link but in a different way. It began life as a pub, The Fox, merged with a works social club Dunlops and now the factory was gone. It was an independent pub again.

'Who's driving home?' Vinny asked.

'Do you want to drink?' asked Helen. 'It's still early. I don't mind,' Vinny replied.

The pub was empty of regular customers. The only punters were those arriving in black.

'Okay, you can drive. I'll have a drink,' said Vinny. 'Let's see if we can get you a shandy,' he said to Charlie.

Vinny and his group entered. There were more people in the pub than at the crematorium. The atmosphere was relaxed; the jukebox was playing. Claire had a table near the end of the bar. Joe knew most people and shook hands as he moved through the pub.

As they entered, Claire approached Jaime. 'Everyone is talking about what you said.'

'It was the truth,' Jaime said.

'Well, thank you. It was lovely. The audio was weird. It wasn't easy to hear my dad's voice today on social media,' said Claire.

'I'm sorry. I didn't share the sound file. I gave it to the police because of the stuff on it,' Vinny said.

'No, don't worry. He wanted people to know. That's why he got it to you. He knew you would do the right thing. I heard about the dog, as well,' said Claire. 'That was disgusting. I can't believe anyone could be so low.'

'Yeah, that was nasty,' Helen said.

'Do you know who did it?' Claire asked.

'Well, we don't have cameras or anything, but a neighbour gave us a pretty good description of Gary Mac.' said Vinny.

'It was a lovely service, Claire. Did you pick the music?' Helen asked.

'Thanks, yeah.'

'Okay, let me get you guys a drink,' said Joe, finally joining them.

Vinny moved towards the bar. 'I'll bring your drink over,' Vinny said to Helen. He followed Joe to the bar. 'These are on me,' Vinny said as he held out his money to get the attention of the barman.

'No arguments from me,' said Joe.

After delivering the drinks, Vinny found Anne and Jaime.

'Any news?'

'Yeah, we've had the full forensic toxicology report. We knew there was morphine in his body, but there was also fentanyl, a lethal amount.'

'That proves something is going on, doesn't it?' Asked Vinny.

'No. The police are still saying it was accidental. There is a history of this stuff being added to heroin by dealers. We have no proof it was intentional.'

Thirty minutes later, Vinny, Joe, and Jaime were still at the bar. Charlie had found some other youngsters and was at a separate table when Macca and Gary entered. They moved easily through the pub.

Claire joined Helen, Sharon, and Anne. The four women now stood chatting in a circle. Vinny crossed the bar with a new drink for Helen. 'Here you go.' He rolled his eyes in acknowledgement of Macca's presence.

Helen leaned over and squeezed his arm in support.

The next person to enter was DC Crowley. He moved through the drinkers to Claire. 'Excuse me, ladies. I just wanted to offer my condolences. I won't be staying.'

DC Crowley left. Helen nudged Vinny to look out of the window. He hadn't come alone. He stood chatting outside the pub to two uniformed coppers next to a squad car.

Macca made his way over. 'Claire, I'm sorry about Sam, whatever has happened the last few days and despite the rumours.' He looked directly at Vinny as he said this, then turned back to Claire. 'I'm sure you know Sam was my friend and comrade since…since God knows when.'

Claire replied, 'I know, but there has been a lot going on.'

Macca turned to Vinny. 'You've got some cheek coming back

to Speke, spreading all this shit about me. You think I had anything to do with this?'

'You don't own this estate. This is my dad's funeral, and Vinny was invited,' Claire said.

'Will no one rid me of this turbulent priest?' said Vinny.

'What the hell is that supposed to mean?' asked Macca.

'Stochastic violence,' said Vinny.

'For Christ's sake, Vinny,' Helen spoke directly to Macca. 'It means that you didn't have to do it yourself because your thug of a son did it for you. All he needed were the signs and messages from you.'

Gary Mac, who stood next to his father, now moved forward to stand in front of Vinny. 'You be careful what you say. I've had enough of you.' He jabbed his finger into Vinny's chest.

Claire put herself between Vinny and Gary Mac. 'And some of us are more than sick of you. Strutting about the place like you own it.'

'Careful, Claire,' said Macca.

'Careful, my arse. You're going to regret messing with my dad, both of you.' Claire pointed at father and son.

Other drinkers had gone quiet. Even the Jukebox was between songs. The silence was strangely focused as people stared at father and son.

'Gary, come on, I think we should go,' said Macca.

'I think that's a good idea,' said Vinny.

Gary Mac turned quickly and threw a jab at Vinny. Vinny moved just enough, and the blow glanced off the side of his temple. Claire's right hand flew through the air and landed with a heavy slap, Gary's head snapped to the right and his cheek turned red. Before he could respond Macca grabbed his son by the jacket and pulled him towards the door. Macca's head hung low as he finally got his son out of the pub.

Helen and Anne came across to Vinny.

'What the hell was all that?' asked Helen wide-eyed.

'You finally stood up to him,' said Jaime.

'Not me mate, I think Claire just put both of them in their place.'

'Was that the guy we went to see?' asked Charlie.

'Yeah,' said Vinny.

'Well done, Popeye.' Charlie grinned.

'That's enough out of you.' Vinny rummaged in his pocket and pulled out a few pound coins. 'Here, go and play the machine.'

'Sure, thanks, Dad.' Charlie wandered over to a games machine in the corner.

'I guess that's been building up for a long time,' Claire looked embarrassed. 'Listen.' The jukebox kicked into life as the McNally's and the tension left the room. 'One of my dad's favourites, Sam Cooke.'

'A change is gonna come,' said Helen.

'You might be right about that.' Joe nodded to the end of the bar.

'Who is that?' asked Vinny.

'Beep,' replied Joe.

Chapter Thirty-Five

Vinny

Two weeks later
Monday, July 11th, 2016

Vinny followed his Sat Nav, although this was unfamiliar territory, it was the place that made the city. North of the centre between Vauxhall and Scotland Road and adjacent to the river and the docks, this is where Scouse, as a culture and a people were born.

The Gerard Majella Courthouse, in Boundary Street, looked like a school in the middle of a housing estate. This was home to the Coroner's Court. A collection of well-kept municipal buildings surrounded by a metal picket fence. Opposite were a small parade of shops, a sandwich shop, a grocer's and a hairdresser's, and the other sides of the square by small red brick houses. This was the place where the details of sudden, unexpected, or suspicious deaths were examined.

Vinny found a place in the visitors' car park. Joe pointed across the houses. 'On the docks down there by the river, that's where we started.'

'Who is this we?' asked Helen.

'The Liverpool working class, the mix of English Protestants, Irish Catholics, and Welsh Methodists, that make up the core of the dockers, carters, and tradesmen who teemed about these streets. The barefoot diseased slummies. Liverpolitans and Merchants Lived in Georgian Liverpool, we survived in the courts and basements, the rooms and cellars of private landlords.'

'Sounds like fun,' said Vinny.

'You shouldn't joke. If some had their way, we'd be going back there too.'

'Well, not today.' Helen put her arm through Joe's and walked him toward the entrance.

Security staff directed them to the courtroom. The corridors and rooms were clean, well lit, and furnished in the style of lawyer's offices, all dark wood and plush upholstery. Helen's shoes rang out on the marble effect floor. The waiting area was busy. Court officers marched to and fro with files. Everyone was smartly dressed. Vinny spotted Anne and Jaime. Anne was in deep conversation with a large, official-looking woman. Jaime noticed them and nodded. He touched Anne's arm, and she looked across and waved. She gestured for Vinny to wait.

'Shall we go over?' asked Anne.

'No, Anne knows we're here.'

'This place gives me the creeps,' said Joe.

Vinny watched Anne in conversation. Her hair was tied back with a burgundy ribbon, and she wore a black trouser suit with a burgundy jumper underneath. Vinny admired her style. There was no doubt she was still an attractive woman. Her light brown skin glowed next to the burgundy. Jaime looked like her husband. Vinny knew he wasn't, but they looked good together. He smiled. It would be a good match.

'You ok?' asked Helen. 'You look miles away.'

'Yeah, I was.'

Anne ended her conversation and crossed the waiting area. Jaime stayed where he was.

Vinny looked toward the entrance in time to see Claire arrive. 'Ok, we have a room set aside.' Anne led the way back along the corridor toward the entrance, meeting Claire on the way. Anne led them into a room. A long table was surrounded by chairs.

'Isn't Jaime coming?' asked Vinny

'He has something else to do,' said Anne.

'This is very nice,' Helen said.

'For family and friends of the deceased,' said Anne.

'You seem to know your way around,' said Vinny.

'I have been in contact with Pam for a couple of weeks now.'

'Pam?' Helen asked.

Claire pulled out a chair and sat down. 'Pamela Jones, the Coroner's investigating officer. She's really nice.'

'Yeah, she's been a real help. If we get anything from today, it will be with her help.'

'What about the police?' asked Joe.

'Less so.' Anne spread her hands. 'Everyone should take a seat. It should only be a couple of minutes before the court is ready.'

'Court, does that mean lawyers?' asked Helen.

'Anne is my representative,' said Claire.

Anne explained. 'An Inquest is an investigation into a death of unknown, violent or unnatural causes to find out who the deceased was, and where, when and how they died. '

'A fact-gathering exercise?' asked Vinny.

'Yeah, the Coroner makes "findings of fact" about who the deceased was, when and where they died and the medical cause of their death. The Coroner can also reach conclusions, natural causes, accidents, suicide, or unlawful killing. There are other things like traffic accidents and misadventure. But for us, the options will quickly be whittled down to two accidental or unlawful killing. I think suicide will be ruled out. The police will argue about the case for an accident. It is our job to show that it was unlawful.'

'Can you do that asked Vinny?'

'The lady you saw me speaking to was Pam, Mrs Jones. She will be briefing the Coroner now, on what we expect to happen.'

'Who are all the people?' asked Helen.

'Not sure. Inquests are public, so people can come in off the street. I did see one reporter. You have court officers, police. There are quite a few people involved. Everyone ready?'

The morning passed slowly, the air in the room became thicker as the day wore on. The Coroner an elderly woman, fitted the old school building; her cut-glass headmistress accent stood out among the various shades of Scouse. Vinny was surprised to see DI Cooper at the back of the room. DC Cowley was at a table near the front and had reported on his findings of the night of the overdose. The forensic toxicology report had been introduced. That it was an overdose that killed Sammo was not in question. It was also accepted that there was a lethal concentration of Fentanyl found. Anne had occasionally asked questions in order to clarify events. She now questioned DC Cowley.

'DC Cowley, you reported that you attended the scene at 11.45pm. Is that correct?'

'Yes.'

'And after examining the scene, your conclusion was that it was an accidental overdose, and you released the body for transfer to the Mortuary at the Royal Liverpool. Is that correct?'

'It was my assessment that it was an accidental overdose. There was no note, nor was there any sign of struggle to indicate anything else.'

'So you authorised the release of the body?'

DC Cooper's eyes flashed across the courtroom, Vinny watched as Anne followed his look toward DI Cooper at the back of the room.

'DC Cowley, is it the case that you authorised the removal of the deceased?'

'No.'

Anne shuffled her papers and pulled out a sheet of A4. 'In fact, the signature authorising the removal of the deceased is Detective Inspector Cooper, is that correct?'

'Yes, that's correct.'

'Is DI Cooper based in the Speke station?'

'No.'

'So how was DI Cooper alerted to the situation?'

'I called him.'

'Now why would you call an officer based in Merseyside Police HQ for a death by accidental overdose?'

'I had received a memo a week or so earlier advising that anything related to Mr Samuel Maddows should be reported to DI Cooper.'

'OK thank you, DC Cowley.'

Anne turned to the Coroner. 'Excuse me, Ma'am but the officer in question is in attendance today. Can I call him as a witness?'

The Coroner lowered her glasses and checked her notes. 'Can DI Cooper make himself known?'

There was a hum of voices, and people looked around. DI Cooper at the back of the room stood.

'Here Ma'am.'

'Would you please come forward, Detective Inspector?'

'Can we find a chair for the officer?' The Coroner asked, and a court official quickly brought one forward. DC Cowley moved aside to make room.

'Thank you, Ma'am.'

Vinny whispered to Helen, 'Here we go.'

Anne began. 'DI Cooper, can you explain to the court your position within Merseyside Police?'

'I am a Detective Inspector.'

'Isn't it true that you are a Detective Inspector of the Special Branch?'

'No.'

'Can you tell the court the department in which you serve?'

'Special Investigation Squad.'

'Excuse me, was the Special Investigation Squad previously

known as The Special Branch?'

'Yes, it was.'

'What is the remit of the Squad?'

'To operate between the criminal police and the security services to protect the British public, particularly in regard to anti-terrorist activities.'

'Is it true that you circulated a memo for anything regarding Mr Maddows to be reported to you?'

'Yes.'

'Why?'

'We had received information that Mr Maddows was threatening to reveal information that would be a risk to national security.'

'From whom did you receive this information?'

The DI looked uncomfortable. He shifted in his seat.

'Can you tell the court who provided this information?'

'It was anonymous.'

'After attending the scene of the death. Did you initiate a murder enquiry?'

'No, I did not.'

'Did you record a death under suspicious circumstances?'

'No, I did not.'

'How did you record the death of Mr Maddows?'

'An accidental overdose.'

'So you receive information that Mr Maddows may be about to release information that is a threat to national security. You circulate information that you should be informed if he appears on the radar of Merseyside Police. He is found dead a week later and you attend the scene and record the incident as an accidental overdose?'

'Yes, that is correct. An overdose is an overdose, a tragedy for all involved, but unfortunately, not uncommon.'

'Did you request a forensic toxicology report?'

'No, there was no evidence that there was anything other

than heroin involved.'

'How were the police alerted to the situation on Dymchurch Road?'

'The ambulance service notified the police.'

'Do you know who made that emergency call?'

'As far as I know, it was a neighbour.'

'Detective Inspector, do you know the name Brian Palmer?'

'I have heard it, yes.'

'Did you visit the home of his parents recently?'

'It is possible.'

'Why is it possible?'

'The name sounds familiar, and it is very often it is part of my job to visit people's homes.'

'Did you identify the neighbour who made the 999 call?'

'No, I did not.'

'Did you canvas the neighbours to find out who made the call?'

'There was no need.'

'Where was Mr Maddows found?'

'In his living room on the sofa.'

'Inspector, how could a neighbour have known Mr Maddows was in danger and call 999 without being in the room with him?'

'I don't know.'

'Thank you, Inspector.'

Anne turned to the Coroner. 'With your permission, I will introduce two items of audio evidence. The first is part of a recorded message left by the deceased. The second is a recording of the emergency call on the night of the death of Mr Maddows.'

The Coroner addressed a court officer. 'Have the items been logged?'

'They have Ma'am.'

'Then you may proceed.'

Before the Storm

'This is part of a recording left by Mr Maddows a few days before his death. I would just like to identify two people mentioned in the recording. The person referred to as "Macca" is Councillor Steve McNally, and Gary Mac is his son Gary McNally.'

Anne pressed a key on her laptop and Sammo's voice filled the room.

I got out of the military, but I couldn't get the military out of me. Macca stayed for a while, but the peace process came soon after. We thought it was over, finished. But the families wouldn't let it go. Year after year, they probed and asked. Now the shit is hitting the fan; a couple of weeks ago a new report said there was collusion between the security forces and the killers at Loughinisland. They didn't name names, but I can.

I told Macca I'd had enough. I wanted to tell people I needed to get it out of my head, or at least stop hiding it, lying about it. He wasn't happy. Told me no one would believe a junkie. He might be right, but I don't give a shit anymore.

Things have been getting pretty crazy. I don't know if Gary Mac has said anything, but the kids are being a pain in the arse. I think they all look up to him. Banging on the door all hours of day and night. Throwing rubbish in the garden. One of them on a bike lifted his shirt so I could see he had a gun stuck in his waistband. Can you fucking believe it?

I think he's letting me know what life will be like if I do say something. All you need is one person to call you a grass. To be honest, the council wants the house back anyway, so fuck 'em.

I don't know what you can do. I just think people should know… Maybe they do know and don't care. But I need to stop hiding shit. You know what I worked out? When we hide stuff, it's not hiding it from the world. We are hiding from it. I need to come out of hiding. If I am going to sort myself out, I need to face things I have done. Being around Claire is the hardest thing you can't love and ignore the pain. We can only hide it if we don't feel it. But you know that. What the fuck, eh Vinny? Will anyone even care? If something happens to me, at least you will know why.

Anne turned to the Coroner, 'If something happens to me you will know why. It is clear that Mr Maddows knew he was in danger.'

'Thank you, Ma'am, on behalf of the family we would like to call a witness, Mr Brian Palmer.'

The Coroner looked to the court officer. 'We have been notified, Ma'am.'

DI Cooper stood. 'Excuse me, Ma'am but we have not been notified of any other witnesses.'

The Coroner looked to the court officer, who looked to the Court Investigator.

Mrs Jones stood. 'Ma'am, we are under no obligation to inform the police. Given the sensitive nature of the evidence of this witness, I placed him under the protection of the court.' Mrs Jones sat down.

'I object, Ma'am.' DI Cooper was still standing.

'Please sit down, Detective Inspector. There are no objections to these proceedings, and this is my courtroom. Mrs Jones has followed the correct procedure for the protection of witnesses and we will hear the testimony of Mr Palmer.'

'Thank you, Ma'am.' Anne looked to the door. There was muffled chatter.

Helen turned to Vinny. 'Did you know about this?' Vinny shrugged. All eyes in the courtroom had followed Anne's and as the tension mounted, the door opened, and Jaime entered, leading Beep into the courtroom. The court officer sprang into action and with the help of others placed another table and two chairs opposite the Coroner. Jaime and Beep took their seats.

'Can you give us your full name and address?' asked Anne.

'Brian Palmer, 124 East Damwood Road, Speke.'

'Mr Palmer, I would like to play a recording for you and the court. If I may? The second sound file.'

The Coroner nodded, 'You may.'

There was a click and then static before a female voice announced, '999 emergency. Which service do you require? Fire, ambulance, or police?

'Ambulance, 72 Dymchurch Road, Speke, my mates dying.'

'Can you tell me what happened?'

'Get an ambulance here quick- he's going blue…'

There was a sharp click, and then the static returned.

'Was that your voice, Mr Palmer, calling 999 for an ambulance for Mr Maddows?'

'Yes, it was me.'

'How long did you know Samuel Maddows?'

'Years, since we were kids.'

'Excuse me for being so direct, Mr Palmer, but we are here to establish the circumstances of his death. You were a partner in the deceased's drug-taking activity?'

'Yeah, we were both using, but he got off the gear for a while.'

'What is your status now, Mr Palmer?'

'I'm clean. I haven't used since that night.'

'What happened that night?'

'I gave him the gear. He shot up, and I was all ready to go next, but I saw he was in a bad way.'

'Can you describe what happened?'

'He was on the sofa and injected. He leant back or kinda fell back. You know his head and everything. I could see his eyes moving behind his eyelids. That shows he's getting the hit, and he went off, all relaxed like, and that's how it normally is, for as long as it lasts, you know.'

'So why didn't you inject? That was your plan?'

'Yeah, I was about to, but he went limp, his eyes stopped twitching, he kinda fell sideways. I reached out to push him back up, but he was heavy, then I saw he wasn't breathing. There was nothing and his lips started going blue, his skin changed colour. That's when I knew he was dead. He overdosed. He was in a coma. Or dead…'

'My first thought was this must be good shit. My second thought was he's fucking dead. I called the ambulance and then got out of there.'

'Where have you been since then?'

'Hiding. Keeping my head down. I heard the police were looking for me, looking everywhere, and I knew Gary Mac would be too.'

'Thank you, this next part is very important for the Coroner to hear. You will not get in trouble now. You are under the protection of the Coroner's Court. All we are interested in is the truth.'

'Mr Palmer, did you know the heroin you gave to Mr Maddows that night contained Fentanyl?'

'No, no idea, absolutely not.'

'Where did you get the heroin?'

'From Gary McNally.'

'I want to be clear. You got the drugs taken by Mr Maddows that night from Gary McNally?'

'Yes.'

'Did Mr McNally say anything?'

'He said we should enjoy it because it was his special mix.'

'His special mix?'

'Yeah, that's what he said.'

One last question, Mr Palmer, how much is a shot of heroin?

'Depends, but a wrap, ten, fifteen quid, depends who's got it, how good it is.'

'And how much did you pay that night?'

'Nothing. He said it was a freebie as long as I shared it with his dad's old mate, Sammo.'

'Thank you, Mr Palmer.'

Chapter Thirty-Six

Anne

Monday, July 11th, 2016

Anne turned to the Coroner. 'Ma'am we have heard in his own words that Mr Maddows was in fear of his life because he was about to talk about his activities in the armed forces in Northern Ireland. We are not asking for judgement on those activities or what he was about to reveal. DI Cooper has given evidence that he was aware that Mr Maddows was about to share sensitive information. We know from the emergency call that Mr Palmer was present with Mr Maddows at the time of the overdose and we have his testimony the drugs that killed Mr Maddows came from Mr Gary McNally and were his "special mix."'

'Ma'am I think we have provided enough factual evidence to show that the death of Mr Maddows was not accidental, but was in fact unlawful.'

Anne sat down next to Claire. Claire reached out for her hand.

The Coroner lifted the glasses that hung on a chain around her neck and examined an A4 sheet in front of her. 'Is that all the evidence we are expecting?' she looked over her glasses at the court officer.

'It is Ma'am.'

'Then we will take a fifteen-minute adjournment.' The Coroner stood, the court officers followed her, prompting everyone to do the same. 'What do we do?' Helen asked.

'Not sure,' Vinny waved to Anne, who made her way across.

'Great job,' said Helen.

'You kept that quiet,' said Vinny.

'Thanks, we had to. People were looking for him. We couldn't risk word getting out.'

Vinny looked around before asking. 'So, where's he been?'

Anne leaned in and lowered her voice. 'In Jaime's.'

'Since the pub?' asked Joe

'He was scared,' explained Anne. 'There is someone from the Chronicle here. I can't see McNally surviving on the council after this.'

'I'd better be getting back.' Anne left and joined Claire back at the front.

The room was filling up again when the side door to the Coroner's office opened.

A minute later, the room was quiet as The Coroner began to speak. 'In English Law, unlawful killing is a verdict that can be returned by an inquest in England and Wales when someone has been killed by one or more unknown person. The verdict means that the killing was done without a lawful excuse and in breach of criminal law. The facts of this case lead me to the conclusion the death of Mr Samuel Maddows was an Unlawful Killing. The conclusion of unlawful killing, in this case, must lead to a police investigation, with the aim of gathering sufficient evidence to identify, charge and prosecute those responsible.

There were some claps and a few gasps. The Coroner stood and left the court. Vinny lost track of Anne and they waited as the room cleared, then left.

Outside the courtroom, Anne waved to Vinny. 'This way.' She ushered Vinny, Helen, and Joe out through a short corridor to a back entrance. Jaime, Claire and Beep and Mrs Jones were already there.

Claire gave Mrs Jones a hug. 'Thank you for your help.'

Mrs Jones shook Anne's hand. 'If you are ever looking for a job, give me a call.' She went back inside the building.

Joe offered his hand to Beep. 'That took some guts.'

'Couldn't let them get away with it,' he replied.

'Well, we've got the truth. Next step is justice,' said Claire.

'There are many who never get the truth,' said Helen.

'I know.' Claire turned to Anne. 'I don't know what I would've done without you,' she hugged Anne, then turned. 'Without all of you.'

Joe put his hand in his pocket and pulled out a gold chain, inch by inch. In the afternoon sunlight, the watch glistened.

'Is it really the one?' Jaime asked.

'Open it and see,'

Jaime reached out and let the watch settle in his hand. He felt around the rim and placed his nail under the edge, flipping open the cover and there inside was an engraving; *Faugh A Ballagh*. Jaime held the watch for a minute before handing it back to Joe.

Joe handed the watch to Beep. 'Here, you keep it.'

Beep's eyes widened. 'Why?'

'Vinny told me the story of what happened across the water. My grandfather took this watch off a dying British officer nearly a hundred years ago. I think he always regretted it. The watch was never mine or my family's. The only thing we ever wanted was our country back, and who knows, we might be closer to that now than ever.'

'The motto inside is from the Royal Irish Rangers. It means "*Clear The Way*"' said Vinny.

'Maybe this can clear the way for you to stay off the gear,' said Joe. Beep smiled.

'Clear the way to prosecuting those bastards,' said Claire.

'Clear the way to the pub,' Vinny laughed. 'Who fancies a pint?'

Chapter Thirty-Seven

Macca

Thursday, 2nd July, 1981

Macca stepped over the low wooden gate, careful not to rattle the latch. He marched up the path and darted into the entry. Quick and quiet. The light was fading. Looking down the end of the street, he could see the sun disappearing beyond the houses into the river.

The streetlights were on, the orange glow fighting the remains of the day. Kids had been called in, football and skipping were over, the street fell quiet. TVs blared behind curtains up and down the road. Hale was better than Speke because they had more, much more, cash, even jewellery, but the walk from the estate was dangerous. The bizzies knew kids from Speke going to Hale at night were not out visiting friends or family. This should be easy. Macca relaxed in the entry, safe in the knowledge he remained unseen from the street. The path ran between the two houses, giving access to the back gardens. At the end, there were two gates at forty-five degrees to each other. He moved down the entry cautiously; he knew there were no dogs next door.

Sammo was somewhere in the street and would give a whistle if anything looked out of order, so there was no rush. This was about patience and nerves.

Before the Storm

Old man Doyle turned out the light in the living room and made his way upstairs. Macca watched as the light from the living room went out. He moved down the entry to the back gates. The old man would be in the bathroom above. Macca looked up and saw the light through the window. He should wait until this light went out, too, but fuck it, he liked the danger. He grabbed the top of the gate, which wouldn't budge. Locked. He pulled himself up smoothly and eased on top of it. He was just feet away from the bathroom window. The light went out. Macca dropped silently to the ground.

The back door was half glazed, four square panes above waist height. He tried the door, but it was locked. The bottom left window in the door had a crack. Macca's lucky night. He pulled a pair of socks out of his pocket and slipped them over his hands. A precaution learned watching Kojak and Columbo, as police in Speke didn't bother fingerprinting for burglary. He pressed against the crack with his elbow pushing firmly, then relaxing, pushing, then relaxing. Each time the glass moved, it separated from the putty holding it in place. Another push, harder this time, and a new crack appeared. Now he could push and pull a triangle-shaped piece to loosen it, until he could lift it out of the frame, and discarded it on the grass. Macca guessed the old man would be in bed by now. Macca rolled up his sleeve, he slid a hand, then an arm, through the gap in the glass. The key sat in the lock halfway down the door. Macca turned it and let himself in. His eyes had adjusted to the darkness. The kitchen was tidy; a single cup and plate were on the drainer next to the sink, a knife and fork in a glass next to them. The air was still. A dog barked in the distance, sounding an alarm for better-defended homes.

The kitchen table was against the wall. Macca reached for a shelf above it. He picked up the first of three tins, turned the lid, and his fingers went inside. Sugar. He emptied it out onto the floor. The second tin held tea bags. Maybe he would be lucky with the third. Biscuits. He took a bite of one and let the others fall. He picked up a tea towel from the drainer.

Mr. Doyle coughed and turned over. The bed creaked as he tossed and turned, seeking comfort. Macca opened the living room door. He knew these houses well. They were all the same, and he had been in this house with Helen. A cupboard occupied the space under the stairs in the hallway. Everyone had an utilities cupboard, and everyone had a lecky and gas meter. Shillings fed the meter until the money changed. Now they were ten pence pieces.

He crossed the room quickly when he heard the cough from above. He wasn't worried. If the old man came down, he could be out the door in seconds. Small padlocks fixed the coin collection tin under the meter. Macca pulled out his screwdriver and wedged it through the gap. A strong twist and the loop of metal holding the padlock bent. The padlock would hold, the collection tin was weaker. One arm of the loop snapped off with barely a sound. Macca slid the padlock off, laid the tea towel down on the ground and eased the collection tin from its place. The coins slid out with tinkles, a sound Macca loved. He repeated the exercise with the gas meter. Holding the corners of the tea towel, he enjoyed the weight of coins. He was happy. Everything was still and quiet, nothing stirred. He put the tea towel down, stood in the living room, and spun, smiling, with his arms extended. He bent down, picked up the tea towel, and tied the corners together, closing it tightly. The kitchen door was open, and he could see straight out to the back garden. His way out was clear, but he didn't take it.

Another cough from upstairs. He moved toward the hallway and opened the door. The front door faced the stairs. He leaned down and placed the tea towel filled with coins on the bottom stair. He placed a foot on the first step. He stood still and stopped breathing. He could hear the laboured, rasping breath from above. He climbed the stairs, each squeak and creak a challenge. His nerves were tingling, his stomach turning as he reached the landing. The old linoleum floors were slippy and curled at the edges. To his left was the bathroom and ahead he could hear breathing. Could he do it? Could he open the door? He would be down the stairs in no time if the old guy woke up. What was the point?

He pushed the door with his fingertips, surprised how easily it floated open. Before him was an old metal frame bed. From just outside the bedroom door, he could see the old man on his back, the blankets pulled up to his chin, his chest rising and falling steadily.

The moon must have appeared from behind a cloud because a beam of light pierced the darkness, and a glint caught his eye. On a nightstand in front of a framed photograph of a man and woman smiling, something was shining, reflecting the moonlight in a soft yellow glow. He crept forward, finding his rhythm with the rising and falling breath. His heart raced. He was inches away from the old man and a couple of steps away from what looked like a small, round case of some kind.

The air burst with a sharp snort as the old man made a noise like a pig. Macca lunged forward and grabbed the object. The man's eyes flashed open, and he raised his head. A bestial 'Aargh' burst from his mouth with spittle and snot.

Macca's left hand pushed the man's chest back down.

'Aargh,' a more piercing and frightened sound came next.

Macca moved his left hand up and pressed it down over the man's mouth. The old man struggled to speak. Arms flailing, he clawed and scratched at Macca's hand.

Macca slipped the watch into his pocket and pressed down with both hands covering the man's mouth and nose.

Macca looked into the bulging terrified eyes.

The End

Acknowledgements

I've always had a desire to write, but for a long time thought I would never achieve my goal of becoming a writer. I owe an enormous 'Thank you' to Ted and James from Northodox Press who accepted *Under The Bridge* for publication. Writing may be a solitary task but publishing a book is a collective achievement, and involves all those who help along the way. Leila Kirkconnel and Clare Coombes gave invaluable advice in the drafting stage. I appreciate the work Northodox colleagues do in proofing and editing. Thanks are also due to readers Maria Hunter, Jo Peggrem, Rhi Foynes, Meeta Tailor, and Paul Cooney.

I also want to acknowledge those working-class authors not yet published and encourage them to continue. I started to write a biography of my dad when I was sixteen, up in my bedroom on the Dymchurch estate in Speke. I wrote about half a page. I knew my dad came from Ireland and my brother died there. I wanted to write my dad as a hero, not because he was, but because I somehow wanted to pay him back for making that journey across the Irish Sea. My dad was a worker, a painter and decorator and my mum worked part-time at Evans Medical all the time I was at school. What made me a writer was trying to change in fiction, what I couldn't change in fact. I wanted to celebrate the lives of my dad, my mum, and my dead brother.

The thread that runs through the Liverpool Mysteries is

Before the Storm

the understanding that the only solution to the problems we face as working-class communities. Will come from those communities, people like my mum, my dad, my brother, my sisters, my aunties, and cousins -us – asserting our interests, our history and ourselves to renew the broken society we have. Humanity and solidarity expressed through action are the keys to our future, irrespective of colour, sexuality or nationality. For those who are looking, I hope my writing not only expresses some of the pain and suffering we go through but also points to the collective solutions on offer.

Return to where it all began with
Under the Bridge.

**Keep reading for an exclusive extract of
the updated edition.**

JACK BYRNE

UNDER THE
BRIDGE

BOOK ONE IN THE LIVERPOOL MYSTERIES SERIES

Chapter One

Michael

The bone poked out of the mud and into Michael's life.

'Whoa, stop, stop!' Michael, the site caretaker, waved his hands above his head and shouted over the grinding diesel engine.

The digger emptied its load on a growing mound of damp earth, a strip of blue tarpaulin hanging from its scoop. The bone disappeared, reburied immediately. But Michael knew he had seen it and started digging through the soil, his fingernails becoming clogged and his hands cold as he dug deeper.

'What's up?' The driver killed the engine and climbed down from the cab.

'I saw a bone.' Michael was determined to find it now.

The drizzle came in waves, sweeping in from the Mersey and across the building site, leaving dew drops on everything it touched.

The foreman shouted, 'Why you stop?'

'Paddy 'ere reckons he saw summat,' said the JCB driver.

'Michael, what you see? Why you stopping job?' Istvan turned to the driver. 'Get back on machine.'

Michael's fingers dug through the congealing mud to reveal a hard, brown shape. 'Here it is.'

'Fucking dog bone. Get back to work.'

Michael ignored him and pulled the earth aside to reveal a long shaft. 'This is no dog bone - this is a man's.' He looked round as other workers gathered. 'Check the trench to see what else we got down there,' he said.

'Who you think you are, CSI? You are caretaker - get back in shed.'

The driver joined Michael. He grabbed a shovel and jumped down into the shallow trench. 'Here, this is where it come from.'

He scraped away the soil as a growing band of workers watched.

Istvan was losing control of the situation. Flashes of blue appeared in the ground, and the driver bent and tugged at the plastic sheeting. Another worker joined him, and they began to prise free the plastic, pulling and tearing it.

'Careful there.' Istvan leaned forward, now as intent as everyone else.

The site was quiet as work stopped, and people gathered around. There was something there, wrapped in plastic sheeting. 'That's enough, back to work, everyone,' Istvan ordered in vain.

'Go on, lads,' Michael urged.

He wanted to see what was there. If it was human, Christ. This was Raglan Street - he knew this street. This is where the builders' yard was back in the day.

The two men in the trench climbed out. Leaning back in, they wiped away the loose soil and got a grip of the tarpaulin from each side and heaved. There was a ripping sound, and both men fell backwards as a cloud of soil exploded into the air, a mud-covered skull in its midst.

'Bingo,' shouted Michael.

Chapter Two

Vinny

Vinny reached for his phone. *Bollocks. Twenty minutes to get there.* He couldn't afford to be late, not today. Today, everything holding him back would end. A son he never saw, an average history degree, and part-time work in a crappy shoe shop, all of which had reduced his finances and his reserves of optimism to zero. His clothes were laid out: ironed jeans and a smart polo shirt. Not over-formal. He wasn't a geek. He had debated a collar and tie but rejected it. He was dressed and out in ten.

Panic and hope were two butterflies that fluttered round in Vinny's stomach as he cycled along the busy streets of Liverpool, rehearsing his lines in this audition for life. He dodged and weaved through the mid-morning traffic. Sweating, he pushed himself up the wide spare avenues of Toxteth until he reached the narrow, crowded streets around the University. He had done his preparation; he knew his arguments. He didn't want to mess this up. The building he was heading for wasn't among the lifeless concrete structures or the new steel and glass blocks. As he flew along the pavement of Hope Street, he could see his destination - the glorious red brick creation poking out behind the modern funnel-shaped Catholic cathedral.

He dismounted, patted down his wavy brown hair, and smoothed out his jeans. As he was bending to lock his bike to the street barrier, a tall, dark-skinned woman approached him.

'Can I give you a flyer?' her accent was broad, rich, and not local.

Vinny looked into her bright eyes. She wore a multi-coloured band around the black hair that topped her slim face and sharp features.

'Sure.' He took the leaflet.

'Do you work for the University?' she was advancing, clipboard in hand.

'No.' He didn't want to get into a discussion.

'A student?'

She was persistent, he would give her that.

'No. Look. Sorry, but I've got to get inside.' He was moving away from her as he said this.

'The student union supports us,' she declared.

'I have to go.'

He didn't wait for a reply. He scanned the leaflet as he edged his way through other campaigners and took the three steps into the building. *Justice for Cleaners.* He did something he would never have done if Anne were with him. He scrunched up the leaflet and tossed it in a waste bin just inside the double doors. He checked his phone. *Bang on time.*

Vinny walked through the high arched main entrance into a wide atrium and felt the cool air on his face. The contrast between the busy street outside and the cathedral-like interior was immediate. *Wow*, he thought, *this is where I belong.* He looked up to the richly decorated ceiling rectangles of deep blue with red and gold borders. The wide-open space below had a polished floor, and blood-red ceramic tiles covered the walls up to the first-floor level. Not an easy place to clean, he realised, thinking of the "Justice for Cleaners" woman. A heavy balustrade ran round a first-floor gallery supported by columns dressed in the same deep red tiles. He scanned the room list of plastic letters and numbers on a brass stand. He found her. *Dr A Sheehan, room 4B.*

The brass nameplate shone yellow-gold with age. Tiny, almost invisible swirls indicated years of assiduous polishing. Vinny knocked lightly and waited before inching the door open. The heavy oak door swung too easily on its hinges, opening faster than he'd intended.

The first thing he saw was a crucifix. The body hung heavily with arms outstretched, sinews and muscles strained, a crown of thorns with sharp points sticking out at the world or embedded in the skull of the drooping head. Rivulets of deep red blood were streaking down the pained, angular face. *Fuck*, Vinny thought.

'Yes?' someone from within called out.

He opened the door wider. 'Sorry, Sheehan? Professor Sheehan?'

The woman behind the oak desk looked busy, distant, turning away from the computer screen to face him. 'Yes?' she said again.

'Vinny, Vincent Connolly. I have an appointment.'

'Ah, come in, Mr Connolly.' She checked her wristwatch and smiled.

Entering the room, he closed the door behind him and made his way over the carpeted floor to the chair facing the broad oak desk.

'I'm sorry, forgive me. I get so carried away at times. Is it Vincent?' she asked, pushing her glasses high on her head - they balanced precariously on her bunched-up hair.

'Yes. It's Vincent.'

He hoped the formality would equate with gravitas. He took a deep breath to try and settle himself, and sat upright, leaning slightly forward.

'So, Vincent.' She started looking through papers on her desk. 'How can I help you?'

'I raised the idea of investigating Irish immigration to the UK after the Second World War. I have the emails here.' He rifled through his bag.

'Ah, yes, that Mr Vincent Connolly. No need…' With a wave of the hand, she released him from his search. 'I remember.' She smiled, leaning back in her chair, her arms resting on the black leather.

Before the Storm

On the shelf behind her head, he could see a number of her titles, including her most celebrated work, *The Making of Modern Identity – A History of Liverpool*.

Doctor Sheehan's voice was soft and melodic. He couldn't quite work out the accent. 'Go on. I'm listening.'

Vinny took a breath and launched into his practised spiel. 'There is a wealth of material available from the 1840s and '50s on the effects and consequences of the famine and mass emigration from Ireland. There has, however, been very little research on the scale and impact of changes since then. Everything seems to stop around World War Two. Some of the largest changes in the structure of Liverpool have been since that period: the slum clearances, the building of new housing developments on the edge of the city. This was all happening when there was a shortage of labour. This shortage was partly filled by returning troops, but it also required an influx of Irish workers.'

'Okay, that's a fair point, and although I think some people are beginning to look into this, you are correct; it's an under-researched area. Can I ask what your interest in this is? Are you Irish?'

Vinny allowed himself to relax back against the chair. 'No personal interest,' he said. 'I just think it's an area rich in potential. It's a period when a lot was going on. The city was changing, not only geographically, but culturally. It's also when the Scouse identity was being developed.'

'Connolly is an Irish name, isn't it?' she asked.

'I guess so, but I was born here,' Vinny said.

'So, you are English, Irish, and Scouse?' she asked.

Vinny thought for a moment. He had never heard it put that way before. 'Does it matter?' he asked.

'Not to me,' she replied. 'But you may find it does to you.'

Keep reading at Northodox.co.uk

JACK BYRNE

ACROSS THE
WATER

BOOK TWO IN THE LIVERPOOL MYSTERIES SERIES

NORTHODOX PRESS

HOME OF NORTHERN VOICES

 FACEBOOK.COM/NORTHODOXPRESS

 TWITER.COM/NORTHODOXPRESS

 INSTAGRAM.COM/NORTHODOXPRESS

 NORTHODOX.CO.UK

SUBMISSIONS ARE OPEN!

WRITER &
DEBUT AUTHOR   [ ]

NOVELS &
SHORT FICTION   [ ]

FROM OR LIVING   [ ]
IN THE NORTH